SADDLED WITH TROUBLE

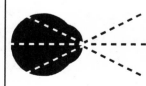

This Large Print Book carries the
Seal of Approval of N.A.V.H.

SADDLED WITH TROUBLE

MICHELE SCOTT

THORNDIKE PRESS

An imprint of Thomson Gale, a part of The Thomson Corporation

Detroit • New York • San Francisco • New Haven, Conn. • Waterville, Maine • London

LIBRARY OF CONGRESS CATALOGING-IN-PUBLICATION DATA

Scott, Michele, 1969–
   Saddled with trouble / by Michele Scott.
     p. cm. — (Horse lover's mystery ; #1)
     ISBN-13: 978-0-7862-9473-2 (lg. print : alk. paper)
     ISBN-10: 0-7862-9473-6 (lg. print : alk. paper)
     1. Horse trainers — Fiction. 2. Large type books. I. Title.
   PS3619.C6824S24 2007
   813'.6—dc22   2006103027

Published in 2007 by arrangement with The Berkley Publishing Group, a member of Penguin Group (USA) Inc.

Printed in the United States of America on permanent paper
10 9 8 7 6 5 4 3 2 1

To Mom and Dad,
who nurtured my love of horses.

ACKNOWLEDGMENTS

I want to thank my cousin and lifelong horse enthusiast Jessica Hanson for helping me with the research on this book; my friend and horse expert Nikki Shea for being a first reader; Bob Avila and Dana for allowing me to come up to their amazing facility and meet some gorgeous animals (Rocky included); Brian Davis of the Santa Rosa Police Department; Mike Sirota for his continued dedication to me and my writing; my agent, Jessica Faust; and my editor, Samantha Mandor. I also have to give a big thank you for all the support to The Cozy Chicks — Karen MacInerney, Maggie Sefton, Diana Killian, and Heather Webber. It's great to be a part of such a wonderful group of talented writers and friends.

ONE

Michaela Bancroft didn't hear her sworn enemy walking up behind her until it was too late.

"Working overtime?" Kirsten Redmond said.

Michaela whipped around in her desk chair, where she'd been sitting for thirty minutes going over finances. She immediately stood up. "What do you want, Kirsten?"

"I know you received some very important papers early this afternoon from our attorney, and I'd like them signed, sealed, and delivered as soon as possible, so that Brad and I can get on with our lives."

Michaela brushed a patch of dirt off her Wrangler Jeans. She'd been working with the horses and out in the barn all day and knew that her appearance wasn't remotely close to Miss Glamour Puss's here. The thought caused a flutter of discomfort. "You amaze me. What, do you have your little hair-sprayed, fake-bake, plastic Barbie doll-looking friends spying on me? Because it truly is a wonder how you know every little detail of my life. Or maybe you're screwing the mailman, too. Does his wife know? What, did he give you a call as soon as he delivered the papers?" She hated sounding so bitchy. God, why couldn't she just turn her back and ignore Kirsten?

"You're such a bitch."

That was why. Not that she *was* a bitch, but Kirsten and Brad had sort of pushed her into that category and she was living up to it, at least at that moment. "Yeah, well, it takes one to know one. Now, be a good girl and run along and play dress up or paint-your-nails with your girlfriends. Okay?"

"At least I *have* friends."

"Oh, that hurt. And, you probably have some real quality conversations with them. You know, about important subjects like what color hat and boots you'll wear to this year's Miss Rodeo Pageant. C'mon, Kirsten, give up the dream. You're a bit too old for the crown and from what I know of rodeo queens, they have a lot more class, know how to ride a horse, and have a brain. Oh yeah, and they're what, usually about five years younger than you are?"

Kirsten frowned. "I was Miss Rodeo of Indio, you know."

"Yeah, five years ago. I think I do remember. Wasn't there some article about the Coachilla Valley being desperate for entrants?" Michaela smiled sweetly, knowing she was getting the best of Kirsten.

Kirsten stomped her foot. "At least I've got Brad and you don't, and as soon as you get those papers taken care of we can start planning our future and I can start thinking about what color to paint our nursery. We want *lots* of children."

"I feel sorry for those kids." Michaela's stomach tightened and she clenched her fists.

"Just sign the papers."

"Just go away. Bye, bye." She waved at her. "Some of us have important things to do."

Kirsten stood her ground, planting her light pink Justin boots into the dirt. Her long blonde hair hung loose down her back, and her overly made-up face caused her to look aged and brittle for someone who couldn't be over twenty-five. She shoved her hands into her plastered-on jeans, belted in by a bright silver belt buckle — her Miss Rodeo Indio silver belt buckle.

"Listen. I've asked you to leave nicely. I don't have time for your games. Trust me, I

11

don't want Brad within fifty feet of me. Why you feel the need to annoy me like this is very confusing. *I've* moved on."

"Great, so you'll sign the papers?"

Michaela sighed and forced a smile. "The papers. Yeah, well see, those divorce papers aren't your concern. It's really between Brad and me."

"Not really. We want to get married. Brad just got a new truck. A Ford F-350. It has a backseat. We got the backseat for when we start having babies. And, trust me, it won't be long."

Anger rose from Michaela's gut and rushed straight to her brain. "As I told you, I don't want Brad back at all. Here's the problem, though: Brad owes me a lot of money from debts incurred by him, and I want that money. When I get it, I will sign the papers. Maybe he should think about returning the truck."

"*I* bought the truck. And, Brad would be able to pay you off on *your* debt if your uncle hadn't fired him."

"That debt is *our* debt, not just mine. And, as for my uncle Lou firing Brad, that was cut and dry: Brad wasn't showing up for work even before Lou discovered what was going on between you two, but once he did and showed me the proof, Brad never even phoned Lou. I don't think my uncle had much of a choice, other than to let him go."

"Whatever. You are so gonna be s.o.l. if you don't make a move quick and sign the paperwork." Kirsten did the hair flick thing, a sign of her disdain for Michaela.

All it did was make Michaela want to laugh. "Let me give it to you in simple speak. Brad is an adulterer, so I will sue him to my heart's content until he pays me back every dime, and something tells me that the judge is going to be on my side. Or, how about this? I just won't sign the papers *ever* and all those babies you're talking about having will automatically have a stepmommy."

"You can't do that!" Kirsten whined.

"Watch me." Michaela was aware that she really couldn't. After all, it was California, and she knew she only had thirty days to sign the papers or contest the decree before she defaulted. She was banking on Little Miss Hot Pants not being exactly well-versed in California state divorce law. But, surely Brad's lawyer was, and no matter how Michaela tried to play it, she'd likely be *forced* to sign those papers. She also knew that she would probably have to sue Brad for what he owed her in medical bills, and rumor had it he was going to file bankruptcy, which meant that she wouldn't ever see a penny from him. The lawyer fees alone in taking Brad to court would put her out of business. She knew Brad was living off Kirsten, so why not sign the papers and be free of him, her, and the whole mess? Because *they'd* stuck it to her and she wasn't about to let them get the best of her. Not yet, anyway.

Kirsten turned on her heel in a huff and marched out. Michaela walked out of her office and peered outside the breezeway, watching Kirsten roar away in her red convertible Mustang GT, kicking up dust all the way along Michaela's drive. Talk about trouble. Michaela shook her head and let out a long sigh. What she'd ever seen in Brad Warren was beyond her, because anyone who could fall for a tramp like Kirsten was not a man she would ever want to be involved with. But she had been, and as Mom always liked to spout the age-old adage, "You made your bed," now she'd have to lie in it.

She turned and headed back to the barn to say her goodnights to all the horses down the row. She stopped at the end — at Leo's stall. Her ten-month-old colt glanced out, then returned to his dinner. Michaela had big plans for the little guy. She'd nurtured him from the night he'd been born last March and for a time it had been touch and go. She hadn't known if he'd make it . . .

The early spring night still had a chill in the air. Michaela held a thermos of coffee in her hand as she curled up on a cot inside her office, checking on her mare every hour or so and listening intently for any sounds that might echo down the breezeway, alerting her that the time had come. Cocoa, her brown Lab, lay at her feet, snoring. Michaela had put a blanket over the aging dog. Usually by this time of night the two of them would be sound asleep in the house.

Her mother, after calling earlier, stopped by and brought her some homemade chicken noodle soup and coffee, aware that Michaela would be keeping vigil into the wee hours. It didn't matter how many foals Michaela had seen born in her thirty-two years. It never ceased to amaze her.

Around 1 a.m., as she drifted off to sleep, a thud woke her. She hurried into the stall. The mare eyed her from her straw bed.

Michaela went inside and knelt down beside her, stroking her face. "I know, girl. It's okay. You're all right. You're all right."

Little Bit let out a groan and lifted her head, groaned again, and laid it back down.

"Easy, easy. You're doing good. Good girl."

The mare's water broke and wet her underside. This was it. Michaela went around to Little Bit's backside. The front hooves came first, and then the long spindly legs, revealing black legs like Little Bit's. Next, a tiny face with a small star on it poked through, and with one final push the foal slid out, slippery and covered in the birthing sac, which with Michaela's assistance came right off. She took a hand towel from her jacket pocket and wiped the foal's nostrils and eyes. The foal struggled, laid back down and struggled again. Michaela wiped the tears from her face. The miracle of life.

Little Bit groaned again and Michaela noticed that she was having a hard time lifting her head to look at her baby. She watched for seconds before she realized what was happening with her mare. A lot of blood — everywhere. Oh God. Wait! This was all wrong. Oh God, no! She was hemorrhaging. Somehow she'd been torn inside during the birth. Michaela pulled her cell from her coat pocket and called Ethan Slater, her vet — and longtime friend. Growing up around horses and being a rancher's daughter, she knew that there wasn't a whole lot she could do, and it was unlikely the vet could either. She was losing too much blood, too fast to get her into surgery, and Michaela cried as she gently stroked Little Bit's face, willing her to live and in some way hoping she was alleviating any pain the old girl felt.

Ethan pulled in fifteen minutes later. But it was too late. Little Bit had died, quietly bleeding out as Michaela held her and whispered to her. When he opened the stall door, he reached his hand out to Michaela and she took it. He pulled her up and hugged her. "I'm sorry, kid. I'm really sorry." He let go after a minute and looked at her with his intense green eyes. "We've got work to do now. She's gone, but *he* has a chance. C'mon. Go to the truck and in the right side of my vet box are packages of Foalac. You'll find a bottle there, too. Get them out and follow the mixing directions. I'm going to move him, so you don't have to see her like this. Okay? Now, go unlock one of the open stalls and slide the door for me."

Michaela knew that the timeline they had to get the colt to feed was about one to two hours, but the sooner they could get a grip on things the better, just in case there were further complications where he was concerned. She was so grateful for Ethan's no-

nonsense, methodical ways. She wanted to fall apart. She loved that mare. Hell. Thank god, Ethan knew exactly how to handle the situation *and* her.

She nodded and followed his orders, leaving the stall as he went to pick up the colt, who weighed about seventy pounds. Michaela had lost animals before, but the pain was always just as intense. But she'd never lost a mare this way, and of all her horses, she'd had a real connection with Little Bit. She had an inside joke with herself about how she'd wished for years she was more like her mare, who had no problem at all getting pregnant.

She took the supplemental food and mixed it as Ethan tended to the colt. She brought it back in the large bottle he'd told her to grab. Ethan asked her to set it to the side. "Let's get him up to drink. We don't want him choking." Together they helped the colt get to his feet. Michaela grabbed the bottle and handed it to Ethan, who took it from her and stuck it into the colt's mouth, teasing him a bit at first with it, allowing him to get used to the feeling of the rubber nipple. The baby gummed it, but soon his pink fleshy tongue wrapped around it, and as sucking noises escaped from his mouth, Michaela felt her body relax. She stood on the other side of the colt in case he lost his balance on still-wobbly legs. That night, she resolved to see him through, to see him grow strong and healthy. She'd named him Peppy Leo after his great-grandsire Mr. San Peppy and great-great-grandsire Leo San, both of whom had been huge cutting horse champions, and because her colt was as strong as a lion. And he had *survived.*

"Good night, champ," Michaela said to him. She turned out the breezeway lights and headed toward the house, knowing that in a little more than two years her colt would indeed be a champion. As resolved as she'd been to save him that night ten months earlier, she was just as committed to her vision for him — and herself — now. Kirsten might have taken Brad from her, and the bank might come after her, and who knew what else might happen, but no one could steal her dream from her — the dream she knew would become a reality.

Two

Michaela opened the back door to her ranch-style house, which led into the laundry room. The house, located in Indio, California, amid the Coachella Valley, had been built in the early 80's and was badly in need of an update. Michaela and Brad had bought it with the horse facilities in place a couple of years after they were married, almost a decade ago. Her plans to bring it into the twenty-first century would have to wait until the debts were paid off.

She breathed in deeply. The smell of fabric softener and detergent filled the air. Unbelievable. Camden had actually been doing laundry. Huh. Surprise, surprise. She had come to believe that Camden simply went through clothes until she didn't have any left and then went out and bought more.

Michaela pulled her boots off, not wanting to track mud through the house. Shania Twain's "Whose Bed Have Your Boots Been

Under?" blared from the family room. God, why *that* song?

A little farther away the blender in the kitchen whirled at full throttle, probably mixing the contents of a powerful concoction — tequila, lime-aid, and more tequila. Michaela shook her head as she headed to her room to shower.

Cocoa, who recently had made it to her tenth birthday, lifted her head off her doggie bed and wagged her tail. Michaela bent down and patted the dog's head. "Hey you, you lazy girl. I see how it is, as soon as the sun goes down you hightail it back inside. By the looks of it, I'd say Miss Camden has been letting you dig into the doggie treats again. I'm going to have to scold her." Cocoa just kept on wagging her tail.

Michaela checked her voice mail:

"Hi, sweet pea, it's Uncle Lou. Give me a call back. I was wondering if we could have breakfast in the morning." She smiled. Uncle Lou was definitely one of her most favorite people.

But the smile faded when the next message came on. "Michaela, it's Kirsten. You better sign those papers, or else we're gonna have big problems."

Michaela flipped a finger at the machine. Why did she let that little hooker get to her?

"Ooh look at me, I have fake boobs, collagen lips, lipo on my ass, and I'm Miss Rodeo America," she said out loud, her head bobbing from side to side in an exaggerated fashion.

"News to me."

Michaela spun around to see her best friend and newly acquired roommate, Camden standing, in the doorway, margarita in hand. She tossed back her latest colored locks — flame red — and held out a glass of the concoction. "I gotta tell you that if those are fake boobs, your plastic surgeon did a shitty job, because girlfriend, you're about a B cup. And, for God's sakes who would pay five thou for a measly B cup?"

They both laughed.

"Let me guess: The evil babe who the *shithead* robbed from the cradle has been bugging you again."

"Yep."

Camden held out the margarita. "Drink on me?"

"Nah. Thanks, though. It's been a rough day. The evil babe came by and gave me a piece of her mind. I don't think a margarita will cure this girl's blues."

"No. But a shot will, and I am not taking no for an answer. Now, c'mon." Camden grabbed her hand.

"I need a shower."

"Ten minutes more won't hurt. If I can stand you smelling like a horse, then you can wait. Live a little, and don't let this stuff get you down. You'll be old before you know it and then you'll be dead and you'll be saying, 'Damn I should have had more tequila shots with my best friend.' "

She held up her hands, palms out. "Fine, I give up. I know better than to argue with you. Besides, maybe you do have a point." She followed Camden into the kitchen. "But don't you have a date with Kevin tonight?"

"Nope. He's taking clients to dinner. I'll be seeing him tomorrow. He's taking the day off and we're going to spend it together." Michaela frowned, and Camden added, "I know you don't care for him."

"It's not that. I don't know him that well, really. I just didn't like that he was kind of a jerk to my uncle when he wouldn't sell him his property."

"He can be pushy, I admit that, but he backed off when Lou told him he wasn't interested. He's moved on to other projects."

"I know, but be careful, okay? Get to know this one a bit better than the last one before he slips a ring on your finger." Michaela had a right to be concerned that her friend would rush into another relationship. Her recent split from her third husband, Charlie Dawson — a big-time financial advisor — had left her in a lurch. Seems Charlie knew exactly how to work the financials to his benefit and Camden was out on her butt and wound up at Michaela's front door needing a place to stay, until she could find a place of her own to rent or buy. That had been six months ago, and as far as Michaela knew, Camden hadn't done any house shopping as of yet, only man hunting. She kept insisting to Michaela that Charlie would settle with her, because she hadn't signed a prenup, and then she'd get into a new house. But Michaela really didn't care. She enjoyed her friend's company and wild ways, so far removed from her own behavior, but entertaining nonetheless.

"What, you afraid you're gonna be stuck with me forever? That you'll have to install a revolving door for your divorcée friend? Won't happen, worrywart. I'm gonna find me a real man who can take good care of me and me of him. Who knows, it might be Kevin, it might not." She shrugged. "Now, let's have that drink."

Ten minutes turned into twenty and before long an hour had passed and Michaela had filled up on two of Camden's cure-alls, though refusing to down the shot. She didn't think she could handle the booze straight. "You know that SOB has a new truck," Michaela said. "A Ford F-350." She shook her head. "Kirsten tried to tell me that she bought him the truck. Please. Does it say sucker somewhere on my forehead? Jerk probably hid some money away that I didn't know about — maybe he hid some cash in a safety deposit box or under the mattress, or better yet under, his *girlfriend's* mattress. He's such a jerk, and that little trophy he hangs out with is a piece of work." Oh boy, the alcohol was certainly going to her head.

"You know." Camden pointed at her. "It's not like you aren't gorgeous. I don't know why you always say *she's* the trophy. She's no prize. Brad lost the prize and I bet he knows it. Look at you. Oh, and I might add that you have a brain, too. A commodity Kirsten definitely lacks."

They were sitting on the couch in the family room. Camden took her by the shoulders and turned her to face the mirrored wall behind them. "Just *look* at you."

"Oh yeah, look at me. Real prize. I've got horse crap on my jeans, and my hair is pasted to my head from sweat. Yep. I'm a real prize."

"Shut up." Camden stood with her empty margarita glass. "Want another?"

"Nope. I think I've had enough."

As her friend walked into the kitchen to pour herself a refill, Michaela turned back to the mirror. She pulled the rubber band from her blond hair, letting it down, and studied her reflection. Twenty-two was ages ago; well, ten years to be exact. Although her boobs were small, they were still perky, and her hair wasn't bleached blond like a *Playboy* model — or Kirsten the rodeo queen — more of a sandy color, long and thick, too. That was a good thing. But, those damn freckles that the sun liked to exaggerate still gave her that "I'm the cute girl next door" look. At least her eyes were something; she really liked her eyes. They were nice — warm, hazel, garnered-lots-of-compliments eyes. Who needed fake anything, anyway? Botox was rat poison! And plastic boobs could rupture. Yep, *natural* worked just fine. A little more sunscreen and a Miracle Bra, maybe, but the other stuff — forget it, and who could afford it anyway? Damn if she could.

Michaela moved to a barstool at the counter, watching Camden pour some more margarita.

"It would be kind of fun to do something

nasty to him, wouldn't it?" Camden asked.

"Who? Brad?" Michaela shrugged. "Yeah, I suppose it would. I'd love to do something to that stupid new truck of his. I'm sure he loves the thing."

"Ooh, like key it?"

Michaela gave her a look. "Nasty and mean are two different things. I don't know if I could go that far."

"You're a prude."

"Are you calling me a goody two-shoes?"

"If the shoe fits."

"Shut up. Pour me one more of those. Tell you what. Since we're in no shape to drive, I'll carry out a dirty deed to give Brad a nightmare to contend with." Camden rubbed her hands together. "On one condition." Michaela shot her index finger up.

"This is going to be good, isn't it?"

"We've gotta do this on horseback."

"Oh, sister, you expect a lot from a friend. You want me to get up on one of those filthy beasts?"

"Um, Camden, I doubt it would be the first filthy beast you've gotten up on top of."

Camden started to protest, then said, "Okay, you may have a point. So, you're willing to take a chance on putting my drunk ass on one of those animals and venture out in the dark?"

"Yep. Besides, I know you. You're barely buzzed. Me, on the other hand . . . phew, you make a strong drink. I'll put you on Booger. He's push button. I'd put a baby on him and trust him."

"Great. I get to ride a horse named Booger. The fact that I am even doing this is *so* not me."

"Who knows, you may like it."

They took their drinks out to the barn, where Michaela saddled up the horses. "Okay now, come here and give me your left foot." She clasped her hands together.

"What?"

"Put your foot in the stirrup here. Grab the saddle horn here with your left hand, and the back of the seat of the saddle with your right hand and step up in the stirrup and swing your right leg over the rear end of the horse and sit in the saddle."

"God, Michaela, I had no idea I'd have to do a flipping gymnastic stunt."

"Aren't you the girl always bragging about her flexibility?"

Camden sighed. "Fine. Let's do this before I change my mind." Michaela got next to her and helped to give her a boost up. Camden squealed as she swung her leg over and nearly came off on the other side.

Michaela helped her get adjusted. "Oh shit, shit, shit. Get me off. Get me off now!"

"No. Now trust me. Hang on. That's all you have to do. Hang on."

"No shit, Dick Tracy, you think I'm about to let go?"

Michaela grabbed a trash bag filled with the *contents* they needed and put them inside a saddlebag. The saddlebags tied on, Michaela put her left foot in the stirrup and swung her right leg over the mare.

"Showoff," Camden muttered.

They headed over to Brad and Kirsten's place, which was only a couple of miles away. It took some time because Michaela had to keep in mind that Camden hadn't been on a horse more than three or four times in her life. Every time she glanced back to see how she was doing, she could see by the light of the full moon that Camden wore a mask of fear. She tried to make small talk, but Camden was hanging onto poor Booger for dear life. Her hands were both around the reins and saddle horn so tight and from what she could tell it also looked like Camden had poor Booger's girth or mid-section in a vice. It was lucky Booger was exactly what she'd said he was — one mellow fellow — because a horse who wasn't so well broke would have been having a fit with Camden on board.

The lights were on inside Kirsten's house. Was that laughter? Yes it was. Oh, how nice for them. They were having a grand old time.

Kirsten's place was a modest ranch-style home with a few acres of land. There were a couple of horses out in a small pasture. One whinnied at the sight of newcomers.

"Shhh. Shut up," Camden whispered.

Michaela pulled slightly on Macey, her mare's, reins. The mare stopped, as did Booger. "Uh, Cam, they don't understand shut up. Besides, horses whinny at times. They won't think anything of it, even if they can hear what's going on out here. Sounds to me like they're having a party."

"Hmmm. I think you're right. Well, good, because we *are* the party crashers. Still want to go though with it?"

Someone inside cranked the stereo up another notch. It was playing Faith Hill and Tim McGraw singing "It's Your Love." Michaela peered through the front window and saw what looked to be Brad and Kirsten dancing. He had *never* danced with her. Jerk. "Oh yeah, I am so ready." Michaela dismounted and led Macey over to a hitching post next to the pasture. The other horses trotted over. The same noisemaker let out another "How do you do," and Michaela realized that time could be of the essence if he didn't pipe down. After enough whinnies someone would surely take a peek, and she wanted to be certain they were long gone before that happened. She wrapped Macey's reins around the post, and walked over to Camden.

"Okay, you always want to get on and off on the left side, so bring your right foot out and back around, then kick your left foot out of the stirrup — kind of lean over the saddle with your body and basically step down and off."

Camden did as instructed and landed on her butt. "Like that?" she asked, a smirk on her face.

"Not quite. You'll have a second shot at it later though, when we get back home. Now come on, get off your ass. We've got a treasure for Brad."

Michaela retrieved the trash bag and the two of them, quietly and quickly, all the while trying not to giggle at their immature antics, snuck up on Brad's brand-new red Ford F-350. She opened the driver's side door, knowing the moron wouldn't have locked it, sliced open the bag with her pocketknife, and shoved the contents under his seat. Boy, was it was going to be a real pain getting it cleaned out. "Nothing like the aroma of fresh manure to take away from that new car smell."

She tossed the bag down and grabbed Camden's hand as they ran back to their horses. She quickly boosted her friend up, who this time managed much better, and then she got back up on Macey. They rode off, cracking up the whole way home, making Camden loosen up, and actually enjoy riding Booger. Their laughter didn't stop even after they'd put the horses away, got cleaned up, and wound up on the couch with a bag of popcorn in front of the boob tube. "What I wouldn't give to see the look on his face."

"Oh God, I'd love to see him get in that truck and start smelling the smell and then he'll have to get out and when he looks under the seat, he's gonna die," Camden said.

This put them into another fit of gut-wrenching laughter. Yes, as childish as it had been, it did feel really, really good. Facts were that Brad had left for the much younger Kirsten after Michaela had spent the last few years trying to get pregnant. With Brad's support they'd sought out fertility specialists and Michaela had given herself shots daily in the abdomen in hopes of conceiving. She'd gone through the expensive in vitro process twice, and the day she was prepared to go through it again for the third time, Brad's infidelities had been brought to light. Now, there were a stack of bills from doctors on her desk and every time she looked at them, she couldn't help but be reminded of what Brad had done to her. Worse than sticking her with the bills, was his total deceit. But tonight was the first time she didn't feel a ton of anger toward her ex. Funny how a stupid teenage-type prank made her feel a bit better.

Michaela finally made it off the couch and into the shower she hadn't taken all evening. Then, finding Camden sound asleep on the sofa, Cocoa curled up on the floor next to her. Michaela decided to leave the two of them there, covering Camden with a blanket and patting her old dog on her head a good night. As she settled into bed, exhausted, her phone rang. She looked at the clock on her nightstand: a little after eleven. Her stomach sank. What if it was Brad or Kirsten and they'd seen her and Camden? No, caller ID said that it was her uncle.

"Hi, Uncle Lou."

"Hi. I didn't hear back from you tonight. Did you get my message? I thought I'd better check in and make sure you're okay."

"I'm fine. I did get your message. Sorry. I was a little busy."

"No problem, sweet pea. I was only concerned because I know that you've had some rough times this past year."

"Thanks. But I'm fine. Really. In fact, I'm doing, uh, really well." She loved the way he'd called her sweet pea ever since she could remember. Her father always called her pumpkin, and that made her feel good, too, but Daddy also knew how to spank and send her to her room, or ground her when she needed it. She loved him for his sense of fairness. But Uncle Lou was the spoiler. He'd never had any kids of his own, so spoiling Michaela was one of his favorite things. "You want to grab breakfast in the morning with me, right?"

"I do. There are some things I need to talk about with you." He cleared his throat.

"Uncle Lou? Are you okay? You sound . . . I don't know. Tired?"

"I'm fine. Working a lot, that's all. I'm having a hard time unwinding these days for some reason. I'm getting old, and riding the animals every day is starting to wear on me."

"You are not getting old," she said. "Sixty-one is a spring chicken."

They both laughed. "I don't know about that. I'm feeling like a cooked goose. You get to bed now, and I'll see you about seven-thirty over at The Dakota House."

"Ooh, sounds good." Her stomach rumbled just thinking about the yummy breakfasts The Dakota House specialized in, especially considering that all she'd had tonight was a liquid diet. "I can't wait. Sleep well."

"You too, sweet pea."

Michaela hung up the phone. Something in Uncle Lou's voice bothered her. What was it? The sound of exhaustion? At first she thought maybe that was it, but, no. Resignation? Maybe. Defeat? Yeah, it did sound like that, but about what? She yawned. Whatever was eating at Uncle Lou, she resolved to get to the bottom of it tomorrow over a ham and cheese omelet.

THREE

The next day Michaela rose early and handled all of her morning chores before going to meet her uncle for breakfast. She suffered a bit of a headache from last night's fun, but it didn't take long to wear off as she went about feeding the horses and cleaning out the stalls.

Leo came up and nudged her while she changed his bedding, replacing the day-old shavings that had begun to smell like urine with fresh ones that made the air smell like sawdust. "Hi, you," she said. "What's wrong? You're not hungry this morning? You want to play?" She rubbed him on top of his forelock — the piece of mane hanging between his ears and down onto his face. He was such a beautiful animal — bay in color, a dark reddish brown with jet-black stockings going up past his knees, and an almost black mane and tail. He had a smidge of a star, almost like a crescent moon on his face, and his large brown eyes reflected an intelligence Michaela knew was indicative of a winner.

Leo turned back toward his food. She finished up his stall, and went into the office to see what was on tap for the day, after breakfast with Uncle Lou. It looked as if the vet was scheduled to come out and do some routine checks. She wondered if it would be Ethan or his partner. Had Ethan returned from his rafting trip? He'd suddenly taken off over two weeks ago without telling her he was leaving, and she'd been angry with him for it since. Ethan had been staying at her uncle Lou's place for a few months because his fiancé, Summer Mac-Tavish, had broken off their engagement the night before their wedding. After Ethan left on his sudden trip, Michaela's mother mentioned to her that she'd heard he and Lou had had an argument. Michaela asked her uncle about it, but he wouldn't say much, just that they'd had a difference of opinion. It had bugged her since her mother had told her, and she planned to ask him about it if he was back today. She couldn't help but wonder if the argument had been over Summer herself, because Summer was Uncle Lou's accountant. And frankly, Michaela was a bit surprised that Lou had kept

Summer working for him. Especially considering the way Summer left Ethan. Lou had been close with Ethan since Ethan was a kid, and Michaela figured that it probably hurt her friend that the man who really had been the closest thing to a father Ethan had ever known had kept Summer on.

After doing her chores she checked the clock: past seven. Time to go and meet her uncle. Camden wasn't on the couch when she went back inside to change. She must have moved in the middle of the night and made her way to her bed. She decided not to bother her. Camden drank twice as much than Michaela had last night and would probably feel much more the worse for wear this morning.

She beat Uncle Lou to The Dakota House and ordered a cup of coffee. The place smelled so good — a mixture of cinnamon, coffee, and bacon filled the air. She melted back into the vinyl booth and watched people come and go from the restaurant, which was decorated with various Indian "artifacts." Twenty minutes later she started to fidget as there was no sign of her uncle. It wasn't like him to keep her, or anyone for that matter, waiting.

She dialed his cell phone. It went straight to voice mail. She called the house phone.

No answer, only a machine. She waited another fifteen minutes and tried again. Same thing. This was just plain screwy. She paid for her coffee and decided to drive over to her uncle's place to see what was up. He couldn't have forgotten. But maybe he'd simply slept in after his late night. It wasn't like him, but *that* tone in his voice last night hadn't sounded like him either. Had he been drinking? No. He hadn't come off like that. Granted, he liked a drink in the evening, but he was not known to booze it up.

A few minutes later she pulled into the luxury-style Diamond Bar Z, Lou and Cynthia's ranch. There wasn't much activity. Usually Dwayne, their assistant trainer, or Dwayne's cousin Sam, who also helped train, would be out working horses, and their ranch hand Bean — his nickname, because he was as skinny and lanky as a green bean — might be around. That was doubtful though, as Bean was notorious for being late. He was a bit slow. As a kid he'd fallen off a horse onto a rock and suffered a brain injury. Lou had taken him in years ago and given him a job.

Lou's truck was there. Cynthia's Mercedes wasn't. Strange. The big truck and trailer were both gone. Then Michaela remembered that Dwayne and Sam were probably hauling horses out to Vegas for the National Finals Rodeo. If she remembered correctly Uncle Lou said they were planning on pulling out for the rodeo yesterday, around noon. Dwayne competed in calf roping. Her uncle used to be involved in team roping, but with age had slowed down and now busied himself with the training and his responsibilities as the breeding manager. Michaela had made plans to trek over and see the rodeo over the weekend. Dwayne had given her free tickets, which were hard to come by, and Camden, who was going with her, had some connections at The Bellagio, so they were set with a nice room at a great rate. Michaela liked to watch the events; her friend liked to watch the cowboys. It was sure to be an entertaining weekend.

She got out of the truck and was greeted by her uncle's golden retriever, Barn Dog. "Hey, boy. Where is everyone?" She patted the dog, which licked her hand. "Some help you are." She laughed. "What's this? Paint?" She probed Barn Dog's fur near his collar. Maybe creosote. Lou used it to keep some of the horses from chewing on the wood pasture fence.

She headed toward the barn expecting to

find her uncle there. Maybe one of the horses was sick. "Uncle Lou?" Her voice echoed through the breezeway. No Lou, but she did get a few whinnies as horses popped their heads out. None of them were eating. She looked at her watch. After eight. They hadn't been fed? Lou always fed them. Even though he had hired help, it was something he'd done for years. "Lou? It's me, Mickey."

She heard Loco pawing the ground in the last stall. Uncle Lou kept his multichampion cutting stallion a few stalls away from the other animals. Although a good stallion, he was still a stud, and he did have a mind of his own. A gorgeous blue roan in color, Loco came from great bloodlines and had earned almost almost three hundred thousand dollars in winnings. The horse was truly her uncle's joy in life.

"Hi, big guy," she said as she approached the stall. He lifted his head and snorted, his eyes wild. "Hey. What's wrong?" He was acting really off. His coat gleamed with sweat. And . . . what was that smell? Not horse sweat, but rather coppery. What the *hell* was that? She wrinkled up her nose. Was one of the mares in season? She doubted it. Lou knew better than to keep a mare in season in the same corridor as the stud. "Loco, what is . . ." Her voice faded as she peered into his stall. She stumbled back and grabbed hold of the stall's bars to keep from falling. Bile burned her throat. She swallowed hard and blinked several times. *"No, no, no!"*

The latch on Loco's door was undone; she whipped it open. The stallion bolted past her and out of the breezeway. She ran over to her uncle, who lay facedown in the straw — impaled on a broken pitchfork sticking through his back. She lifted his hand — cold. Her own hands shook uncontrollably as she dropped his to the ground. A scream caught in the back of her throat. She gasped and fell into the straw, pushing herself away from Lou. She brought her hands to her face, her voice catching up with her anguish as her horrified scream echoed through the breezeway.

FOUR

Uncle Lou was dead. Michaela's hands hadn't stopped shaking over the last hour since finding him, and the trembling had spread through her body. Even though the morning sun hit her face, she'd never felt so cold in her life. Would she ever be warm again? Would her stomach, all knotted, ever stop feeling like she wanted to throw up? Doubtful, after what she'd seen. She figured that her eyes were red and swollen from crying so hard.

This could not be happening. It could not be true. Why would someone do this?

She wiped the tears from her face and watched from the porch as more police pulled into the ranch. After she'd made the 911 call, a cruiser showed up, and within minutes was followed by detectives. A CSI team was now there, and the coroner was on the way. All sorts of people swarmed the property, taking photos, collecting evidence.

She'd been instructed by one of the officers to wait on the porch; someone would be over to speak with her. The poor horses in the barn were going nuts with all the commotion. Their whinnies resounded across the ranch, and they had to be starving. Michaela cringed listening to their distress, rested her face in her palms and sobbed. Again, the thoughts of who could've done something like this — *and, furthermore, why?* — raced through her mind.

"Miss Bancroft, would you like some coffee?"

Michaela looked up and squinted, blinded by the sunlight, to see one of the officers standing over her. He held out a foam cup. She took it from him, nearly spilling it, wrapping both hands around it to try and stop them from shaking.

The cop sat down next to her. "I'm Detective Jude Davis. I'd like to ask you a few questions."

She nodded.

He pulled out a small notepad and pen from inside his tweed sports jacket. "Your call came in around quarter after eight this morning. What time would you say you got here?"

"About five minutes before that."

"Did you notice anything unusual?"

"I noticed it was quiet." She set the coffee next to her on the step and took a tissue from her pocket. "I'm sorry," she said and sniffled, trying hard to keep from crying again.

"I understand. You say it was *quiet*." The sunlight caught his blue eyes, causing him to squint. He took a pair of sunglasses from his pocket. "Can you tell me what you mean by that?"

"Yes . . ." She paused. "Okay." She was having a difficult time finding words. This wasn't a conversation she could accept, much less even believe she was part of. "Usually in the morning there's a lot of activity with animals being fed. Sometimes my uncle might be on the tractor cutting grass or in the arena working with a horse."

"That's not what you found this morning?"

"No."

"What brought you here in the first place?" He raked his hand through his wavy blond hair.

She explained what led up to her finding Uncle Lou.

"Do you know anything yet? What happened?" she asked, as he continued writing in his notepad.

"We don't."

She shook her head. "I can't believe it. I don't know why . . ." She raised her soggy tissue. He pulled a clean one from his khaki slacks. She tried to force a smile, but instead broke down again. She realized Cynthia was not there and through her sobs she asked, "Do you know where his wife is?"

"Yes. We were able to locate her at the gym. She's on her way back here now."

"God, poor Cyn."

"You were close with your aunt and uncle?"

"I see them all the time. I'm usually over once a week for dinner. I help Cynthia prepare it and my folks join us, too. Uncle Lou stops by my place quite a bit." Michaela took a hasty sip from the coffee.

"And his wife . . . Cynthia? I take it since you don't refer to her as your aunt that she is a second wife?"

"Yes. They've been married for several years now. My aunt Rose died over ten years ago from breast cancer and my uncle met Cynthia a year or so later."

"Uh-huh. Were they having any problems that you knew about?"

"Oh, no. Cyn loved my uncle, and he worshiped her."

"Is this Mrs. Bancroft? Your aunt, or I mean, Cynthia?" He pulled a small photo

inside a small plastic bag, marked EVI-
DENCE

"Yes, it is. Where did you get that picture?"

"It was in your uncle's wallet, which we
found in the corner of the stall near him."

"Oh." Michaela didn't know what else to
say. "Do you know if there is anything missing? Maybe someone was trying to rob him
and it went bad?"

"I can't determine that as of yet. I'm not
certain what all he carried in his wallet. I
can say it does look fairly intact, though.
There was some cash and credit cards. We
won't rule out anything, though."

She nodded. It would be difficult to
believe that someone would try and rob
Uncle Lou while working on his ranch. A
random robbery didn't fit well for her
either, and she could sense that Detective
Davis reflected that thought.

"She's much younger than your uncle,
isn't she? Your aunt? Cynthia Bancroft."

Michaela hesitated before answering. She
could see where Detective Davis might be
headed with this line of questioning, but he
had it all wrong. Cyn really *did* love Uncle
Lou. Sure, her own family had wondered
when Lou had introduced all of them to
her and learned that she was twenty-five
years younger, but over time it was easy to

see that she loved him dearly, that she was good-hearted and down to earth. "Yes, that's true. She's only a few years older than me. Why? What does that have to do with anything?" She set her cup down and crossed her arms.

"Ms. Bancroft, I have a job to do. I have to ask these questions. I know the timing isn't great, but it's necessary."

Michaela shrugged. "They didn't have any problems that I knew of." She thought briefly about the conversation she'd had the night before with Uncle Lou — the way he'd sounded. She'd meant to get to the bottom of it today. Were he and Cyn having some type of problem, or did he *know* that someone wanted him dead?

"Are there others who work here?"

She nodded. "Dwayne Yamaguchi is the head trainer and is assisted by his cousin Sam, but the truck and trailer are gone. I assume they took horses over to Las Vegas, probably yesterday."

"Why would he do that?"

"The National Finals Rodeo begins this weekend and Dwayne will be competing. I think the guys planned on heading out yesterday, and Bean would be the one sort of running things here with my uncle."

"Bean?"

"I don't know his real name. He's a tall skinny guy."

"What does he do here?"

"He's kind of a caretaker and ranch hand, helps out where he's needed."

"You haven't seen him around this morning?"

"No. I'm not surprised though. He's, um, well, he has some mental problems."

"What do you mean mental problems, exactly?"

"Well, it's not like he's crazed or dangerous. He's a bit slow. He had a head injury as a kid. In fact, he really acts like a child in a lot of ways."

"Why did your uncle keep him around then?"

"Bean is good with the animals. He's very conscientious about them and he looked up to my uncle, kind of like an older brother. I think he's probably not too much younger than my uncle."

"Do you know where he lives?"

"No. I don't. Cynthia might know."

"All right. Thanks. Anyone else work here that you can give me some information on?"

Michaela sighed. "Well, Summer MacTavish does the books for my uncle. She's the ranch accountant, but she's not here daily. I believe she comes in once a week to do payroll and accounts receivable. I'm really not certain of her schedule."

Another cruiser pulled up. Michaela saw Cynthia in the back.

When it stopped she got out and came running to Michaela. "What happened? They said . . . they said that it's Lou. That he's . . . Is he, Michaela? *Is Lou . . . ?* Did someone . . ." she cried. Her taut face lacked its usual olive glow, now appearing almost alabaster against her brunette hair.

Michaela's stomach twisted and she closed her eyes, hoping the words would come. Instead, she wrapped her arms around Cynthia. "I'm sorry, I'm so sorry," she whispered.

Wracking sobs overtook Cynthia and Michaela couldn't contain her sadness any longer. They held each other for long moments and cried. Michaela didn't want to let go. Maybe if they stayed like this, she'd wake up and it would all turn out to be a nightmare. It had to be that — some horrible dream — or a joke. She felt Cyn waver and start to lose ground. The detective took her elbow.

"Mrs. Bancroft, why don't you come sit down inside the house and we can talk."

A shrill whinny sailed through the wind. "Oh, God. Loco," Michaela said.

"Loco?" Davis asked.

"My husband's stallion. He's out? Oh no! You have to get him!" Cyn wailed.

"He ran out when I opened the stall, when I saw . . ."

"You found him? *You* found Lou?" Cyn stared at Michaela in disbelief.

"Ms. Bancroft, why don't you see if you can find the horse? I'm going to take Mrs. Bancroft inside. There are a few more questions I need to ask."

"No. I'm going with her. I have to go with you, Cyn. You can't be alone right now."

Cynthia shook her head. "Go, please. Lou would be . . ." She sucked in a deep breath. "He'd be devastated if something happened to Loco. Please Mick, find the horse."

She could see the pleading in Cyn's brown eyes and knew she was right about Lou. He'd loved that animal probably as much as he loved anything in the world. Still, it tore at her heart to leave Cyn in the hands of the police, with no one to comfort her. Loco whinnied again in the distance. She had to go and find him. He might hurt himself.

The detective escorted Cyn into the house. Michaela turned and set out to find the horse, avoiding the many officers doing their job. She started for the tack room but thought twice. She didn't want to disturb what the officers were doing, and more than that she couldn't bear to see Uncle Lou again. She doubted that the police would allow her through anyway.

She went to her truck, knowing she had a halter and lead rope in the back, one of those things she always carried. She then approached the house, realizing there was no way she'd be able to capture Loco without some type of handout. She opened the front door. How many days had she entered this house and found Uncle Lou in his den reading the paper or having a whiskey sour, his favorite drink? Today, even though she knew that Detective Davis and Cyn were inside, an eerie silence and a pressure pervaded the air. A heaviness that she'd never sensed before. This place had always felt like a second home to her. Today it just felt empty — a balloon filled with sadness, ready to burst.

She found the cop seated at the kitchen table and saw Cynthia standing over the sink, vomiting. She placed a hand on Cyn's back, rubbing it. After a minute, the woman splashed water on her face, then turned and faced her. "Did you find Loco?"

"I haven't had a chance yet."

"You have to find him. You know that Lou

would be beside himself."

"I know. I came in to get some carrots and see if I couldn't lure him back."

"In the fridge."

Michaela went to the crisper and took out a bag of carrots. She turned again to find Cyn back over the sink.

Davis motioned for her to follow him to the front door, where he said, "She's very distraught, obviously. I'll be here for a bit and I still have some more questions to ask you. We have a lot of work to do. I've got all of your information I think, so if it's fine by you, I'll come by your home so we can talk."

"Of course." She left the house and went to track Loco.

She spied him near the back pasture. He stood outside the fence with a mare butted up to him. Both horses were going crazy, stomping their feet, pawing at the ground and squealing at each other. Loco put all his weight into the fence, trying to break through. This was not going to be easy.

She held out a carrot to him. He sniffed it, snorted, and tossed his head about. The mare arched her neck, reaching for the carrot. Michaela waved her arms at the mare and made a hissing sound to chase her off. If she could get her out of the picture it might be easier to get Loco. The mare pranced about five steps away, tail in the air, and then came back. She flung her arms again. This time the horse took off down the fence, Loco close behind. The scenario went on for several more minutes until Michaela got smart, caught the mare first and led her back to the breeding arena.

She then put to practice the technique she'd learned from both her dad and uncle — called patience. For several minutes she stood ten or so feet away from the stud. He finally became curious about the handout she had offered and slowly came toward her until he got close enough for her to slide the halter over his face. Patience and persistence paid off — virtues both Dad and Uncle Lou repeated to her time and again.

It was difficult to lead Loco because he knew the mare wasn't too far away. She could've used a chain right about then, to have laced through the halter — it would've helped to control his unruliness. He pulled on Michaela, who felt as if all the strength had gone out of her: despair taking hold and not letting go.

They made it down to a set of corrals, but a mare and foal were too close by and she knew they'd have to be moved. She released Loco into the corral, not having any other choice, then went about maneuvering the mare and foal out into the pasture. She hoped she'd be able to get a hold of Bean and tell him to get to the ranch ASAP, because Cyn couldn't take care of the horses. If she couldn't reach him, she'd have to come back over that evening, put all of the horses back where they belonged and feed them.

After making sure the animals were okay, she walked to her truck. Bean stood there leaning against Uncle Lou's old green Chevy work truck, which she knew he allowed Bean to drive just around the ranch. He didn't look well at all.

"Um, hello, Miss Michaela. A policeman told me I had to stay right here because something bad happened to Mr. Lou. What happened? Do you know what happened?" He wrung his hands. "Why are the policemans here? What happened to Mr. Lou? I got here and they were here. The police. They would not tell me where Mr. Lou is and they won't tell me where Mrs. Lou is either. Do you hear that?" He pointed to the barn. "The horses keep crying and they sound hungry. I want to feed them. Where is Mr. Lou?"

She reached out and touched his shoulder. He shrank away from the contact. "Bean, Lou had to go to Heaven today and he's not coming back." She nearly choked on her own words.

"Why did he go there?"

"Listen, I know this will be hard for you to understand, but Lou won't be back. Heaven isn't a place where we go on vacation. It's a place where we go when . . ." She bit the side of her lip, then sighed and finished what she was saying, "We die. Heaven is a place where we go when we die, and Lou died this morning."

"I don't believe you." Tears sprung up in Bean's eyes as Michaela recognized that he realized she was telling him the truth. "I want him to come back."

"I know. Me, too."

He wiped sweat from his graying brow. Bean was probably about fifty but looked a lot older. Hard years in the sun had weathered him with deep crevices on his face, and what hair was left on his head was completely gray.

Someone cleared his throat behind her. "Ms. Bancroft?"

She turned around to see Detective Davis. "Yes?"

"I need to speak with Bean here, now. I'll be in touch shortly. You can go on home. Mrs. Bancroft is resting, so I'll be stopping by your place or giving you a call in the next few hours."

"Sure. Okay. Bean if you need anything, please ask me."

Bean didn't respond, but rather stared blankly, tears still streaming down his face. She didn't know if he was going to be all right.

As she pulled out of the ranch she looked in her rearview mirror to see a distraught-looking Bean talking with the cop. She prayed Davis would go easy on him.

By the time she made it out onto the road, her tears flowed freely again. She sucked in a breath and drove to her parents' house. They had to be told.

FIVE

Michaela's parents lived fifteen minutes away. She drove down the long gravel road bordered by barbed wire fence on either side, and overgrown grass and weeds swaying in the early winter breeze. Everything had begun to turn the color of straw, giving it an almost cold, desolate feel. The house she'd grown up in came into view — a cozy stone cottage style — nothing special to most, but to her it was still home. She noticed a piece of the fence was down and figured her dad must have been out mending it earlier because his materials lay across the driveway.

She stepped out of her truck and wrapped her arms tighter around herself as the wind picked up and bit through her, bringing with it the smells of fresh-cut hay and earth, chilling her further with the reality setting in that she was alive and Uncle Lou was not.

Her folks obviously hadn't heard her coming, because as she neared the house she could hear them through the kitchen screen. Her father was yelling, something he didn't do often. Michaela's body tensed. She couldn't hear what they were saying. Could the police have already called? No, her father was definitely hollering at her mother.

". . . dammit, Janie. My holier than thou brother is not always right, you know." She heard her dad say as she opened the door. They stood in the circa 1975 family room with flowered velvet sofas and oversized table lamps on oak end tables set on avocado green shag carpet. Mom with her hands on her hips, Dad with his arms locked across his chest. They turned when they saw her.

"Michaela?" her mother said concern in her voice. She always knew when something wasn't right with her daughter. "What is it?"

Her father, Benjamin Bancroft, uncrossed his arms, the angry flush of red draining from his face, and hurried to her. "You've been crying. What in the world is wrong?"

"I need to talk to both of you. Sit down, please."

Dad's eyes widened. Michaela noticed that his hand was bandaged. "What happened?"

"Oh, I hurt it this morning, working on a section of the fence. It needed new barbed wire."

"Looks bad," she replied, seeing some blood stain the bandage.

"No. I'm fine."

"What is it, honey?" her mother asked. "What's troubling you?"

"Sit down, please." Taking a deep breath, she told her parents everything. Apparently the police had not yet informed them. Her mother cried in disbelief. Her dad just sat there, stunned. No tears, nothing.

Finally he asked, "What about Cynthia? How is she?"

"Not well."

"I'm going over there."

"Maybe you should wait, Dad. The police are investigating and to be honest, I don't think us being around is such a good idea."

He looked down at his injured hand and rubbed it. "No matter. I'm going."

"I am, too," Janie Bancroft sobbed.

"No. Wait here," her husband said.

"Benjamin, you won't tell me what to do."

"I'm going, too," Michaela insisted. She looked at her father's hand again. "Dad, that thing is pretty bloody. You sure you're okay?"

He nodded, looked down at his hand and back up at her.

"Go change the bandages, Benjamin. A few minutes won't matter," his wife said.

That was Mom — practical, devoted, and deeply religious. Michaela knew how her mother would get through this: the way she did with every upheaval in her life, through her faith. It always awed Michaela, but Janie Bancroft had to be the strongest woman she knew, and this family would need that strength right now.

Michaela watched her father disappear down the hall to do as he'd been told.

Her cell phone rang. Janie was grabbing her sweater from the front hall closet. Michaela was shocked to hear Ethan Slater's voice on the other end. She'd forgotten that a vet was coming to her place that morning for a routine visit. Ethan had obviously returned from his trip and was on call.

"I know you're obviously out and about, but I think you may want to get back over here, Mick."

"What? Why?"

"It's Leo, kid. He's colicing and I need some help with him. I've shot him with Banamine and now I need to oil him."

"Oh, no. I'll be right there." She hung up and told her mother what had happened.

"Go, honey. There's nothing you can do right now. Your father and I need time anyway, and we need to get ourselves over to Lou's, see what happened, what we can do. I think it best if you take care of the colt."

"Oh, Mom."

"Go. I'll call you if we need anything."

Michaela hugged her and headed home. God only knew what else might be in store. She was all cried out at this point. Her mind whirled in a mixture of total confusion: her beloved uncle lay dead — murdered — in his prize stallion's stall, Ethan was keeping something from her — she knew that because of his abrupt disappearance on his rafting trip — her parents were fighting, and if she didn't know better, her dad seemingly *also* had something to hide. She could have sworn he'd been lying about how he'd hurt his hand. Benjamin Bancroft never was a good liar, and her intuition said that he hadn't told her the truth about his injury. *Why?*

And now Leo was colicing. This could be bad. Michaela knew that colic was one of the leading causes of premature deaths in domesticated horses. It presented itself as abdominal pain and usually manifested from some type of impaction in the intestine. If Ethan hadn't come by, then chances were that Leo would be gone now. Catching colic in the early stages was one of the only chances for a horse to survive. Hopefully Ethan had caught it soon enough. She didn't want to think about losing her baby right now.

Ethan had already started medicating him, but oiling the colt would not be pleasant. Michaela knew she'd have to help Ethan get a tube down into Leo's stomach. Hopefully the oil would cause the impaction to move through his intestines.

She pulled up next to Ethan's truck and got out. He was in the stall with the colt. "Hi," he said. "I'm sorry to have to track you down. I've kept him on his feet and had him walking. I don't think he's been down too much."

That was a relief. If Leo had had much of a chance to lie down, he probably would have started rolling, twisting his intestine, and that would mean a costly surgery that was not always very successful.

"The Banamine should be kicking in," he said. Michaela knew from growing up with Ethan — who'd always wanted to be a vet — and helping him study for his finals during vet school, that Banamine was used to help alleviate the pain. "I was thinking I could give him a little ACE to ease him further while we tube him, but he's got a good nature about him and I don't think he'll give us too much grief."

Michaela nodded and took the lead line. She faced Leo, holding the rope tightly under his chin, lifting his nose in the air. Ethan began to slide the plastic tube up into one of his nostrils and down his throat. Leo stomped the ground and tried to shake his head, but Michaela kept a tight grip on him. Once the tube was down into his intestinal tract, Ethan was able to pump the oil through. Leo didn't put up much of a stink. After finishing with the tube, they took him out of the stall and walked him around for some time to keep him from lying down to roll.

"I think we caught it in time. Good thing. He's a beautiful animal, Mick, and I know what he means to you." She nodded; her face grew taut and she felt the tears starting again. "Hey, hey, it's going to be okay. He'll be fine. We just have to keep a watch on him, but like I said, it looks like we caught it just in time. So relax now, okay? Let's get him in the stall and see if he'll eat some bran."

Michaela couldn't respond. Ethan put Leo

back as she got a small bucket of bran for him. She poured it into his feeder; he started to eat it.

"See, look at that."

Michaela choked back the grief tightening her chest. Ethan put a hand on her shoulder. For the first time since she'd arrived back at her place, she really looked at him. Green eyes, sun-kissed, sculpted cheekbones, a crooked nose — due to a kick from an angry horse — faced her.

"What is it, Mick? What's wrong?"

She covered her eyes. Her body started that uncontrollable shaking again.

"Mick, you're scaring me. What the hell is it? Is it your dad?" She shook her head. "Brad? Is he giving you grief again? I can talk to him and make him leave you alone. Believe *me,* I'd get some pleasure out of doing that."

"Lou was . . . murdered this morning!" She blurted it out and as she did, the impact of the reality hit her hard. Her knees buckled.

Ethan held onto her. "Oh, my God. Oh, my *God.* Mick, no, no . . . Jesus, how, who . . . what in the hell?"

Sobs wracked her body as she shook in his arms, unable to speak. When she finally did she could only tell him what little facts she knew.

"*You* found him?" he asked, stunned.

She nodded.

"Ah, Mick. God, I wish I could do something. I'm sorry. I'm really sorry. I don't know what to say. Is there *anything* I can do?"

"No." She pulled away from him. "There's not."

"I can't believe it. Oh, man." He shook his head. "I was by there yesterday to talk to him."

"You were? Why?"

"I needed to talk to him about something."

Tears running down her face, she crossed her arms. "Ethan, why did you go on the rafting trip without saying anything to me? Why did you leave Lou's ranch? Did he kick you off?"

Ethan sighed. "Let's not go into this now. You need me, I'm here, and learning this is like getting sucker-punched."

She saw his eyes water. He turned away. "I'm sorry. The last thing I want to know is that you two had a fight, but you have to tell me. What was going on between you and my uncle? I asked him after you left and he wouldn't tell me either. When I spoke with him last night, something seemed to be troubling him, and now, knowing you went there, I have to wonder if it was *you* on his mind, and if so, why."

"Wait a minute, you think I could have something to do with this? With Lou being killed?"

"Of . . . course not."

"Why the interrogation, then? I didn't hurt Lou. He treated me like a son and I loved him." Emotion caught in his throat. "I would've never hurt that man, and just because we had differences between us doesn't mean a damn thing." His voice rose. "It's true we've been best friends since we were kids, Michaela, but I don't tell you *everything.* What Lou and I had between us needs to be kept there for now. Leave it alone and trust me. I wouldn't hurt him *or* you. For God's sake, don't you know me better than that?"

Michaela took another step back. She *thought* she knew him, but there was a rage combined now with a pain in his eyes she'd never seen before. Her body ached. She closed her eyes. He pulled her into him again. "Trust me, *please.* I can't tell you what happened. Not yet. When I can, I will."

She shrugged him off. "Fine."

Ethan's pager beeped. He read the number. "It's the hospital." He went to his truck and called in. A minute later he came back. "I've gotta head over there. I did emergency surgery on a mare this morning and now there's a problem. I'll be back to check on Leo . . . and *you.*"

"We'll be fine."

Michaela went back into Leo's stall and stayed with him long after she'd heard Ethan drive away. She wondered where he was staying these days.

She finally made it inside the house. Camden wasn't home. No telling when she'd left or where she'd gone. Probably a spa day or shopping spree. In a way it was good she wasn't around. Michaela wanted some solitude. When Camden did show up, she knew she'd have to relay the horrific events all over again, and she wasn't sure if she was up to it. At the moment numbness had set in — thinking or feeling just seemed too damn hard. The energy to retell the events of this morning would be too much to bear right now.

She took a long hot shower, pulled on a sweater, and as the sun began to set she poured herself a glass of wine. She turned on the TV to try and take her mind off of what had happened, but it was all right there on the news. An attractive local newscaster relayed the story of how Lou

Bancroft, well-known rancher, had been found murdered at his ranch that morning. A pitchfork stabbed through his back. Oh no. That was the last thing she wanted to hear or see. She turned the TV off and tossed the remote.

Those were not the images she wanted to remember her uncle by. What she wanted was to hold his hand again, like she had so many times when she was a child. He had great hands — tough, strong, dependable. When she'd been little and he'd taken her to horse shows or the county fair he'd held her hand tight, letting her know that he was going to make sure she remained at his side. Aunt Rose would tell him to relax, that no one was gonna steal little Mickey, but Uncle Lou would guffaw at that remark and he'd say, "You're right, Rose, because I'm hanging onto the kid!"

She wiped her tears away and finished off the wine. Time to head back out and check on Leo. She urged Cocoa to come along with her.

At the barn, Michaela peered in on the horses before going to get another bucket of bran for Leo. She unlocked the tack room door and stopped. Leaning against the frame was the pitchfork she used for changing straw. She gasped when she saw it, her mind flashing back to Lou, the broken-off pitchfork sticking out of his back. It was like a stab in her heart. The tightness in her stomach came back and she felt woozy, her thoughts spinning with the memory.

Her stallion Rocky whinnied and brought her back to reality. Thank God. *Don't think about that, not now. Stay focused. Do what you need to do.* She went inside the tack and feed room. Scents of grain, saddle soap, and leather wafted through the air, and she breathed them in. She opened the can where she kept the bran. *Dammit.* Empty. She'd made a mental note earlier when she and Ethan had given Leo some, to go down to the feed store and get another bag of it. Maybe there was some in the trailer.

"Come on, Cocoa." Her dog stood her ground. The hair on Cocoa's neck rose as she seemed fixated on something at the other end of the breezeway. "You are such a silly old girl," Michaela told her. At times Cocoa could behave like an old woman who has had too much gin — brave and stupid, as if she needed to pick a fight with some- one. "It's probably a rabbit. Let's go. C'mon." Cocoa growled. "For God's sake, come on." She patted the side of her leg, and the dog finally fell in line as they walked over to the garage, where she'd parked the horse trailer. She found a half a bag of bran up in the storage area. Good. She'd drag it over to the barn in the morning. For now she scooped out a half a bucket's worth and walked back to the barn.

She poured it into Leo's feeder and watched him eat. After he finished she took him for a short walk. She headed back to the tack room to get the blankets out and put them on the horses for the evening.

At the door of the tack room, she stopped. Something was wrong here. She stepped back. Her pulse raced and her heart beat madly against her chest as she realized that the pitchfork, which had been there only an hour earlier, was now gone.

Six

The barn spun in a mixture of browns and beiges. Michaela braced herself against the tack room door and tried to regain her composure. Think, *think.* Her hands shaking, she reached for the phone and started to dial 911, but what the hell would she say? *"My pitchfork has been moved?"* Maybe she could tell them someone broke into her place. *No.* That wasn't necessarily true, but someone *had* moved the pitchfork. She hung up the phone, yelled for Cocoa who dragged herself in, closed and locked the tack room door, then dialed the number to the police station and asked for Detective Davis. When she told him what had happened, he assured her he'd be right over, and to stay put. She hung up the phone and waited, looking at Cocoa, and for a brief moment she wished she had a Doberman instead of a Lab. Especially when she thought she heard something. There it was again. *Shit.* Someone was walking down the breezeway. One of the horses whinnied. Michaela looked around for a weapon. Nothing. Shit, shit, shit. Oh jeez, whoever was there was probably here to, to . . .

"Mick, are you in here?"

She threw open the tack room door and yelled, "Dammit, Ethan, don't you ever do that to me again!"

He stopped. "What are you carrying on about?"

"The pitchfork . . . and then walking down the breezeway. What were you thinking? Are you trying to scare me?" She trembled and her face burned. Here she'd gone and called the cops, and it had only been Ethan all along.

"The pitch . . . Girl, I have no earthly idea what you're talking about. What have you been smoking? I just got here. And since when did bumps in the barn ever put the hairs up on the back of your neck?"

She glared at him. "What do you mean you just got here?"

He looked at his watch. "Uh, well, pretty much just that. I pulled up a few minutes ago. I was coming to check on Leo, the next thing I know you're going psycho chick on me." He put an arm around her. "You okay? I'm sorry, dumb question. Of course you're

73

not okay. You're shaking like a leaf, kid. What is going on?"

She told him what had happened.

"Are you sure?"

"Yes I'm sure. I know what I saw." She backed away and studied him for a second. "You don't believe me."

"No, it's not that. I think you've had a real difficult day and our minds can play all sorts of tricks on us when we're dealing with stressful events."

"Bullshit! It isn't stress. It wasn't my mind playing tricks on me. *That pitchfork was moved.* It was right here" — she smacked the wall — "and now it's not."

"Look, I apologize. I believe you, okay? And, because of that, I'm not letting you stay here alone."

"I'm not alone. I've got Camden."

He shook his head. "She'll do you a helluva lot a good now, won't she? What's she going to do if some maniac comes through your door? Throw a pair of stilettos at him?"

Michaela couldn't help but smile. He had a point. "I got Cocoa here."

"Uh-huh. You'd have better luck with your margarita-drinking, high-heeled, society-wannabe pal at your side than that old girl."

"That's not nice."

He shrugged.

"I don't need you staying here. You'd drive me crazy and Camden would drive you crazy and the next thing you know we'll all be snapping at each other. Not a good idea."

"Stubborn and foolish. That's the way you've always been."

"Look who's talking."

"I'll stay out here in the tack room, keep an eye on the colt, and if any trouble happens to come your way, I'll be within screaming distance. Just be sure to do one of those horror film-types, you know, a Fay Wray scream, and that way I'll know you're not joking."

She had to admit that having Ethan close by would be a comfort. No. She wavered for a second. She'd learned the hard way that men were not dependable. But, Ethan was different. They'd known each other since before they could each ride a bike, much less a horse. Was he really different, though? He was the same man — supposedly her closest pal — who'd taken off less than a month ago on a river-rafting trip without telling her or calling her while away. What had he been up to, alone on that trip?

"You can't sleep in the tack room. It's not exactly comfortable."

"In case you hadn't noticed, I don't need a five-star hotel. I just slept on the ground in a pitched tent for weeks, Mick. I think a cot in the tack room would suffice. Besides, half the time I'm woken up in the middle of the night to take calls."

She started to reply, but the sound of a car door closing sounded outside the barn. Detective Davis entered the breezeway. "Ms. Bancroft?"

"Hello, Detective."

He walked toward them. "Good evening, Mr. Slater."

Michaela glanced at Ethan. Davis must've already spoken with him. Was he a suspect?

Ethan nodded. "Evening." He turned to Michaela. "I'm going to grab a few things, and I'll be back."

"Don't worry about it. You needn't come back. We'll be fine."

"Stubborn." He shook a finger at her. "I *will* be back. If for nothing other than to make sure Leo is doing okay."

"Where is your stuff anyway?" Michaela asked, curious about where Ethan had been staying since he'd returned.

He hesitated. "Summer's place."

Before she could respond, Ethan hurried out. *Summer's* place? His ex-fiancé? The same Summer who stood him up at the altar a few months ago? The one he'd been loyal to and had even gotten her the job at Uncle

Lou's as his accountant? Oh boy, did they have something to discuss when he returned! She'd surely give him a piece of her mind.

"Ms. Bancroft," Davis said. "Do you want to tell me what happened here?"

"It's okay, you can call me Michaela. Why don't we go on into the house?" She rubbed her arms. "I'm cold. I can fix us some tea or coffee."

"That would be fine. But before we do that, you said something about a pitchfork being in one place and then not being there later?"

"That's right. Follow me." She led him to the tack room. "I needed to go over to the horse trailer and see if I had any more bran for my colt, and when I came back the pitchfork, which had been right here, was gone. I did notice my dog seemed to be bothered by something outside the barn. I figured it was a rabbit."

"But the dog didn't bark?"

"No."

Davis nodded. "Okay. Why don't you show me around and we'll see if anything else looks out of place. Let's retrace your path as far as when you first came in to the tack room and spotted the pitchfork."

"Sure." She walked him through everything from the moment she'd entered the barn.

"You've got quite a crew here." He nodded down the aisle of stalls at the horses. The more curious ones peeked their heads out at the newcomer.

"They're my life. Keep me sane. Horses are good for the soul, you know." She'd remembered Uncle Lou often telling her those exact words from the time she was a child. He'd been right. "They're constant. There for you. Always."

"I can see that."

"Do you ride?"

"Me?" He laughed. "Hardly. Once, actually."

"Where was that?"

He stopped for a minute and shoved his hands in his pockets, kind of looking away from her. "Uh, Barbados."

"Barbados?"

"Yeah. One of those expeditions, you know, trail rides."

"But in Barbados?"

He shifted his weight from one foot to the other. "My . . . honeymoon. I was on my honeymoon."

"Oh, right. Honeymoon. How nice."

They walked outside and headed toward the horse trailer about fifty feet away.

Michaela squinted her eyes as they neared, then gasped. "Do you see that?" She reached out to touch the pitchfork leaning against the horse trailer, its metal spikes shining reflectively from a beam of light showering down off the top of the barn.

Davis grabbed her hand. "No. Don't touch it. I need to have it dusted for finger-prints."

"Sorry." She pulled her hand away and for some odd reason felt heat rise to her face, obviously angry over her faux pas. Or was it? For a brief second she couldn't help feel Davis's grip sending something electric through her. She took a step back, suddenly a bit dizzy. Her feelings had nothing to do with Davis, she reassured herself. Instead, it was the realization that somebody had been on her property and had either been play-ing a cruel joke on her, or had intentionally planned to do her harm. Yeah, that's all it was.

Michaela sat down on the step. The sad-ness she'd felt earlier still lingered, but now shared space with an overwhelming sense of fear.

"You okay?" Davis asked, pulling a pair of latex gloves out of his coat pocket.

"Tired. That's all." Michaela noticed, as he slid the gloves over his hands, that he wasn't wearing a wedding ring. Huh? What about that honeymoon in Barbados . . . ? Lord! What was wrong with her? Why in the world did she care if this guy was married or not? He was the detective on her uncle's murder case, for heaven's sakes, and now he was checking out a threat on her property.

He bent down next to the pitchfork and picked up a wrapper, holding it up to the light.

"What is it?" Michaela asked.

"A wrapper for chewing tobacco," he replied.

"Chewing tobacco?"

"Yep." He took another small plastic bag from his coat pocket and placed the wrapper in it. "Anyone you know around here chew tobacco?"

"No."

"Maybe Dr. Slater?"

"Definitely not." She stood up.

"Okay. I'll take it with me, too. Doubt it will tell us much, but you never know."

"So where do you think it might have come from?"

She shook her head. "That I don't know. It makes sense that whoever moved the pitchfork might have been the one to leave the tobacco wrapper. But that doesn't seem too smart to throw it down."

"No." He sighed. "But it could have dropped out of someone's pocket and they might not have seen it."

"Makes sense." Michaela felt a shiver run down her spine with the repeat thought that someone might have been watching her from outside the barn while she fed and took care of the horses, waiting for a deliberate moment to do something to spook her. Or, what if that person had planned to do something more than spook her, but had gotten scared when Ethan pulled in? She didn't like this at all. "Do you think whoever was trying to frighten me — which, I assume, is what someone was trying to do — could also be my uncle's murderer?"

"I don't know. But can you think of anyone you and your uncle knew that might have some type of, uh . . . well, is there anyone out there who might want to get even with you for something?"

She sighed and nodded. "Maybe I do. Let me pour you that cup of tea. This might take a while."

SEVEN

Michaela hadn't thought about it until Detective Davis mentioned the possibility of revenge. And, it clicked that maybe there *was* one person out there who wanted to get even with both her and Uncle Lou. The thing was, she knew how this might sound, because she knew exactly how it sounded to herself — not good.

Davis sat at her kitchen table sipping his tea. Camden still wasn't home. Where the heck was she? Must still be out with Kevin Tanner. Hadn't she told her last night they were spending the day together? Looked like day had turned into night. Camden sure was spending a lot of time with him lately.

She sat down across from Davis. He twisted the mug back and forth between his hands. "Good tea."

"Thanks." She took a sip and it warmed her insides. "Here." She opened the top of the cookie jar that sat on the table. "They're not homemade — Oreos. Kind of a vice for me."

He smiled. It was a nice, warm smile. Comforting. "I have a sweet tooth, too. I better not, though. Ms. Bancroft, you said that there was someone who might have something against you and your uncle."

"Please, like I said, you can call me Michaela," she interrupted.

"Okay, Michaela, who are you thinking of?"

She leaned back in the wooden chair. "Possibly my soon-to-be ex-husband."

"Really? Why is that?"

"Brad is a cheat and a liar. Something my uncle Lou always knew and tried to warn me about. But, you know the saying: 'Love is . . .' "

"Blind." He finished the sentence for her.

"Right. Brad and I were married for nine years. We married young. I was right out of college, and there were some good times — a few, maybe." She forced a smile, trying to convince herself of this as much as she was Davis. "But then Brad became really involved in the rodeo circuit."

"Aren't you as well?"

"No. When we were married, I would go to the rodeos, and I still like to go and watch the big National Finals Rodeo held out in

Vegas each year. I did use to run barrels as a kid."

"Run barrels?"

"Sure. It's a blast. Your horse running all out and rounding the barrels in a cloverleaf pattern. You know, barrel racing."

"Oh yeah, yeah. I got it. I've seen that before on TV."

She smiled. "I'm sure you have. Anyway, it's my favorite event to watch at the rodeo. In fact, the NFR starts this weekend, and I'd planned to drive out with my roommate, but now that seems wrong to do, considering what's just happened with my uncle."

Davis shifted in the chair. "I understand. Why would your ex be seeking revenge?"

"Like I said, this might take some time to fill in all the holes."

"I've got time." He leaned back in his chair, his blue eyes trained on her.

"Brad rides bulls. Or he did, anyway."

"A bull rider?"

"Yeah, I know, don't say it. Everyone does; you don't look like the kind of girl who would marry a bull rider."

"The thought crossed my mind."

"Well, when we met, bull riding wasn't his thing. He was more into the working cow horse events. But he got the bug. Someone dared him and the fool took the dare. He

84

started riding broncs, and then onto the bulls because the money was great and he got hooked on the adrenaline rush. It also didn't help that he was good at it. Then, he got hurt, broke his hip, and I nursed him back to health. He had a few surgeries, and although he couldn't compete any longer, because it was too painful, it didn't stop him from wanting to go out on the circuit."

"He enjoyed the lifestyle," Davis suggested.

Michaela nodded. "The problem was, or I should say, *is,* that the money he'd earned, he blew partying on the circuit with his pals. I tried to salvage the marriage. I wanted children."

"He didn't?"

"Brad said that he did, promised me he'd be around more and help me grow my business, and that we could start a family. He tried to convince me that it was good for him to be out and about with his buddies, that they were all spreading the word about what a great trainer I was. Even though I don't train horses for rodeo-type events other than some barrel racing, there is quite a bit of crossover communication in the horse world. Plenty, actually, especially because most of us in this part of the industry ride quarter horses." Davis raised his brow and shrugged, and Michaela continued. "A quarter horse is a really great breed — stocky, athletic, good-natured, they tend to be of sound mind, and intelligent. I guess you could say that they're kind of the Labradors of horses, if that makes sense to you." He nodded. "They're a versatile breed. I love working with them."

"Your ex didn't exactly go around touting you as the brilliant trainer, I take it?"

"No. He was too busy with other things."

"And, you put up with that?"

A wave of shame swept through her. She *had* put up with it. "I did, but in my defense as I said, love is blind, or in this case plain stupid. I wanted to believe him and I really wanted kids. He did get me a couple of clients, and that kept me hooked into thinking that he was sort of a manager — the good husband doing his part to bring in the business. Stupid, I know."

"We all want to believe the best in people, I don't think that's stupid at all." In spite of himself, he took a cookie from the jar, bit into it, and set it down. It left a crumb on the side of his mouth. "You don't have any kids, then?"

"No." She didn't want to go there. It wasn't necessary. He just needed to know the facts, and why Brad would have the need to see her uncle dead . . . maybe even her. She couldn't imagine him actually doing it, but one never really knew a person. And, after nine years with Brad, she'd discovered that she hadn't really known him at all. But Uncle Lou had him pegged from the get-go. Why hadn't she listened to him?

"With Brad out *promoting* me, and me supporting him, my uncle Lou became even more wary of him. He didn't trust him. He never thought he was good enough for me, but he'd kept that to himself after I finally told him to drop it." Michaela took a sip of her tea before going on. Cocoa padded over to her, her tail wagging. She reached down to scratch the dog's head.

"Beautiful dog."

"Thank you. She's an old girl, but like tonight, she's obviously still got it, still alert — sometimes."

"I've got a feeling that your uncle may have stopped talking about your ex, but he did something else to prove his point."

"He did. First, he decided to play by my rules and give Brad the benefit of the doubt. He gave him a job at his ranch, helping out with the artificial insemination program my uncle started a few years ago. But, Brad took advantage of the fact that Uncle Lou was *family,* and it didn't take long before he came and went as he pleased. He also thought the job was beneath him."

"Why is that?"

Michaela felt heat rise to her cheeks. "Well, even though the program Uncle Lou ran was a breeding program, as I said, it was artificial insemination, and someone needed to collect the . . ."

Davis held up his palms. "Say no more. Brad was the collector?"

"Yes, but it's not what you're thinking. It's quite technical. They use dummy mares. It's all very clean, but still," she said, not really wanting to continue.

Thankfully, Davis didn't seem to either. "Right."

"Anyway, Brad was blasé about the job. My uncle grew more suspicious of him and had him followed." Michaela stood, walked over to a drawer in the kitchen, and pulled out a large envelope, which contained photos. She handed them to Davis.

"Brad."

"Yes, and Kirsten Redmond."

Davis thumbed through the prints that Michaela had gone over countless times in the past until she'd finally accepted that it was true: Her husband had cheated on her with Miss Rodeo America. She shut her eyes tight for a second as Davis continued scanning the photos. "I'll burn those after we go to court."

"Your uncle Lou had him followed, this is what came of it, and you divorced Brad. I would assume that Brad also lost his job at the ranch?"

"Yes."

"Do you think Brad wanted to get even with Lou for having him followed, thus causing your breakup?"

"Partly. But Brad did plan to divorce me."

"Then what gives?" Davis patted his leg and Cocoa came over to him. "I like dogs. I've got a Lhaso Apso."

She laughed. "That's not a dog."

"Oh, so you're one of those people who believes a dog is only a dog if it's big and loud. He may not be big, but I assure you he's loud." He grinned.

"I'm kidding. I like all dogs."

"Right. So, what happened with you and your ex?"

"Brad and I had been married nine years like I said. We were three months short of our ten-year anniversary when I filed for divorce."

"Let me guess: You were the breadwinner, and he knew by waiting the full ten years it would make him eligible to receive spousal support for a very long time."

Michaela couldn't help but laugh at the way he'd put it, but yes, that was exactly how she'd felt when one of Brad's ex-cronies told her of his devious plan. The laughter felt good for a moment. How could she laugh today, or any day ever again, for that matter? She'd found Uncle Lou only that morning with a pitchfork through him. She shook her head, hoping to cast that image from her mind. Doubtful that could ever happen. "You know a bit about California divorce laws."

He nodded. "He was banking that he wouldn't get caught cheating, could divorce you after ten years, and you'd be stuck paying spousal support."

"Exactly. But he did get caught, thanks to my uncle, and now it's hopeful a judge will take a look at that and things will go in my favor. Now, he's making all sorts of claims that we were separated while he was out having the time of his life, and that I'd kicked him out. His girlfriend harasses me to no end. She enjoys calling me, insisting that I sign the papers he had some moronic attorney devise. I read over them last night. He wants to settle with me. I love that. Crazy. But the best is we have a pile of medical bills that our insurance refused to pay, and he's basically skipped out on his portion of the obligation. I've even heard he's going to file bankruptcy. So, I'm stuck with that. But, I will hold out signing any type of papers that benefits either one of them."

Davis shook his head. "Did he plan to marry this rodeo queen? If so, the gravy train would have come to a halt, even if he hadn't been caught in the act."

"I don't think so. Brad is greedy. He's the kind of guy who likes his cake and wants to eat it, too. My gut tells me that Kirsten was a fun fling and he never thought I would find out about it. I do think he planned to leave me though, after the ten years was up. Things with us had ceased to be fun, and Brad obviously isn't one with too much depth."

Davis nodded. "I went through a divorce a few years ago."

That explained the no ring on the finger. "Not fun. Do you have children?"

"One. She's nine. My ex and I have joint custody of her."

"That's great. I mean, not great you have to share your daughter like that, or that you're divorced, but that you have a child." She swallowed hard.

"You think that it's possible your ex blames your uncle for everything?"

"I think it's possible."

"I'm going to need to speak with your ex-husband. Can you give me his information?"

"Of course." Michaela stood and went into the kitchen. She took out a pen and paper from her odds-and-ends drawer and wrote down Brad's address and phone numbers, then handed it to Davis. His fingers brushed her hand. On purpose? She didn't think so, but oddly enough — and maybe because she didn't want to be alone — her stomach fluttered at his touch. She tried to ignore it as he stood and shook her hand.

"I know it's been a rough day for you. I'll have a cruiser come by. But you should be safe enough here, especially with Dr. Slater around."

"Oh, no. He's not my boyfriend, if that's what you're thinking. I've known Ethan forever." That sounded brilliant. Why did she feel the need to clarify their relationship to the detective?

Davis nodded. "I thought you'd like to know, we have an officer stationed at your uncle's ranch."

"That's good. Thanks. Um, how is Bean?"

"Mr. Chasen?"

"Is that his last name?"

Davis nodded. "Sylvester Chasen. He's fine. We questioned him and let him go on his way."

"Oh." She wanted to ask Davis more about Bean, but had the distinct feeling he wasn't going to tell her anything.

"I was also able to get a hold of Dwayne Yamaguchi. He's coming back from Vegas tonight to help Mrs. Bancroft out. And, uh, Sylvester, or I mean Bean will be back in the morning to work, I believe. Again, thank you for your time. I'll be in touch."

As he started out the door, Camden breezed in past him and said, "Hello."

He nodded and continued on his way, Camden's eyes following him like a cat toying with a mouse, as he closed the door. She turned and faced Michaela. "Hot damn, look at you, finally moving on. Tell me, I have got to know, who *is* the hottie?"

"You don't really want to know," Michaela replied and burst into tears.

EIGHT

Camden loaned her shoulder to Michaela and after a couple of hours she was all cried out — again. They now sat in silence on the couch.

"I'm sorry, sweetie. I can't imagine what you've been through today, and I'm sorry that I wasn't here for you. I wish you'd called me, I would have boogied back here."

"I know. The day has gone by in a blur. It all seems so surreal. There are moments when it feels like it *didn't* happen, and I actually smiled when that detective was here, but then the reality hits and I feel so horrible. I can't explain it." She lifted her head, and the room spun slightly — the combination of exhaustion and lack of any decent food.

"Who do you think could have done this?" Camden asked.

"I don't know, and I don't know why either. Lou was such a good man. He didn't have it in him to hurt anyone. His gentle hand with the horses, his demeanor . . . You knew him. He was solid, decent." She shook her head. "It makes no sense to me at all."

"He was one of the good guys, Mick. I feel lucky to have known him, although I don't think he ever had much tolerance for me." Camden laughed.

"That's not true. Uncle Lou liked you."

Camden waved a hand at her. "Please, we both know that I am not quite as down to earth as your uncle would have liked, especially for someone in your life."

"Okay, so maybe you were a bit flamboyant for him. But he appreciated you. I know that."

"No matter. I liked him and I know how much he loved you, so we were both on the same page there. But again, who do you think would want him dead?" At that moment a knock at the sliding glass door caused them both to turn. "Ah, Dr. Slater is back in town, huh?" Camden asked. Michaela nodded. "When did he get back?" Michaela shrugged. "I see. Well, better get the door. I'll make myself scarce. You two probably have some talking to do."

Michaela opened the door.

"Hi, Ethan. How was your trip? We missed you around here," Camden said.

"Good. Thanks."

"Did you come to comfort our girl?"

"I did."

"Great. I think she's a bit better. You always seem to have a knack for putting a smile on her face. And, I've probably done all I can for the evening. I'll let you two talk. I think she could still use some company."

Michaela cleared her throat. "Hello, guys, I'm right here. I'm not a kid, you know. I love how much you care, but come on."

Camden rolled her eyes. "There she goes again with that 'I'm-so-tough' act. Don't let her fool you."

"I won't," Ethan replied.

"Night all, and Michaela, if you need me, I'm just down the hall."

"Sorry I'm late," Ethan said. "I checked on Leo a minute ago; looks like things are moving along fine in his gut. I'm pleased, because you know colic can be rough. I wish I could have helped you more today with him," he said, taking a seat in one of Michaela's leather chairs opposite her tan sofa.

"I told you that you didn't need to come back here."

"I know what you told me, but since when do I ever listen to you?"

"Good point." She plopped back down on the couch. "Are you gonna tell me why

Detective Davis was by to talk to you and what had you so upset with Lou?"

"No. Not right now." Ethan rubbed his temples. "Honestly, I can't tell you anything until I find out a few more things myself."

"What the hell are you talking about? You're really starting to irritate me, Ethan."

"Well, you wouldn't be the only woman I've heard that from tonight."

"Oh, no, no, no, do not tell me," Michaela said. She took one look at him and knew. Dammit, the man was a glutton for punishment. "You and Summer?" It all came back to her, Ethan rushing off to his ex-fiancé's house.

He nodded.

She would've shaken him if she'd had the energy. "Tell me, please, that you and Summer are not getting back together. It is *not* what I want to hear. Do you know how bad she is for you? What a *bitch* she was to you? My God, Ethan, she left you the day before your wedding. What are you thinking?"

Ethan took her hand. "Mick, Summer is pregnant."

Nine

"You dumbass. Tell me you're kidding." Michaela shook her head and stared at Ethan to see if he was telling the truth. This was not the time to joke. He looked down, and when he looked back up at her with those green eyes of his, she could see there wasn't any lying going on. Nope, he wasn't yanking her chain. "What were you thinking? Wait a minute, let me rephrase that: What were you thinking *with?* Hmmm? I'll say it again: You are a dumbass."

"I don't need a lecture. I know all of this already. I know everything you're going to say to me."

"Oh, really? What? Isn't Summer the woman who left you high and dry after you saved for a year to give the princess her perfect wedding? She's a user, a loser, and she'll do nothing but hurt you, Ethan . . . Hasn't she done enough already? For all you know she isn't even telling the truth.

You know this woman's MO. She just loves to play you and when she thinks you're over her, she hooks you back like a dumb puppy dog."

"Michaela!"

When she looked at him this time, his eyes were moist. "Like I said, I know all of this. But it's true. She is pregnant. I went with her to the doctor, and I can't . . . I just can't abandon . . ."

She sucked in a breath of air, her mind clouded over with the events of the day, and now Ethan's revelation. She could strangle him. But she softened at the look in his eyes and the words she knew he couldn't express. She took his hand. "Ethan, I know what you were going to say. I do. But look, this isn't about your father. I know you, and if the kid is yours, you will be there and be a great dad. But you don't have to get sucked back into Summer's drama." Ethan had never known his father. His mother had told him that their relationship wasn't long lived and once he found out she was pregnant, he took off. Then, he died in a car accident shortly thereafter. He and Michaela rarely discussed it, but the few times they had, it was obvious the pain Ethan felt from it. He'd once told her that he'd be the kind of dad a kid could count on. He'd always be there for any child he had, and she believed him. But, why did he have to be having a baby with Summer? What a cruel joke.

"I have to stick by her. I would never abandon my child, or Summer in her condition."

Michaela shook her head again. She couldn't take much more of this. "You know, women raise babies on their own all of the time. You can still be the dad. But at least promise me something."

"What?"

"You won't marry her without really thinking about it."

"I agree, Mick. But, I feel like a kid deserves a family. A real family, with his mom and dad together." He put his face in his palms and sighed deeply. "I want to do the right thing, and I was going to marry her before she left me. I don't know. I really don't know right now. She's angry at me anyway for coming back over here to stay the night."

"I'm sure she is. We're not exactly bosom buddies. You need to remember, marriage is for life. At least for someone like you, and I don't want you to be miserable because you made the wrong choice. I . . . care about you." She felt herself slipping and simply didn't want to deal any longer with the horrors of the day. Standing, she brushed off her jeans. "I'm sorry if I was hard on you. It's been . . ."

He wrapped his arms around her. "I know it's been difficult and I'm sorry my timing isn't great. You've always been there for me. It was selfish of me to come to you with this right now."

"That's what friends are for. We have needs during the craziest of times. I suppose it's what makes us human." She glanced up at the clock. Almost ten. "I've got to go to bed. I'm beat."

"I'm going to crash in the tack room. I'd like to be able to keep an eye on Leo."

"You said that he's fine and I think he is. Why don't you head back to Summer's? You said that you were staying there again, right? I mean . . . when you left earlier, you inferred that anyway."

"I've got some stuff there and yes, I've been there off and on since I came home. I stayed at my office last night. But tonight, if it's all right with you, I'll stay here. I think Summer and I both need some space to try and figure things out."

"Of course, but take the couch at least."

"I'll be fine."

"So, at least you haven't set up house yet with her?"

"She wants me to."

I bet she does. Summer knows she had a good thing. "Yeah, well, you can stay here as long as you need to, as long as you promise me you'll think about this thing with her. I'm begging you."

"I told you that I would. I promised. I'll pinky swear if you want."

She laughed, remembering how when they were kids they would always pinky swear on secrets of the utmost importance, like the time they were playing with Ethan's G.I. Joes in Ethan's backyard, and they'd taken a gas can from his mom's garage and dug a trench, placing the figures down in it, pouring the gas into the trench and lighting it on fire. What they hadn't realized was that their fun and games would "backfire," as they just about caused Ethan's house to burn as a *poof* of flame shot out from the fumes and caught one of the trees in the backyard on fire. It had been horrible at the time, and they were questioned by Ethan's mom and her parents but they'd pinky sworn never to tell, and to this day their parents figured they'd done it, but because there was room for doubt on their innocent-looking faces, they hadn't been punished.

"No need to pinky swear. I believe you."

"Thanks for the couch, but I think I'll

camp in the tack room. That way I'll be close to Leo and you won't have to worry. Did that cop find out anything?"

"We found the pitchfork out by the bales of hay . . . and a chewing tobacco wrapper."

"That's odd. Have you hired any help lately? Someone who might chew?"

"Nope. I am an island unto myself. In other words, with the lawyers tying things up between Brad and me, I'm too broke to hire help."

"Well, you know that I'll be here if you need me."

She kissed him on the cheek. Tears stung her eyes as she walked down the hall. She didn't know if the tears were for Lou, the thought that Ethan was about to make the biggest mistake of his life, or for the fact that a manipulative woman like Summer was pregnant, and she was still paying bills to doctors who, no matter what they'd put her through, hadn't been able to make her fertile.

TEN

Michaela slipped out of her jeans and donned a long T-shirt. She brushed her teeth and splashed her face. No time for nightly rituals. She could hear Camden's muffled voice on the phone in the next room.

She picked up her own phone and dialed Lou and Cynthia's number. A man answered. "Oh hi, Michaela. It's Dwayne. Sam and I pulled back onto the ranch not too long ago. I cannot believe this. I plan to stay here with Cynthia until she feels it is okay for me to leave and go back to the rodeo. Bean is here, too."

Dwayne Yamaguchi was one of the best working cow horse trainers around and he'd worked for Lou for almost eight years. He was also quite the calf roper. Not Michaela's favorite rodeo event — maybe it was something about running down the calf and flipping him over and tying his hooves. Although her dad and uncle always told her that it wasn't cruel. Ranchers did it all the time. And, Dwayne was one of the best at his sport.

His cousin Sam, a *paniolo* — a Hawaiian cowboy — had come over from the islands a couple years after Dwayne had joined on with her uncle, to help out temporarily, and wound up never going back. He wasn't the rider that Dwayne was. He carried quite a bit more weight on him than his younger cousin. But from everything Michaela knew about him, Sam did a good job with the horses.

"Thanks, Dwayne, for coming back. Is Cynthia okay?"

"As good as you might expect. You know, she had a terrible blow, losing a loved one. Lou was a good man. Did not deserve this fate. She is resting now."

Michaela could hear him choke back emotion as she felt it rise again in her own throat. "I was hoping to speak to her. But it's good she's sleeping."

"You going to come by in the morning for a coffee, right? Maybe she be up to talking then. I hope I can get back to the horses in a day or so. Lou would want that."

"You're still going to ride?"

There was a pause on the other end. "You

know, Michaela, I run it through my brain the whole drive home about what is right thing to do, or how it looks if I am still in the rodeo. I talk about it with my cousin Sam on the drive and he say to me that Lou was a cowboy. He was a horseman. He did not raise the animals and make investment in them without want of an outcome. He raised champions and I have to go and get a championship again. You know that is what he would have me do. Sam be right. I have to ride."

Dwayne was correct: Uncle Lou had never been a glass-half-empty kind of guy. "You're probably right. Yes, I'll stop by in the morning."

"Good. Get some rest and we will talk tomorrow."

Michaela hung up and turned off the light. She sat in the dark for several minutes, trying to clear her mind of the image of Uncle Lou lying dead on Loco's stall floor. But she couldn't. After a few minutes she decided to get a glass of water.

She passed Camden's room and could hear her still talking. Probably to Kevin. She reached for the doorknob, thinking she'd say goodnight, but before she could turn it, her friend's words came through the door.

". . . with him gone it will be a lot easier acquiring that land. I understand you don't want to look suspicious, but I seriously doubt it. You've been trying to get your hands on that property for a while now. Besides, you don't exactly have a killer instinct. You know how to get people eating out of your hands. It's one of the things I love about you. But we both know just what a killer you are, don't we?" Camden laughed. "Listen, I better go, I need to check on Michaela. Today has been rough on her. Tomorrow night? Yeah. Sure. Well, maybe I should stay home and take care of her. No, she won't want to come. Even when she isn't down in the dumps she's not exactly a party girl. Okay, I'll try. You're right, maybe it would help. Yes, and it would be good if she had a different impression of you. I know. I won't. Okay, sweetie. I'll talk to you tomorrow."

Camden hung up the phone. Michaela hurried back to bed and slid under the covers. A few seconds later she heard her door open. Camden whispered her name and stood over her. She reached out and rubbed Michaela's arm. "Poor kid. Get some rest."

After Camden left she lay awake for quite some time, her friend's conversation playing over and over again in her mind. She *had* been talking to Kevin. The way it sounded, they were talking about it being much easier now for Kevin to get his grubby hands on her uncle's land. Granted, Camden hadn't mentioned her uncle's name, but it made sense. The scenario about the killer instinct, the land being easier to acquire, all of it. Her stomach took a turn for the worse as she couldn't help wondering: Did her best friend have something to do with her uncle's murder?

ELEVEN

Ethan was gone by the time Michaela made it out to the barn the next morning, but he'd fed the horses and left her a note that said he'd stop by later on or give her a call. She knew she'd been hard on him the night before, but she wanted to protect him from getting hurt again — if that was at all possible.

She decided to head over and check on Cynthia, but first she needed to stop by her parents' place. They hadn't called last night, and she'd figured that maybe they had been so caught up in their own grief that they couldn't muster the energy. Whatever it was, she needed to make sure they were all right. She also knew she had to work her horses. Dwayne had hit it on the nail last night: Lou would expect nothing less from her than to move on, take care of her animals and keep working toward her goals, which the two of them had discussed time and again. Still, she knew it would be painful.

Camden was making coffee as Michaela walked in from the barn.

"Want some?" she asked. Her naturally curly hair was frizzed out from sleeping on it, and she wore a pair of men's black silk boxers, which Michalea assumed belonged to Kevin, and a T-shirt that read MASTER OF MY DOMAIN.

Only Camden. "No," Michaela replied curtly. "I'm going over to see my folks and then Cynthia."

"Oh. You want me to come?"

Michaela shook her head. "I'm fine."

"Okay. Well if you need me, call. I think, I'm gonna stay around today. So I'm here for you." She paused. "You know, hon, I was talking to Kevin last night."

"Were you?"

"Yes, and we thought it might be good for you to come out with us tonight. We'll have some Mexican food, maybe a few drinks. Why don't you ask Ethan to come along?" Camden raised her brows. "If I didn't know better, I'd say the two of you could wind up together . . . but what do I know? Look at *my* last three marriages."

"Exactly." Michaela was about to say something even more smart-assy and bring up the fact that her new boyfriend looked

110

like a pretty good suspect in her uncle's murder, especially since he'd tried to purchase Lou's land not too long ago and had received a big fat no from Lou. But something stopped her. "Maybe I will go out with you tonight."

"Good," Camden replied, wide-eyed. "That's . . . great. I'm telling you that getting out will be good medicine. It will. You'll see."

Michaela said goodbye and headed to her truck. Tonight wasn't going to be about good medicine, but rather about fishing for answers. Maybe she'd get into that brain of Kevin Tanner's and find some hint that he might have been behind Uncle Lou's murder, or — and this was a thought she hated entertaining, but after last night had no choice — to see if she could also figure out whether or not Camden had somehow been involved.

Another car stood parked next to her mom's Trail Blazer. It took her a minute to recognize it, but she quickly realized that it belonged to Detective Davis. Something made her uneasy about him being there. Though likely routine, she just didn't like the idea of her parents being questioned by the police. Stepping out of her own vehicle she could smell her mom's famous cinnamon rolls. Janie Bancroft enjoyed cooking and always made major meals for her family, but in times of stress she went into overdrive. Michaela was sure to find a kitchen filled with baked goods and casseroles. For all she knew, her mom had been up all night cooking.

She came into the kitchen through the back door. Her mother and Davis were seated at the table, each with a cinnamon roll and a glass of milk.

"Hi, honey. Good to see you. Get a roll and come sit with us. I understand you've met Detective Davis already," her mom said. She fiddled with the cross around her neck, a habit she had when she was nervous. "I insisted that Detective Davis have a cinnamon bun. I fixed a little bit of food, I guess." Her face appeared strained, as if she hadn't slept, and her eyes were bloodshot. She *had* been cooking. There were brownies, the rolls, cookies, and when Michaela opened the refrigerator door to get a glass of milk she found it filled with a fruit salad, two covered casseroles that, if she guessed correctly, were a taco casserole and a lasagna. Oh boy, Mom was taking this really hard. She'd expected that to happen with her dad, but her mom was always the grounded one.

"Mom, who's going to eat all of this?"

Her mother shrugged. "I'm sure Cynthia could use some, and after the funeral there will be plenty for all who come. People loved Lou, so I suspect there will be quite a large number of folks. I think we should have the reception here. I think it'd be too much right now for Cynthia to deal with. I told her that yesterday that we would take care of the arrangements for a reception, but I'm not certain she heard me. Poor girl. She's beside herself, as expected. So having people here after the funeral, I think would be a nice idea, and as you pointed out, we'll have plenty of food."

"It's a lovely gesture, Mama." Mom was acting nervous, but it wasn't every day that a detective sat in your kitchen, trying to solve the murder of a loved one. Michaela looked at Davis, who smiled. "Good morning, Detective." It irked her to see him sitting in her mom's kitchen all warm and fuzzy like, kind of like a flipping cover of *Good Housekeeping.* Then again, she knew her mom, Janie Bancroft, was one woman who didn't take no for an answer. More than likely she'd practically shoved the roll down the poor man's throat.

He nodded. "Ms. Bancroft. How are you?"

113

"That's to be determined."

Davis stood. "Mrs. Bancroft, I should be going. Thank you for answering my questions. I may have more as the investigation progresses and as I said, I do need to speak with your husband again." He handed her his card. "Please have him call me."

"Certainly," Janie Bancroft replied.

Michaela noticed that her hands were trembling as she took the card from Davis.

"Thank you for the rolls and milk. It was completely unnecessary, but certainly delicious, and very kind of you."

"Oh, gosh," her mom said, a pink hue coloring her cheeks. "My pleasure, Detective."

"Thank you. And, I can not express how sorry I am for your loss." He turned to Michaela. "You, too."

She nodded. "I'll walk out with you, if that's okay?"

"Sure."

Michaela led him out the front door. "What did you need to talk to my parents about?"

"Some routine questions, similar to what I asked you." He reached into his jeans pocket for his keys to his charcoal Ford sedan. "When they were over at your uncle's place yesterday, we didn't get enough time to go over a few things."

"Right. And, my dad, you have to come back and talk to him some more?"

"Yes. He's not home right now."

"He comes and goes. Sometimes my mom and I can't keep track of him. Did you find anything out? About the pitchfork with the fingerprints, I mean?"

Maybe his green eyes, and his smile, and the gentle way when he talked with people had something to do with the way her stomach kept fluttering. He was an awfully good-looking man. As that thought came to mind, she immediately chastised herself for even thinking it. Here her uncle had just been murdered and she was noticing how handsome the detective working on his case was. Right now, she hated herself for that and decided the one and only reason she felt this way around him was that he was a police officer and that in itself can make a person nervous, cause a twitter in the gut.

"Not yet. It may take a day or two. Sometimes longer, depending on the lab. As soon as I know something, I'll call you."

"Thanks."

He placed a hand on her shoulder. "I promise I'm going to do what I can to see to it you and your family get some closure. I'll be in touch."

Michaela watched as he drove away. God, she hoped he was right. She rubbed her shoulder where Davis had touched her, and for a few seconds found herself lost in thought. Why had he done that? It wasn't like an intimate type of touch but one of comfort really, and honestly, she couldn't help feeling comforted by him in the brief second that he'd placed his hand on her. Dammit. She could not, *could not* have ridiculous fantasies about nice, good-looking detectives! She went back inside the house.

Sitting across from her mom, she picked at her roll. They were silent for long moments. Michaela finally reached across the table and took her mom's hand. "Are you really okay?"

"I think I'm better than your dad. He's a wreck. And, of course he won't talk about it with me. But that's the way he is. He gets quiet and goes within himself. He's been doing that more and more, even before this happened. Keeping to himself, leaving the place after he's done with chores and being away for a few hours at a time. Some things, like that fence he was mending the other morning when he got hurt, I've been on him to get done for weeks now, but he takes off and doesn't let me know where he's at. And you know I can't get him to carry a cell phone. When I ask him where he's been, he says that he was in town or running errands or visiting Lou or some of his cronies. I don't know, though. I'm worried, and I'm praying that he isn't gambling again."

"Oh, no, Mom. You don't really think that, do you?"

"I don't know, but if he is, Lou's death could send him into a spiral, and we don't have anything to pay back any more debt. All we have is this place, and we can't take a second on it. We did that last time this happened and now we simply can't go that route. With us only collecting Social Security and not being too smart about how we saved for retirement — I guess because we always figured we'd have this roof over our heads — we can't do that. If your father is back at it again, I don't know what we're going to do."

"But, it's been years since he's had a problem."

"It's an *addiction.* You know that."

"Where is Dad now? I'll go and talk to him."

"I don't know. I asked him to go to the store to get me some things and he said that he had a few errands to run before that. I didn't question him much. He's far too upset right now for me to go snooping, and for all I know he's being truthful. He has slowed down, and he does like to visit with some of the men he used to ride with. So, I may be pointing a finger where I shouldn't be."

"I'd still like to talk to him."

Her mom nodded. She stood and cleared the plates from the table, the scent of her strawberry lotion wafting through the air. "That Detective Davis is a nice man."

"I hope he finds out who killed Uncle Lou, and soon. What was he asking you?"

Her mom faced her, brushing off the front of her rose-colored knit sweater. "About Lou, and who he might have had any troubles with. He asked quite a bit about Bradley, too."

"Brad? What did you tell him?"

She pursed her lips. "I told him that . . . the boy is an ass."

Michaela couldn't help but laugh. "Oh, Mom." Her mother never swore, unless pushed hard and very angry. Brad seemed to have that knack with everyone in her family, though.

"It's true. And then he asked quite a bit about your marriage."

"What about it?" The muscles in her neck tightened.

"He asked if I thought that Kirsten was the only one I knew he'd been unfaithful with, and how you felt about Brad and what Lou had done when he had him followed."

"Really?" She didn't exactly care for Davis's line of questioning with her mom. She thought she'd told him everything he'd needed to know about Brad last night. Why had he grilled her mother? Of course, her mom was naïve and trusting, so she would have opened up to Davis.

"I got the feeling that he'll be having a talk with Bradley sometime soon."

"I'm sure he will. Well, I think I'm going to head over to see how Cynthia is doing. I'll call and see if Dad is home when I'm finished there. I want you to get some rest, Mama. No more cooking or baking. Got it?"

She smiled. "Can I knit?"

"Yes. But that's it." She kissed her on the cheek.

On the way to her uncle's ranch, she couldn't help thinking about her dad and what Mom was thinking. Was he gambling again? He'd always played cards, bet on races or sporting events when she was a kid — no big deal. Then, when Michaela was in high school, one of the local reservations had built a casino nearby and he started frequenting the place. It got out of control, from that point, as he began to miss work. At first she thought her mother suspected that there was another woman. Michaela had tried to steer clear from all of it. After all, she was a teenager, spreading her wings and doing things with friends, studying and just figuring out her own life. And, she definitely did not want to think about or know if her dad was having an affair. She remembered when her parents did tell her about his addiction. She almost thought it funny. Like, how could anyone become addicted to playing cards? But she soon learned it was no laughing matter when her mother grew tightfisted with money for her to go to the movies or to pay for horse show entries. Her sophomore year had been rough, as the year prior she'd started to make a name in the horse world with her barrel racing. Then, suddenly, it was yanked out from under her as the Bancrofts had to find ways to pay off her father's debts.

Along with trying to make ends meet, Ben started going to Gamblers Anonymous, which seemed to work. Eventually life settled back to normal in the Bancroft household.

Then, the bug bit Ben again when he'd been invited by some of his pals from the

American Quarter Horse Association to the races at Los Alamitos. He hadn't told his wife about it. It was only months later when he was knee-deep in trouble again, and they couldn't afford Michaela's tuition, that he'd copped to his problem. Michaela had to take out a student loan and get two jobs to get through school. This time, Janie insisted he get help. They refinanced the ranch, took out all the equity, sent him to some high-priced rehabilitation center in Washington. He came home, went to meetings, and as far as Michaela knew hadn't been involved with his vice since then — over a dozen years ago.

She'd have to talk to her dad because she didn't want this weighing on her mother, or herself, for that matter.

The other thing twisting itself in her mind as she drove over to her uncle's ranch was Davis, and his line of questioning with her mom. He was obviously looking into her theory of Brad seeking revenge, and considering Brad a suspect. But she wondered if there was more to it.

It was a disturbing thought, but it still crossed her mind: Davis likely considered her a suspect, too. After all, she'd been the one to find her uncle's body. Her earlier feelings of warmth toward Davis dissipated some, realizing he was probably not being the nice guy to her because he was simply *a nice guy.* She was pretty sure it was a tactic to extract information from her, and it had worked.

TWELVE

Pulling into Uncle Lou's place felt different. It would never be the same again. It was as if his death darkened every corner of the ranch, for this morning nothing looked as green as it always did, or as bright. Even the smells were somehow different when she climbed out of her truck.

Usually there would be plenty of activity going on right about now, with Uncle Lou either in the arena working a horse or fixing something around the ranch. Horses being groomed, at least one in the wash rack after a morning workout, as well as a couple of horses going through their paces on the hotwalker. Not this morning, Her uncle's presence was definitely gone. The sadness filtered back into Michaela's heart and gripped it in a vise. Would she ever again laugh over a joke she and her uncle had shared? Or would this ache remain? How did people overcome death? Sure, it happened every day. People went on with their lives. They had no choice. But how? Now it was her turn to figure out how the process worked. The first thing she realized that morning was that there truly was no way to be prepared.

She tapped on the front door then let herself into the house. She went into the kitchen where she saw Dwayne Yamaguchi standing over Cynthia, who sat at the table looking as lost as Michaela felt. Dwayne's hand rested on her shoulder. He squeezed it as he swung around and spotted Michaela.

"Good morning," he said. He had dark Asian good looks with a blend of his native Hawaii thrown in. There was a scar underneath his right eye from what Michaela had heard was a barroom fight in which Dwayne hadn't fared well. He also sported a tattoo of a Polynesian dancer on his left shoulder. Dwayne was known to have been a bit of a womanizer and partier back in the day. But a bit of age and the horses he worked with seemed to have grounded him, as he spent most of his time working with them instead of drinking and carousing.

Michaela couldn't help wonder if the slight pain she noticed at times in Dwayne's eyes had something to do with the hula

124

dancer on his arm.

"Hi," Michaela said, and walked over to Cynthia.

Dwayne moved away and went into the kitchen. "I'll get you a cup of coffee." He walked around the counter to get the carafe and pour their drinks.

Michaela sat down at the table and took Cynthia's hand. "How are you?"

Cynthia glanced up with her large brown eyes. "I don't know. I feel numb, like this isn't real."

"I know. I really do." They sat in silence for a moment.

Dwayne brought the coffee over to them. "I've gotta go out to the barn and check on a few things. Sam is out looking over one of the yearlings. Say he may want to buy one, ship it back to Hawaii for working the cows. Thinks he's ready to go on home now. Lou's death shook him up. When you're ready to head out, Michaela, why don't you come find me?"

"Sure." He obviously wanted to talk to her but she wasn't sure why. She turned back to Cyn. "You know, if you don't want to stay here, you can come and stay with me. Or, if you want, I can come over here. I hate the idea of your being alone."

Cynthia nodded. "Thank you, but I belong

here and the police have been by. An officer stood guard last night, and then Dwayne came back. I think I'll be fine."

"Sure, okay, but when Dwayne heads back out to Vegas, I can come over."

"Dwayne says that Bean can stay here and take care of the animals."

"Is he responsible enough?" Michaela couldn't help asking. Bean was good with the animals, but could he do the entire job? He was such a naïve man. She recalled with anger how Brad had taken advantage of Bean when he'd worked for Lou. He'd "befriended" Bean, out of what Michaela had come to believe was for self-centered reasons. She figured that he used Bean to cover for him when he left the ranch to rendezvous with Kirsten, and that he also had him do much of the work Brad was supposed to do around the ranch. She found Bean in tears one afternoon when she'd stopped by to bring Brad lunch, and Bean told her that Brad had gone to the feed store for some supplies. She should've known then. When she asked why the tears, Bean had explained to her that he didn't think he could get all the chores done, because Brad had given him some new ones and he couldn't remember all of them. Boy, had she ever wound up with a jerk!

"I think he is. I know he has some problems, but he's conscientious and he loves the animals. He may not always show up for work on time, but you and I both know it's not going to kill the horses if they get fed an hour later than normal. Bean is loyal. Besides, there's no one else to do it right now, until Dwayne gets back. I'm not up to it, and you have your own place to take care of. I'll be fine."

"What about Sam? Can't he stay?"

"He probably could. But you know those two, they're peas in a pod and Sam is such a help to Dwayne when they're out on the road. It'll work out."

"Okay, but don't hesitate to ask. I don't mind helping around here."

Cynthia nodded. She stood and walked to the bay window that overlooked their patio and pool. She sighed. "Come with me. I want to show you something."

Michaela followed her into Uncle Lou's office. Cynthia went behind his desk and opened a drawer, pulling out a file. She handed it to Michaela. "Take a look."

She opened it. "What is this? Lawsuits?" Cynthia nodded. She glanced over the paperwork. "What's going on?"

"That is exactly what I asked Lou the night before he died when he showed them

127

to me. There are six of them, all pertaining to the artificial insemination program. All of those people in the lawsuits are claiming that the foals born to their mares are not Loco's. They have DNA evidence to prove Loco is not the father."

"What? They're saying that Lou substituted another stallion's sperm to breed to their mares?"

"Yes. But it's worse than that. Lou has no recollection of ever sending product to any of these people."

"Then their claims are bogus."

Cynthia shook her head. "I don't think so. They all have signed breeding contracts. That's Lou's signature on the bottom of each, and look, the attorney included photocopies of the back of the checks. That's my husband's handwriting. The odd thing, though, is that Loco's stud fee is $3,500.00 and those checks are each for two grand."

"A bit of a deal." Michaela studied the papers. Cynthia was right. It did look as if Lou had signed the contracts with these people, as well as the back of the checks. "I don't understand."

"Neither do I. Lou swears he doesn't remember signing any of this stuff. And he claimed that he'd never given anyone that type of deal. I wanted to believe him, but how could I? The other part of it is that I can't trace the money to any one of our checking accounts. The numbers on the deposits don't match up. I can't even find a bank that they went into."

Michaela studied the photocopy of the back of one check to see if it listed the name of the bank where the deposits were made. It didn't, but it did have the bank's routing number and indicated that the deposits were made in Los Angeles. "We need to find out which bank uses this routing number here." Michaela pointed to the number. "Once you can find that out, we can locate the bank and branch where the account was open and maybe go from there."

"How do I do that?" Cynthia asked.

"Did you talk to Summer MacTavish about this? Is she still handling the books for the business?"

"She is, but Lou limited her responsibilities somewhat after she left Ethan. You know how he feels when somebody hurts someone he cares about."

"I do know that. What did he stop having her do?"

"Well, he told her that he'd take over running the books on the breeding program. He only left her in charge of accounts receivable and payroll. I haven't had a chance to speak to her yet, because like I said I just discovered all of this within the last forty-eight hours. But it's driving me crazy because I have no idea where these checks were deposited. I'm afraid to say anything to the police, because what if it's true? What if Lou was defrauding these people?"

"You think Uncle Lou would hide money from you and steal from people?" The words coming from Cynthia sounded completely incredulous.

"No. Not really. It sickens me to think about and now we can't figure it out together. The only other explanation that might make sense is that Lou was having memory problems."

"He was?"

"I noticed it about a month ago, and then when he showed me these papers the other night, he said that he'd been to see his doctor, because he felt like he was losing his mind. He was practically in tears."

Michaela took a deep breath, feeling like all the air had been sucked from her lungs. This was unbelievable. Could that have been why he didn't sound like himself the other night? "Are you talking something like Alzheimer's or senility?"

"I have no idea. I'm hoping his doctor will

130

speak to me about it. I'm the one now who will have to deal with these suits, and they're asking for over a million dollars in damages, claiming that the foals they expected from Loco's bloodline could have profited them greatly."

"You think that any of these people who filed these suits could be responsible for Uncle Lou's murder?"

Cynthia shrugged. "It's a crazy world. After looking over all of this, and wondering what was going on with him, I don't know what to think. But they're all located in Ohio. So, if someone from this core group of people is behind it, they would have had to hire someone, and that really doesn't make a lot of sense, because with Lou gone a lawsuit such as this can become even more convoluted." Michaela put the papers back inside the folder. "I hate to ask you this because I know you're in pain, too, but would you mind taking these papers with you and seeing if you can't find out where the checks were deposited? And, what's going on? I don't think I have the strength right now."

Michaela hesitated for a minute. She wasn't sure she wanted to get herself involved in any of this. Seeing the sorrow in Cynthia's eyes and the grief tightening her face, she said, "I'll see what I can find out."

"Thank you."

"What about Dwayne? Doesn't he handle some of the AI transactions, or Sam?"

"No, not really. They're involved in the training and that's pretty much it. It's mainly been Lou. Of course they've helped at times. Everyone has, even me. And Ethan has also helped out when he was here. Lou was about ready to start looking for some more help, and then he received the lawsuits and thought he better wait until things were cleared up. But no one else handled the paperwork. Lou was the breeding manager, after all. I mentioned this all to Dwayne this morning and he was as floored about it as I was."

"Maybe these lawsuits do have something to do with his murder. Or maybe not. Say this is true. I mean . . . I can't believe that it could be, because Uncle Lou was so ethical in everything he did. But if by some chance there was a mix-up with the DNA?"

"I don't think that's likely. We're dealing in large amounts of cash. People want to be assured of protection in case this exact thing were to happen. I'm sure you're aware that the American Quarter Horse Association maintains DNA samples of all the stallions involved in AI, and for the foals to be registered they also have to be DNA typed, if they're bred via AI. And, the claim is the DNA doesn't match. The plaintiffs have all contacted the AQHA and they're backing these people, saying that their claims are valid. I think they could even force us to shut down the operation."

Michaela frowned. She didn't have a clue what to make of any of it. "Do you know if the owners know who the real stallion is to these foals? There were three other studs here at the time these people would have received the product and had their mares inseminated, weren't there?" It could be as simple, albeit, a horrific mixup if one of the other stallion's sperm was sent out to the mares' owners. Loco's fees were some of the more expensive stud fees out there. The other stallions on the ranch were all of excellent breeding, but they weren't Loco, and Michaela could not blame any of the owners for being upset over such a mixup. People wanted to get what they paid for.

"The documents are claiming that there is an ongoing investigation. They also say that in the breeding reports Lou had to file that none of these mares were included. This was supposedly how the owners were first alerted there might be a problem, when they discovered they couldn't register their foals because there was no breeding report on file with their mares' names."

"So, the plaintiffs here have not named the stallion they believe to be the stud horse of these foals?"

Cynthia shook her head. "You know, it may not even be a stud registered with the AQHA. It could be some random horse. I don't know. At this point I think the AQHA is still trying to track the DNA. I fear that on top of everything, we will lose our business and I'll have to pay all of these damages."

"Did Uncle Lou indicate anyone who he thought would intentionally switch containers to be shipped to the mares' owners?"

She sighed. "He did mention Brad. Brad was working here at the time and knew how the program worked."

"But why? Why would he do that, and how would he get a hold of contracts and checks?"

Cynthia shrugged. "Maybe it's as simple as Brad was being plain mean. We all know he's proven himself not to be the most upstanding individual. Maybe he wanted to sabotage Lou, you know, make sure he ruined Lou's reputation. And once this gets out, my husband's memory will be forever tainted in the horse world."

"I won't let that happen. I don't believe Lou could have done anything to hurt anyone. Not intentionally. I'll help you figure this out." Michaela sighed, trying to wrap her mind around all of this. "What about Bean? I know that everything is on a numbering system as far as which stud's sperm is which in the freezer, that kind of thing, and you keep records, but could Bean have somehow gotten things mixed up?"

"Lou didn't let Bean have anything at all to do with the program for that very reason. He could have easily mixed things up."

"Who was the person in charge of sending everything out?"

"At first it was Brad, then Summer on occasion as business picked up and Lou needed the extra help. I did it as well at times. But Lou was the main handler of all of it. We really should have put better strategies into play. That's obvious to me now. Because somewhere along the way, something got screwed up. And as far as the contracts and checks go, it could be as easy to explain that with age my husband could have signed them *and* been having problems with his memory."

"He wasn't old, though. Sixty-one is hardly an age these days where people begin losing it."

"Alzheimer's disease can begin in your fifties."

"You know, I wish I'd known he was having health problems. Maybe I could have helped."

"Your uncle was a proud man. I'm his wife and he didn't confide in me until the other night. But I should have paid more attention." Her eyes welled up with tears again. "I had noticed that there were little things he'd forgotten, like bills that didn't get paid, and one night when Dwayne was out and Bean had already gone home, he didn't feed the horses until I reminded him. But nothing too major. I thought maybe he was working too hard. Or, maybe the blowup with Ethan was eating at him."

"What do you know about what happened between them?" Michaela asked.

"All I know is that right before he left on that trip, he and Lou had a huge argument and it tormented Lou afterward."

"What was it all about?"

"I don't know. I could hear this commotion going on out in the barn. I walked out there and Dwayne was telling Ethan to get the hell off the property."

"What happened after that?"

"Lou followed him, tried to talk to him, but Ethan wouldn't have anything to do

136

with it. He shrugged him off. Lou nearly lost his balance as Ethan pulled away. Lou wouldn't tell me what it was about, and ever since then he's seemed preoccupied, and sad. Something changed; something Ethan told him changed him, but I don't know what. I even tried to get a hold of Ethan to find out what it was, but he never called me back." The phone started ringing. "Excuse me, Mick. It might be that detective or the funeral home. I'm trying to make the arrangements." She started for the family room.

"Sure. Do you have some aspirin? I'm getting a vicious headache."

"In my bathroom upstairs. Oh, your uncle had some Ativan that he was taking for some headaches he was getting. You can try those, if you want. They seemed to help him."

"Ativan is not for headaches. At least I don't think so. I always thought it was for anxiety or panic attacks."

"I don't know. I don't take that stuff anyway, but the doctor gave it to Lou for the headaches. Sorry, I gotta get the phone."

It wasn't like Michaela was a doctor or anything, but she was sure Ativan was prescribed for agitation. Her doctor had recommended it to her when she was splitting from Brad but she'd decided against it. Like Cynthia, she tried to stay more on the holistic route, if possible. But right now, she needed a Tylenol. Why was her uncle taking Ativan? Well, agitation did cause headaches, so what did she know.

Michaela climbed up to the second floor. Their bedroom was very *Home and Garden.* Cynthia had given the place life when she'd married her uncle. She put colors together well and had a knack for making a house feel like a home with earthy warm tones and various floral and equestrian paintings around. It was pretty and inviting. But now the house, too, felt different, just as the ranch had when she'd arrived. She didn't know how Cynthia could stay here. She knew if it were her, she'd want to get away, but maybe it was a comfort thing. Maybe Cynthia needed to be here at the home she'd shared for the last decade with her husband.

In the bathroom, she found the bottle of aspirin tucked away inside the medicine cabinet, next to a bottle of Ativan. She picked it up. It was a refill prescribed to Lou only two weeks earlier. He had two more refills available. What in the world? Her uncle was never one to take drugs, especially not something like Ativan. His headaches must've been horrendous. What was going on in her uncle's life that he was so stressed-out about? She picked up the bottle and read it again. It was prescribed to Uncle Lou by a Dr. Verconti. Huh. She'd thought he'd gone to the same family doctor as her parents had — Dr. Sherman. He must have switched docs for some reason. Goodness, what had been going on here? And how had she not sensed until the night before her uncle was murdered that something was deeply troubling him? The lawsuits? His memory loss? Where was the money for the breedings? And, what stallion was used to impregnate those mares? Why hadn't she seen that her uncle was in crisis? Had she been so wrapped up in her own problems that she hadn't been available to the one person who had always, *always,* made himself available to her?

Starting to tear up again, she reached for a tissue, wiped her face and tossed it away. She missed the wastebasket and bent down to pick it up. Her eyes widened.

"Oh, my God," she muttered. There in the trash was a pregnancy test, and Michaela knew from all those she'd taken in the past that this one read positive. Cynthia was *pregnant?* But how? Uncle Lou . . .

From a conversation she'd overheard

between her parents when Lou and Cynthia wed, she'd learned that Lou had had a vasectomy. Maybe he hadn't gone ahead with the procedure. *Maybe* she was jumping to conclusions. She heard the blood rushing through her ears. But, if it was Cynthia — and it had to have been done that morning, because that blue line would have gone away after several hours — and if Uncle Lou had had a vasectomy; that meant . . . Michaela shook her head. No. It couldn't be, but she knew she would have to find out. Had Cynthia been cheating on her uncle?

THIRTEEN

Cynthia was still on the phone when Michaela came down the stairs. The revelation that Lou's wife was pregnant, and the strong possibility that the baby was not her uncle's, continued to stun her. Again she thought, maybe he hadn't gone through with the vasectomy. That in itself was bad enough. Here Cynthia would be without Lou to help raise a child, though the alternative was worse: the possibility that Cynthia had been cheating. Michaela's mind wandered even further as another thought struck her — could *Cynthia* have killed Lou? If she was in love with someone else, maybe that *someone* else could have done it. No. No way. She would not believe that. She would stick to the hope that Lou had not gone through with the operation. But Michaela knew that to put her mind completely at ease, she would have to check around, and she didn't really want to ask the two people most likely to know: her parents. What a mess.

She left a note for Cynthia saying that she'd call her later. She really didn't want to be there when Cyn got off the phone. This one had to simmer for a while.

She walked out to the barn and spotted Dwayne down the breezeway, putting Loco back in his stall. He waved her over. "How Cynthia seem to you?"

"She actually seemed grounded," Michaela replied. "More so than I would've expected." Or, maybe Cynthia was in as much shock as Michaela was — not only over the murder of Lou, but also about her pregnancy.

"That's her. Strong woman. She get through this. She know that be the way your uncle would want it. But, I think she put up a front right now. I think inside her there's a big piece of her crumbling."

"You're probably right. How about him? How's he doing?" She pointed at Loco.

"Oh, he know something up. He skittish today. Missing his man, you know. Horses sense. They know when something is different. He know. Spiritual animal. Remind me of home. Too bad he can't talk, tell us who did this."

"Any ideas?" Michaela asked.

"Me? No."

"Were you here when my uncle had that fight with Ethan?"

"I was working in the arena. Heard them shouting. I came on down. Man, oh man." He shook his head. "Ethan real unhappy, you know. Your uncle trying hard to calm him down, but it not happening for him. Mad. Real mad." Dwayne's voice had the melodic lilt that could only come from the islands.

"Do you know what it was all about?"

"No. All I hear Ethan say before I told him to leave was that Lou was full of shit. A disgrace, he say. If everyone knew the truth about him, they'd think, so too. Don't know what that meant. Lou was good man, you know. You'd have to ask Ethan. Lou wouldn't talk about it with me."

The problem was, she had already asked Ethan . . . and he wasn't talking either. Dammit. "Right. Listen, besides this thing with Ethan, do you know anything about the lawsuits against Uncle Lou? Cynthia told me that she'd spoken to you about it."

"You know, that be none of my business. But could be that Lou got things mixed up. I don't like to say that, but he try to take on too much in the last few years with this program. I tell him to just ride and train. No need for all the science, breeding non-

143

sense. He get real stressed-out lately, ask me or Sam to pick up a prescription for him. I see him taking the medicine for stress and I worry about him. I say, Boss, why you taking this stuff?"

"Was it Ativan?"

"Don't know the name. Sam picked up the stuff at the drugstore for him and ask him why he needs medicine. He tells us for stress, and we tell him he needs a vacation. Then Lou, says to me, maybe me and Sam be right about a vacation, 'cause he forgettin' all sorts of stuff lately and feeling confused sometimes."

Michaela's headache wasn't going away *at all.* Everything Dwayne was telling her was very disturbing. "I wish he had taken a break. I wish I'd known the pressure he was under with this program. You never had anything to do with the AI program, then?"

Dwayne chuckled. "Nah. Dealing with all that not my thing. Sure, a lot of money in it. A whole lot, but I'm not interested. I think what happened, you want to know, is that the containers got switched somehow. Honest mistake. That's what I think."

"What about the signed contracts and the checks? Do you think Lou really forgot about that money or where he put it? And if he was hiding money, why would he?"

Dwayne shifted from one foot to the other. Something appeared to be bothering him. After a few seconds he said, "Don't know. But, I think maybe I should talk to you 'bout something else you should know, before you find it out another way. Me, I don't plan to say nothing to no one. But someone else might. I have no control in case they go to the police."

"What are you talking about?" Michaela asked.

"Your father." He fiddled with Loco's halter. "Like I said, none of my business. Lou told me the other day after your dad been to see him, they didn't agree on some things. He said they had a falling-out."

"What do you mean? What kind of falling-out? No one said anything to me." Michaela crossed her arms. She didn't care for the tone in Dwayne's voice or the evasive way he was getting to the point . . . or not getting to it.

"Your dad, he gambling again. He been borrowing money from Lou to pay off his debt. I'm not sure, but Cynthia say she don't know where the money is from the checks those people sent for artificial insemination. Maybe your uncle hang on to that money for your dad. Maybe he keep it aside for him. Lou asked me to see into

145

what was going on with your father, how much he owe, and to who. It's not good."

"Oh, no." Michaela sighed. Her worst fear had been confirmed. For a few seconds she couldn't say anything else as a gamut of emotions ran through her. "What, the horses again?"

"Everything. Horse, dog, sport."

"How much is he in for?"

"Over a hundred grand."

Michaela's jaw dropped. *A hundred thousand dollars?"*

Dwayne nodded.

"Did Lou give him any money?"

"I don't know. He told me to find out how deep your dad in first. I told him the other night before I left for Vegas. The night before . . .'"

Michaela held up her hand. "I know."

"Anyway, he say that he'd call up Benjamin and have a heart-to-heart with him. He hope to get him over here the next day."

Michaela took a step back as it dawned on her why she'd first gotten the runaround from Dwayne. Why he'd told her up front that he wasn't going to tell anyone but that the word might get out anyway. She knew what it might look like, and obviously so did Dwayne. "My dad didn't murder Lou because he wouldn't give him the money to bail him out, if that's what you were thinking." She recalled the argument she overheard between her parents when she'd gone to their house yesterday. Her dad had mentioned something about his brother.

"Whoa, no, no, I know that. I don't think anything. I know you love your family and with Lou gone, I figure I need to tell you. Then you could go and talk to your dad. See if you can help him."

"Sorry." She swallowed hard. "But even considering the money my dad owes, that doesn't explain where the money went from the people who filed these lawsuits."

"No. It doesn't."

"Hey, Dwayne." A large man wearing a Hawaiian shirt walked down the breezeway toward them.

"Yeah, Sammy boy, right here. What you need?"

Sam wiped the back of his arm along his forehead, then slicked back his thick, dark hair with his palm. "Phew. Hot out there and I'm working hard. Need a break."

"You not working hard. You just big," Dwayne teased.

"You funny," Sam replied. "Don't go listening to him. Always thinking he the big shot." He smiled, showing a large gap between his teeth. "How you doing, Michaela? Sorry about Lou. Gonna miss him. Thinking I'm going back home. Too sad here, now. When we done at the finals, I'm getting on the plane and going back."

"Can't blame you. I'd go too, if I think I could make a living back home. You know, life much simpler on the islands," Dwayne said.

"And food is better, too." Sam laughed and rubbed his rotund belly, which moved in unison with his laughter. "You come to islands and see some day."

Michaela smiled. "I'd like that."

Sam nodded. He held up his hands. "Okay, cuz. What you need from me? Soon, I gotta go get some lunch."

"Why don't you take out Ginger."

"Ah, good name. Like to cook with it."

"You like to cook with anything."

Sam shook a finger at his cousin. "You watch your self, little cousin. I take you down."

"Get the mare out. She only a few months from popping a new baby. Gonna be a good one out of her and Loco. That mare be of champion lines herself. Girl need some exercise, though. Too fat. Put her on the hot walker and let her work for twenty/thirty minute. Then, let her go in the pasture. Get some strength before that baby drop."

"Okay, cuz."

"Hey, Sam, where Bean?"

"Don't know. Last I see him, he tell me that he needed to get a soda. Shoot, I the one who needs the soda."

"Bean been acting strange. I think 'cause of Lou. I'll find him."

"If I see him, I'll send him to you. Nice to see you, Michaela. My condolences. I better go take care of Ginger and the baby she gonna pop." He clapped his hands together.

She nodded.

Sam ambled away. Michaela turned back to Dwayne. "Speaking of babies, did Lou or Cynthia ever mention to you about wanting kids?"

"No."

"Huh. Okay."

"Why you ask?"

"I don't know. Kind of random question, I suppose. I was uh, just thinking it's too bad they didn't have any."

He gave her an odd look and she took that as a cue to leave before he started putting anything together, because, Michaela now found herself on a quest to discover just who her uncle's killer was.

FOURTEEN

Leaving the barn, Michaela found Bean sitting in the passenger side of her truck. She opened her door and got in, looking over at him. He had a Coke in his hand.

He sat up straight. "Hi, Miss Michaela."

She noticed him tighten his grip around the soda can.

"Hello, Bean. What are you doing in my truck?"

"I think it is a pretty truck and you smell good and I wanted to know if the truck smelled like you do."

Michaela wasn't quite sure how to respond to that at first. She pushed some loose strands of hair back into her ponytail. "Thank you, but I don't think the truck smells like I do."

"No, it does not. It smells like a dog."

Michaela laughed, knowing he was right. Cocoa had spent quite a bit of time riding around in the truck with her over the years.

It had only been in the past couple of weeks that she hadn't been able to jump into the front seat. "I suppose it does. So, how are you doing?"

He chewed on the side of his lip before answering. "I guess I am okay. Sorry I kind of got mad at you yesterday. I did not want to believe you when you said Mr. Lou was dead. It made me mad and sad, too."

"Oh, Bean, you didn't do anything wrong. My goodness, I certainly wasn't upset with you. It's understandable that you're upset. We all are. Dwayne's looking for you."

"Oh. I'm having a soda right now. And." He paused. "I wanted you to know that I don't like to be mean. I was mean to you and I am sorry, 'cause I know you loved Mr. Lou, too. He was a nice man to me. I miss him."

"I know. We all miss him."

Bean opened the door and got out of the truck. "I will see you soon, Miss Michaela. Okay?" He crumpled the can in his hand.

"Sure. Be careful and take care of yourself."

Bean spat a wad of chewing tobacco on the ground. She grimaced. "I didn't know you chewed tobacco."

"I don't."

"But . . . you just spit it out."

"I tried it. I do not like it. Especially don't like it with soda. Doesn't taste real good."

"I imagine that it wouldn't. Where did you get the chew from?"

"Found it."

"Where?"

He shrugged. "I can't remember."

Was he lying to her? She couldn't tell. "You don't remember?"

"No."

"Can I see the container it came in?"

He pulled it from his pocket. It wasn't the brand that Davis found outside her barn last night, but it still made her wonder if Bean had anything to do with scaring her. He acted like a child, but even children had the capacity to frighten people. Some even had it within them to kill. Bean may have been a child inside a man's body. Was he also a killer? "See you later, Bean."

"Sure." He slammed the door of the truck. She winced. *That was really odd.* Was Bean really as vulnerable and naïve as he seemed, or had he perfected an act that in many ways could have helped him cruise through life? The accident that he'd suffered happened when he was a kid. Could his injuries not be as serious as he'd presented? Was he someone who'd learned it was easier to get by, by victimizing himself more so than need be? It was hard to fathom anyone doing such a thing. An even more disturbing thought was, could Bean be off just enough to murder Uncle Lou? Could they have argued over something and Bean lost his temper, left the ranch, then came back after the police arrived and acted as if he had no idea what had occurred? She hated thinking these thoughts about him. But his behavior just now made her wonder. It also made her wonder if she wasn't simply being plain paranoid. She glanced out her window, seeing Bean wave at her as she drove off, more confused than ever.

Michaela checked her watch. No time to mull this over in her mind right now. There were horses that needed exercising and she was way off with her schedule. One point that Dwayne — and even Cynthia, in a sense — had made was that Uncle Lou would not want her to sink into the misery of the situation. Hard to do, but the reality was that animals in training had to be worked.

She used her cell to try and call her dad. Her mom informed her that he still hadn't returned home.

"Do you have any idea where he is, Mom?"

"No, honey, I don't. I'm hoping that he's

only out for a drive."

Doubtful. Michaela had a sick feeling that her father was probably somewhere making a deal with the devil. If he was in as much trouble as Dwayne suggested, he was likely covering his rear. It was also possible that the same question that had crossed Michaela's mind, had crossed her father's: Could someone have murdered her uncle to get back at her father for not paying his debts?

Instead of going home as originally planned, she headed over to Joe Pellegrino's. Joe was a big, slick Italian guy she'd gone to high school with. Joe'd always had a crush on her, which she didn't reciprocate. However, they'd become fast friends after he'd moved from a school at the other end of the valley, where he'd been teased ruthlessly about his size, even though he really wasn't *that* big. A little pudgy, maybe. After all, Joe did like his pasta. Kids at her high school didn't treat Joe much better when he came over as the newcomer, but she'd befriended him because she was also a bit of an outcast. Riding horses was far more important to her during those years, and still was, than the latest designer jeans or hairdo. Ethan had, as always, been her pal as well at the time, but he'd been quite a bit more popular due to his success on the football field. Joe, though not popular at school, kept her in stitches. He knew how to make a girl laugh.

Her mother did not approve of their friendship or his family, meaning that they didn't see much of each other outside of school. Apparently, his family was noted to have Mafia ties around the country, especially a large connection out of Los Angeles. Supposedly Joe was on the up and up with the hardware store he owned, and Michaela wanted to believe that, but really didn't. If anyone had ideas about who her dad was dealing with, it would be Joe. Dad had to have a bookie, and hopefully Joe could help her find out who it was.

A buzzer sounded as she entered the store. The smell of paint, resins, and metal permeated the air. "Be right with you," a gruff voice from the back called out.

Michaela went to the hammer aisle and grabbed a new one. Last week, while changing out some of the nails that had deteriorated on the saddle racks, she'd snapped the old hammer in two when she'd smashed it down on her thumb and in a fit of pain and anger had thrown it against the wall.

"Well, look what the cat drug in."

Joe Pellegrino approached her. He was at

least fifty pounds overweight. The pasta was treating Joe well, or maybe poorly, depending on how you looked at it. He had warm brown eyes with a twinkle in them when he smiled. His chubby, dimpled face made Michaela think of an Italian Pillsbury doughboy. Joe had thick lips, flushed cheeks, and a thick cap of wavy black hair, which always looked shiny and coiffed. All in all Joe looked like the nicest guy in the world. He wiped his hands on his jeans.

"Been mixing some paint back there. How you doing? You look as pretty as always. Sure is nice to see you."

"Thanks, Joe." She waved the hammer at him. "Need a new hammer."

"Came to the right place. You need anything else? Nails, paint, you know I've got all that stuff. Oh, and I've got a great power drill. You want to take a look?" He smiled at her. "Right. I'm sure you don't want to take a look. I get excited over the damndest things, my Marianne tells me, but it's a guy thing." He lowered his voice. "Speaking of men, I heard about you and Brad. That jerk. Sorry, but he is." Michaela nodded and didn't say anything. "We've known each other since we were what, fourteen? You're a good lady. I like you. But you know that. You know, I could make sure your ex gets a little pain in return for all he's caused you. Maybe a little smack upside the head would remind him how to treat a woman."

That did sound like an opportunity not to be passed up. But in all good conscience Michaela wasn't a vindictive woman. "No, Joe. But thank you. Something tells me he's got all the problems he can handle with his new girlfriend."

"Yeah, she's sure full of herself. Came in here the other day, bossing me around, needing a few things. Pain in the ass, that one. Brad deserves her."

"Listen, I don't need you to do any smacking around, but I do need a favor."

"You name it."

"Did you hear about my uncle? Lou Bancroft?"

"Yeah, my friend, sorry. Read about it in the paper. Was gonna send over some flowers and ring you when I got a chance. That's rough."

"Yeah, thanks. This is kind of personal so I'd appreciate it if you'd keep it between us."

"Discretion is my middle name. Whaddya need?"

"It's my dad. He's gambling big-time from what I've heard, and he's in for quite a bit of money. He's got to be working with a bookie. I need to know who the bookie is, and I need to know how much he owes."

Joe frowned. "That don't sound too good to me. You may want to let your pop handle his own problems."

"Joe, he's my father. Just get me a name, and . . ." She looked out the store window.

"And, what?"

"You don't think my uncle's murder could have anything to do with my dad's gambling?"

Joe waved his hands animatedly. He really could've landed an acting job on *The Sopranos.* He had the drama thing down. "Come on, you know that would not be a likely scenario. It wasn't your uncle dealing with the cash. Look, from what I know about the families — and I'm not saying I know anything, because I only know this stuff from the TV and movies — but, uh, you know the families, they don't do that kind of thing. You piss them off, they take care of *you.* Retaliation on a loved one, well, that's not what they do."

Michaela nodded. "Right." She touched Joe's shoulder. "Could you just ask a few questions, see if I can't help get my dad out of trouble and see if anyone knows anything about my uncle Lou?"

"I got some cousins who might be able to

help me out. I'll do what I can. Give me a day. C'mon, let's go ring up your hammer. You still hanging out with that friend of yours, Camden?"

"She's living with me, believe it or not."

"She's a firecracker, that one. I remember meeting her with you, what was that 'bout a year ago at The Dakota House?"

"I think so." The mention of The Dakota House saddened her. She should've had breakfast with Uncle Lou there the day before.

"Hey, if she's not hooked up with anyone, I got a cousin who could use a date. He's a nut like she is. Think they'd have a good time together."

"I'll mention it to her. I better run." She thanked him, but before she could get out the door he stopped her, his large hand grabbing her by the arm. "You be careful, Michaela. You need someone to watch your back, you let me know. You know, old crushes die hard." He smiled and winked at her.

She stood on her tiptoes and kissed him on the cheek. His face turned the color of the red paint he'd been mixing.

She'd try to find her dad later, but for now she was thankful that Joe Pellegrino had never lost the ache in his heart for her.

FIFTEEN

Michaela took Leo a handful of sliced apples. The other horses down the breezeway gave her a curious look, and she was sure if they could speak they'd be saying, *Um, excuse me, what about the rest of us?*

She knew she spoiled Leo, but she couldn't help it. He was her baby, and — if her gut was right — a future champion reining horse, a horse that would make her a household name in the industry. She planned to show him as a three-year-old in the National Reining Horse Association Futurity in Oklahoma City. Leo came from the perfect bloodlines suited for reining . . . an event designed to show the athletic ability of a ranch-type horse with a little added elegance and finesse. Michaela had not ridden in the futurity before and although she had a little over two years to go, she felt certain that Leo was destined to be a winner.

Training him, in and of itself, was a challenge she would relish. She would have to teach him to move in very unnatural ways and perform extremely challenging and controlled maneuvers with grace. They included small slow circles, large fast circles, and flying lead changes — meaning that as he galloped, he'd have to switch the leg leading with each stride — while maintaining the same speed. He'd also have to learn how to do rollbacks, or a 180-direction change turning around on the hind end and continuing motion in the opposite direction, 360-degree spins done by pivoting his body around one hind leg that stays in place and doing it at a high rate of speed, and finally very long, smooth, sliding stops. She patted his forehead. Dream big. That was always Uncle Lou's motto. Dad's was, "Be cautious." Funny how he hadn't listened to his own advice. At least right now it didn't appear so. Gambling, and owing the kind of money Dwayne suggested, was anything but cautious.

She walked to the other end of the barn, took out her seven-year-old stallion Rocky and groomed him. He was a big, beautiful sorrel. She'd taken him to a few events as a four-year-old and he'd shown great promise, earning out a decent amount for his first year on the circuit, but she'd been trying to get pregnant at the time and that's where her focus was. Then her world went to pot with the discovery of Brad's infidelity. Rocky was past his prime now as far as the show scene went. Since she hadn't shown him much over the years, it wasn't likely he could bring a lot of money in stud fees. However, like Loco and Leo, Rocky was from good lines — his full name was Rocky Chex, with his great-grandsire being Bueno Chex. Now her options were to geld him and make a pleasure riding horse out of him, or turn him out to stud and see if he could still help supplement her income. She had to decide soon what to do with him. But for now, Rocky needed his exercise. She threw the saddle on him; the animal shifted his weight and turned his head toward her with a look in his eye that said, *Can't I just go back and eat?*

"No. You can't, but if you're a good boy today, maybe there will be a treat in it for you."

She retrieved his bridle from its post in the tack room and brought it back, sliding the halter off and slipping the bit into his mouth and the headstall over his ears. She led him out of the breezeway, stepped up into the left stirrup, grabbed the saddle horn and reins with her left hand, and swung her right leg over and sat comfortably in the saddle. She adjusted her seat and slightly squeezed her calves into his rib area, cueing him to go forward. He responded accordingly, and headed toward the arena.

Rocky side-passed around to the gate. Michaela reached over and unlocked it, maneuvered him inside, backed him around and shut it. Moments later they were working on conditioning techniques to better their patterns — flying lead changes, circles, and spins. She then pushed him into a full canter with a strong squeeze of her legs, shifted her weight slightly forward and loosened up on the reins. Reining horses, which were typically of the quarter horse breed, shorter and stockier than most of the other breeds — had good heads about them and maintained calm demeanors. But like the thoroughbred on the track, the quarter horse trained for reining was a fierce competitor inside the ring. There were no other horses in the ring at the same time as the reiner — only horse and rider. But it was as if the animal had a complete understanding of what he was bred for and what was at stake — for him — a bucket of grain and a lot of praise from his rider. For the rider, a wad of cash and some major recognition.

For Michaela as a woman, that recognition meant more to her than most of the riders on the circuit, who were men. She wanted to be at the top of her game. She wanted to be the trainer that everyone looked up to: horseman — or in her case, horsewoman — of the year.

The training that went into teaching the horse to turn on his haunches by coming to a sliding stop from a full run, and doing a 180 turnaround immediately taking off the opposite direction, more like an elegant dancer than a thousand-pound animal, made Michaela's adrenaline run at a rapid clip. There was no other high that could compare. To be able to control an amazing beast while at a high rate of speed and while doing such complicated maneuvers, with just slight touches of her legs, balancing shifts of her seat and soft movements from her hand, gave her the same kind of power that she often imagined was what it felt like for CEOs of huge corporations who went in and achieved *the kill.*

"Wow! Nice riding."

Michaela slid Rocky to a stop and turned to see Detective Jude Davis standing at the side of the arena. She wiped the back of her right arm across her forehead, the reins still in her left hand. Heat rose to her face. She worked almost as hard as the horses she rode, and today she'd been so focused on what she was doing that the sweat matted the strands of her blonde hair to the sides of her face.

"Hey, Detective." Rocky stomped his foot, impatient to get back to work. "Relax, boy." She patted his neck. "Surprised to see you again so soon. How long have you been there?"

"Long enough to be impressed."

Now she was definitely more than flushed. "Thanks. What can I do for you? Did you learn anything more about my uncle's murder?"

He crossed his arms across his dark sports coat, which he wore over a crisp white oxford that wouldn't stay too white if he hung around much longer. "No, sorry. We're still checking into several leads."

Michaela urged Rocky over to the side of the ring and dismounted. "Leads? What type of leads?"

He shook his head and his golden hair waved in the wind. "I can't divulge that information; it's an investigation."

She patted Rocky on the neck. He was soaked in sweat. "Then why are you here?" She didn't have time for small talk, and the way her stomach churned while watching

Detective Davis's lips move when he spoke made her uneasy. Men should not have sexy lips, at least not the one investigating her uncle's murder. How could she even watch him speak, and then look into his blue eyes? Worse yet, how could she continue this way? Had grief driven her insane? It simply was not appropriate for her to think like this about Davis. Plus, she needed to keep in mind that his nice guy act, was just that — *an act.*

"Actually I wanted to stop by and see how you were doing."

Sure. "Oh? I just saw you this morning at my mom's, so not a lot has changed since then." She looked down at the ground. "I'm doing okay, I suppose. I figured I better work my horses and try to maintain some semblance of normalcy around here."

"I think that's good. I mean, trying to get back to daily life."

Michaela didn't respond, confused as to why he was there. She shifted her weight from one foot to the other. What did he want?

"Are you sure you're all right?" he asked.

"I'm sure." She wondered if she should mention anything about her dad and his gambling problem, and that maybe his problem had gotten so out of hand that someone sought retaliation by killing his brother. But almost instantly she had second thoughts. That was something she would trust Joe to follow up on, and she needed to see her father and ask him about it herself. "Well, I've got some more work to do."

He nodded and seemed uncomfortable. "You were close with your uncle."

"I told you that. Yes. He was like another father to me."

"He never gave you a reason to be upset with him?"

Where was this going? Her uneasiness about him being there grew. "Of course not."

"You didn't have any recent arguments with him or discussions that might have caused tension?"

Her grip on Rocky's reins tightened. "No. Why are you asking me this? You questioned me yesterday. I told you everything I could. Is there a problem?"

He shrugged. "Only doing my job. I . . . received some information that maybe you were upset with your uncle."

"What?" she gasped. "Absolutely not. Who told you this?"

"I can't divulge that. This is an ongoing investigation. I've explained that already."

She shook her head. "Wait a minute.

You're asking me questions that don't make a whole lot of sense, based on what I can only speculate is some type of twisted gossip. I'd like to know what it is exactly that you were told."

"You told me yourself that your uncle had your ex-husband followed and that was how you found out about his affair."

"That's true."

"Were you happy in your marriage?"

"What? No! How could I have been happy? My husband was screwing around. And, I know my mom told you the same thing this morning. Why all the questions about my marriage all of a sudden?"

"I have to investigate all possibilities. Prior to discovering his infidelity, were you happy?"

"Again, I have to ask you, what is this all about?"

"I'm trying to establish if ignorance was bliss in your situation. Maybe you had what you thought was the perfect life, and it was suddenly shattered when your uncle exposed the truth."

She groaned. Oh, yeah, his nice-guy façade had definitely crumbled right in front of her. "You have got to be kidding me. Now I get it. You've concocted some type of theory, or someone has put it into your head that I was so distraught over Brad's infidelity, that after I had time to let it all settle, I realized how much happier I was with the loser when I didn't know he was getting it on with the rodeo queen. No, Detective, I was *not* happy in my marriage and I was *not* disillusioned, and I did *not* seek a vendetta against my uncle."

He nodded, and she heard him sigh loudly. "This is rather a sensitive topic, but I have to ask."

"Of course it's sensitive."

"No. Um, see, I understand that you and your husband were trying to have a baby."

Whoa! She felt like the air had been sucked out of her. It took her a second to register where he might be going with this. She closed her eyes and shook her head. Narrowing her eyes at him, she said, "What does that have to do with who might have killed my uncle?"

"I have to look at every scenario, Ms. Bancroft."

"Uh-huh. What scenario are you getting at, Detective?" Rocky pawed at the ground and stomped his foot again, feeling as agitated as she did. She would have liked to turn him around and allow him to kick the crap out of Davis at that moment. "Wait a minute." She sat up straight on the horse.

"You're thinking that I wanted a child so badly that I would have put up with Brad's bullshit. Aren't you? And that my uncle took that away from me." Davis didn't say a word. "Sorry, Detective. I may have been a blind fool with my ex, but I am not a sucker, and another thing, I'm not desperate either. I may not be Miss Rodeo America." She shook a finger at him. "But if I wanted a man to have a baby with, I think I could find one who wouldn't cheat on me, thank you very much. Now, if you have nothing more to ask me, I'd appreciate it if you'd leave. In fact, even if you have anything else to ask, I don't care. It's time for you to go."

"As I said, I'm simply doing my job."

Wait a minute. Was he smiling at her? Was that a slight grin on his condescending, smug face? She could have sworn it was! "Right. Well, you're not doing it too well, because I am the last person who would want to hurt my uncle. Goodbye, Detective." Michaela turned away from him and got back up on Rocky. She trotted him over to the side of the arena, hot tears stinging her eyes. Asshole! When she turned Rocky back around, Davis was gone. She tried to regain focus and run Rocky back through his maneuvers, but found herself growing angrier. The horse sensed her tension, and responded in kind, tossing his head in the air and losing his direction. It was time to put him away, and get a grip.

She dismounted Rocky and led him down to the cross ties, where she took his tack off. Then she guided him to the wash rack, where she rinsed him off and brushed him down. She was still reeling from the detective's comments, which felt like accusations.

She let Rocky dry off in the wash rack, while she went back into the tack room and retrieved his day sheet to keep the flies from bugging him and from getting himself too dirty if he rolled, which inevitably he would.

Michaela turned as she heard one of the mares whinny from her stall on the end, then the pounding of hooves from outside. She bolted out of the tack room to see Rocky loose and running free around the ranch. Dammit! He'd yanked himself free from his lead line on the wash rack. That wasn't like him. What had gotten into him? But worse yet, he was taking off over the hill behind her place.

She ran into her office and grabbed the keys to her quad. Normally she wouldn't go chasing after a loose horse on a four-wheeler, but he'd taken off and where he was headed and as fast as he was going, there was no way she'd catch him on foot.

She revved the engine, kicking up dust all around her as she raced over the embankment that separated her property from the dilapidated old dairy farm behind her ranch. She'd wanted to buy it few years back, in order to expand, but the money hadn't been there. And now it was possible a developer was going to come in and build a mini-mall. Once Rocky made it past there, he'd hit the road and she couldn't let that happen. Geesh! She'd had it up to there with chasing loose horses in the last day.

As she came over the hill she caught a glimpse of him. He was still running, but he looked to be slowing down, and he also looked to have a destination. He was running into the old barn.

Michaela slowed the quad down as she approached the building, not wanting to frighten him. She didn't have anything to lure him with. She shut the quad off and slowly and as quietly as possible, entered the barn. Rafters lay strewn across the ground. It was difficult to see due to the haze of dust, kicked up by Rocky. Dust particles sparkled in the beams of light shining through the cracks of the old building, casting shadows around and causing Michaela to feel uneasy.

Rocky whinnied down toward the end of

the barn. She looked around to see if there was anything she could use to catch him with. Another whinny. Michaela stopped. That didn't sound like Rocky. Wait a minute. There were two horses at the end of the barn, and as she came closer she could see Rocky standing outside a makeshift stall, and inside was a mare. They were nuzzling each other and getting awfully cozy. Holy smokes! The horse Rocky was snuggling up to was a mare and she was obviously in season. But who did she belong to? Something was not right here. At all. First thing she'd have to do was get Rocky out of the old barn. Since someone was apparently using the old place to house the mare, they did have a bucket of feed to the side and a halter. She got a scoop together in an old coffee can someone had left inside the bag of grain, and after a few minutes of working at it, she had Rocky haltered and was leading him out of the barn with neither the mare nor Rocky too pleased about it.

"Oh brother, you wouldn't even know what to do with her." It took her almost thirty minutes to get him back over the hill and another thirty to clean him up, since he'd gotten himself filthy on his escapade.

When she was finished she went into the house and called for Camden.

"Hey honey, you're a mess. You better get in a shower if we're gonna head out tonight. I just got back from getting myself a stunner of an outfit. Went to The River over in Rancho Mirage today. I love it there. We should move there. Far more, you know, well-to-do. I had a mojito with lunch, too. Those are yummy. I'm thinking, instead of margis, I need to learn how to make mojitos. Wanna see my new outfit? I was just going to get my shower." Camden came down the hallway toward Michaela, wearing nothing more than a hot pink silk bra and matching panties. Michaela eyed her. "What? I told you, I was getting in the shower when I heard you come in."

"Get dressed. I need your help."

Camden frowned but went back into her room and came back quickly in a pair of jeans and a T-shirt. She followed Michaela out and got into the truck with her, who explained everything to her as they drove the back way around to the old dairy farm. "So, someone's got a horse there? So what?" Camden asked. "Probably a temporary thing. Maybe whoever owns the place is letting a friend use it for their horse. I don't know, but I also don't see why you're so weirded out about it."

"You don't find it strange that someone is

keeping a mare all by herself in a worn-down deserted barn?"

"No. Not really. I'm sure it's what I told you, basic. Someone needed a place to put their horse and they either own the barn or know someone who does. Do you know who owns the place?"

"No. I've heard all sorts of rumors from developers coming and building a minimall to condos, to even the city buying it and turning it into a horse park for kids. But I haven't heard anything in awhile. Of course, I don't keep much track on local current events."

"I'm telling you, I think you should relax."

Maybe Camden was right. It wasn't a big deal. The big deal was that Rocky had gotten loose and acted like a maniac and it was the last thing she needed today. She pulled up next to the quad. "I'll drive it home and meet you back there. I'm going to set her halter back and check on her. Make sure she didn't try and bust herself out of here after lover boy paid a visit."

"Okay."

Michaela got out of the truck, carrying the halter she'd borrowed and walked back into the barn. This time all was quiet. No dust, no noises, and as she came toward the stall — no horse either. Nothing. No feed.

No sign that a horse had been in this very spot an hour earlier. As she started to back out and get the hell out of there, something caught her attention. There on the ground not too far from where the horse had been kept was a pile of clothes and a sleeping bag. What in the world? Who had been staying here? She bent down to look over the pile. There was a small radio, a bag of chips and bananas, and a book. A children's book. Interesting. The clothes were too large to belong to a child, yet the book, a copy of *Peter Pan,* appeared worn. It was obvious there was a guest here at the old farm, and whoever it was could be lurking nearby. It had to be the same person who had taken the mare out of here. Michaela knew she'd better get the hell out of this place.

She set the book down and quickly headed out of the barn, feeling spooked. She jumped on the quad, drove around the opposite side of where she'd been before and turned to head home the back way. That's when she noticed a paper taped to the side of the barn, and even though her adrenaline was running from fear, she had to see what the paper read. It was a permit to build. And, it was issued to Tanner Developments. Michaela's mouth dropped. Camden's boyfriend owned the land.

Sixteen

Michaela went to her office before going back to the house. She was shaken and she didn't want Camden to clue in. She needed to pull herself together, before heading out for their night on the town.

She had to find out who the barnyard resident was at Tanner's newly acquired piece of property and if he was aware that a pretty little mare had been holding down the fort. Who owned that horse? And where the hell was that person now? Michaela wanted to head back to the dairy farm and take another look around, but she wasn't about to go there alone. That would be plain stupid. She'd already accomplished the *stupid quota* for the day. Who could she trust right now to go back over there with her? A frightening thought crossed her mind: She didn't feel like she could really trust anyone at the moment. Everyone she cared for seemed to be hiding something from her.

"Michaela."

She jumped, nearly coming out of her skin as she turned and saw Summer, Ethan's *ex*-fiancé.

Summer was a pretty woman with cinnamon-colored hair, which she usually wore slicked back into a ponytail. Her eyes were an interesting green color, so light that they almost appeared clear. Each time Michaela saw her she was reminded of a Stepford wife. Her skin was dewy with the perfect amount of meticulously applied makeup and she always looked as if she'd just stepped out of a Ralph Lauren catalog.

"I didn't mean to frighten you," Summer said. She fiddled with the knot of a khaki-colored cashmere sweater around her shoulders.

"Oh, hi, Summer. I didn't hear you walk up." This was the last thing she needed right now. Hadn't she had enough for one day? Now, she'd have to listen to Summer's crap.

"Yes, well that's obvious. You've done some wonderful things to the place since I was last here. When was that? I think your Christmas party? God, a year ago — can you believe that? We really shouldn't let time go by without visiting. It's simply not neighborly."

What in the world did Ethan see in this

woman? "Summer, why are you here? We both know that there isn't a lot of love lost between us, so don't carry on about how we should get together more often."

Summer shrugged. "I wanted to tell you how sorry I am about your uncle. I cared a lot for Lou and I wanted to extend my condolences because I know how close you were with him."

Michaela studied her. "Thank you. You didn't have to come out here to tell me that, though. You could have called, but I do appreciate it." She wondered if she should pursue asking Summer about Lou's books. "You were still working for my uncle?" She'd decided to go for it, although with trepidation.

"Some. Lou really wanted to have somebody come on full-time, and I can't do that. I have my own business to run. I did his books on the side to subsidize my own work."

Why was she lying? Michaela knew that Summer had been relieved of most of her duties because of the obscene way she'd left Ethan. And, Lou held a grudge, as Ethan should have as well! "Oh, so your business is taking off? You training a lot of jumpers these days?" Michaela tried to be nice. She knew that Summer had grown up riding warmbloods and thoroughbreds and had done well in the world of show jumping.

"Yes. It's going well, and now with things kind of changing in my world . . ." She ran a hand over her stomach and looked down. ". . . I'm thinking about expanding my business into a breeding program, kind of like what Lou had."

"Huh. You're multitalented." Michaela tilted her head to the side. "I didn't know you bred horses."

Summer let out an aggrieved sigh. "I don't. I would, of course, hire a breeding manager, but I think that Ethan can help me get it off the ground. He's a vet, after all. I'm sure that until I found the right person, he could do it for me."

"Right." Michaela nodded. "Well, good luck with that. Thanks for stopping by. Sorry to be short, but I have work to do."

Something not so deep down told Michaela that this conversation was far from over and that Summer hadn't only come here to pay her respects. She'd seen the woman work her "magic" on her friend, and she had the art of manipulation down to a science. Michaela felt sick to her stomach and decided not to pursue a line of questioning about Uncle Lou's books with Summer until she found out what institution the money from the owners of the mares had been deposited into.

"Michaela?"

"Yes?"

"I am aware that Ethan has confided in you about our . . . little surprise." Again she touched her stomach, and Michaela's did a flip.

"Yes."

"Well, I am very happy about the situation."

"I'm sure you are."

"And I am coming to you woman to woman and asking that you remain neutral. Ethan and I have many things to work out between us, and, I'm not sure how to say this, so I'm just going to."

"Please do."

"I'm asking you to stay out of Ethan's and my business."

Michaela folded her hands together, squeezing them — an attempt to keep from wrapping them around the woman's swan-like neck. "You know, Summer, I could actually do that if you hadn't taken Ethan's heart and ripped it into shreds. The man would have crawled across broken glass for you. Believe me, I don't know why, but regardless, he would have, and I supported his and your relationship because he loved you. But, I'm sorry, I can see right past those pretty green eyes and that Pilates body and the graceful airs that you put on. Ethan is a man, after all, and I think we . . ." She pointed to herself and then to Summer. ". . . both know they don't always think clearly."

Summer crossed her arms over her crisp button-down. "You have some gall. I may have made mistakes in the past where Ethan is concerned, and I am willing to admit that and make changes. He can see that and forgive me. And, do not forget that Ethan and I *are* having a baby together, whether you like it or not. If you want to stay in Ethan's life I would suggest you stay out of mine. In fact, I would go so far as to suggest you support me thoroughly, or you may be sorry. We both know how important family is to Ethan. He would never leave a child, not after what happened to him with his own father."

"Are you threatening me?"

"No. I'm not at all. I am only stating facts. You know, I find something fascinating about you." Summer shook a finger at her. "You're a very controlling woman. You don't want your closest friends to be happy because you've never been able to have that. It's not only Ethan I've watched you try and control. It's that ex of yours, and now your friend Camden. I know Kevin Tanner quite well, and he's told me that you're negative about your friend dating him. Why is that, Michaela? Maybe you should look at that. Maybe it's time you let people go, and have your own life. What's the saying? 'If you love something, set it free . . .' and you know what I think about your opinion of me? I think this has nothing to do with me, and everything to do with Ethan."

"What?"

"It's obvious, Michaela. You're in love with the father of my child. You've been pining for him for years, and it appears that you'll have to continue to pine. Give up the *best friends* act. Ethan is mine. Stay out of our lives."

Michaela's mouth opened to say something. But nothing came out as she watched the arrogant Summer MacTavish leave her barn. A few seconds later she bolted out of the tack room and yelled at Summer as she climbed into her Cadillac Escalade, which had a decal on the back window that read MACTAVISH SHOW JUMPERS. "I am not a control freak! You are! Look at you! You've even gone so far to get knocked up so you can manipulate Ethan! And, I do love him, because he's my friend, and I refuse to stand by and watch you destroy his life! You bitch!"

Summer slammed her car door and drove away. Michaela went back to her office and thought about the words they'd just exchanged. Why hadn't she been able to make a quick-witted retort? Comebacks were not usually a problem for her. Instead, her anger had gotten the best of her and the words came out sounding immature, like something from a seedy talk show. God, what had come over her? And now, she couldn't help wondering if there was any truth to what Summer had said. Was she the controlling type who drove people away? More than that, was there any truth to the idea that she was *in* love with Ethan?

SEVENTEEN

There was no choice for Michaela but to forget the day. At least for now. She couldn't let Camden know that she had a gazillion things running through her mind, including thoughts that Camden or her love interest might have wanted to harm her uncle, or that her own father was gambling again and possibly in debt to the mob, or that she suspected someone was trying to frighten her for God only knew what reason, and that there was even a possibility that the person trying to scare her was also her uncle's killer. Even more than that, she couldn't confide in her friend that Summer MacTavish was pregnant with Ethan's baby and that the perfect princess had come by to tell her to buzz off. But worse was the fact that Michaela wasn't able to ask the woman she'd considered her best friend for a decade now if she did indeed have control issues, and if so, did she push the people she loved away? Normally questions such as these — and honestly, there had never been questions posed for her quite like these — she'd have opened up about them to Camden. For as light-hearted as her pal seemed to be, she also had a good ear and an available shoulder to cry on, plus she'd always been totally frank and honest with her. At least she'd always thought so, and Michaela despised this burning ache inside her that raised doubts about Camden. She hated the thought that all of this could be true, but she really hated that she could even *think* there was the possibility that any of these thoughts were true.

Michaela was applying some blush when Camden walked into her bathroom, a margarita in one hand and a bag from Saks in the other. She swung the bag back and forth. "Here you go. Let's get this party started." She handed the margarita to Michaela.

Michaela set it down on the sink counter. "I think I'll wait until we get to the bar."

Camden frowned. "It's one of my specials. The Cadillac — you know, with a Grand Marnier float on top. Smooth." She took a step back. "Honey, I know sometimes I can be crass and put on a good game face. I know you're hurting, and I'm sorry. I thought maybe a bit of devil's brew might help relax you. But if you're taking it easy, I understand."

"Thanks."

"Now give it back to me. Why let it go to waste?" She smiled, but Michaela knew she was only half kidding. "Okay, since you're not ready for the hard stuff, do me the favor of . . ." She pulled out a black lace camisole, ". . . wearing this. I saw it, and knew it would look absolutely hot on you with a cute pair of tight jeans. You'll have all eyes on you from the minute you walk in the bar. The men will be fighting over you and the women will want to fight you."

Michaela looked at the wannabe blouse. Yes, it was cute in a Frederick's of Hollywood kind of way, and surely it would attract attention, but not the kind she desired. "As pretty as it is, Camden, you know I wouldn't be comfortable in that. I just can't."

"For me? I thought it would be so gorgeous on you. Come on."

She shook her head. "I'm sorry. I wish I could, but you know how self-conscious I get. Look, I know what you're trying to do. You want to make me feel better and I am so grateful, but it's hard enough for me to go out tonight, much less wear something

187

that should really be worn by Pamela Anderson."

Camden waved a hand at her. "Oh pooh, she's got nothing on you. But fine, all right. I understand. Maybe someday, my friend, you will realize just how beautiful you are and start dressing like it. Me? I already know I'm hot property and I ain't afraid to show it. Now, Kevin's driver will be by in about a half hour. I am so pleased you decided to go with us tonight. Where's the doc? Hell, he might as well come, too. I figure he's not going anywhere. I can see it now: You and me in rocking chairs with our margis or one of them mojitos, Ethan nursing sick horses while pushing a walker, while the two of you still try and reconcile the fact that you have feelings for one another."

"What?"

"I'm just kidding. But face it, Michaela, you two can't live with or without one another. You've both got a bad case of unrequited love gone wrong."

"That is not true. That is *so* not true. I've known Ethan since I was three years old. I don't love him and he doesn't love me, at least not in that way . . . and why do people keep suggesting that I have feelings for Ethan?"

"People?" Camden brought the margarita

to her lips, taking a big drink.

Great. She wasn't going to let this go, was she? No. Not in a million years. But, Michaela knew she couldn't tell her about her run-in with Summer or that Summer was pregnant. Ethan had made her promise not to tell anyone, and she was going to prove Summer wrong. She could stay out of Ethan's business and allow him to make his own decisions . . . or in this case, mistakes. But she knew that once she told Camden, the cat would be out of the bag and there would be no going back. "You. I mean, you. This isn't the first time you've made remarks like that, and, well, it's annoying."

"Sorry. I didn't know I was *people,* and I will work hard to refrain from making any further remarks that simply happen to be *the truth.* I may be annoying, but I am always honest, and I would never hurt you." Camden took a step closer to Michaela and reached for her hand. "I love you and you're my friend. You can always count on me. I'll see about working on that annoying part of me, once I go and get dressed to the nines, 'cause honey, this lady is getting lucky tonight. Oh, and in case you change your mind about the blouse, I'll leave it with you." She winked, let go of her hand, and sauntered away.

Michaela didn't change her mind and wound up wearing a pair of jeans — comfortable, not tight — a white T-shirt, and a caramel-colored fitted jacket with a pair of high-heeled Charles David boots — one of the few extravagant items in her closet that were the same color as the jacket. She went to her jewelry box and took out a pair of diamond ring hoops. They were another extravagance — one her ex-husband had given her. One she simply could not see fit to toss or sell on eBay, and when it came down to it, she'd been the one to pick them out. Plus, the facts were that she'd footed the bill in the long run. Therefore, technically, the expensive earrings were not from Brad at all, but a self-deserving gift from her damn self!

But the night he'd given them to her — Christmas Eve three years ago, had been so romantic, so sweet — a memory that she wished she could forget because it reminded her that somewhere in Brad was a man who she'd thought had loved her.

That was history, and to learn the reality of what her life had been at that time — nothing but a lie — had allowed her to look at herself and others in a different light. One that at this moment she wasn't too sure she cared for. She'd become calloused, or at least it felt like it, and there was a part of her that longed for the days when life felt and seemed more simple, when she still had dreams of a family, of the kind of love only seen in the movies or written about in books.

She slid the earrings through the holes in her lobes and stood back. She kind of liked the way she looked tonight. She could actually see the resemblance to Faith Hill that others often mentioned to her, and she was pleased she'd chosen to wear her hair down in loose waves rather than drawn back in her usual ponytail.

"Mick, the car is here," Camden yelled from the other room.

Car. Jeez. Who did this guy think he was, anyway? For goodness sakes, it wasn't as if they were all the rage in Beverly Hills headed to The Ivy. Sure there were places in Indio that had plenty of its well-to-do class but there weren't exactly the Lindsay Lohans and Eva Longorias of the world coming to hang out in their local digs. However, that was Camden. Find the flash and run with it. To Camden that obviously meant Kevin Tanner. Michaela would go along with it for the night, because she was determined to find answers. Answers she hoped Camden's latest flame would supply.

EIGHTEEN

Kevin Tanner waited inside the car as the driver opened the door for the women.

"Oh, my, aren't you dressed to impress," Camden remarked.

"Well, you know what they say, when in Rome," Kevin replied.

Michaela bit her tongue. For a moment she felt like rolling on the ground in laughter, even after her bizarre day and the past forty-eight hours.

Kevin was somewhere between forty and fifty; hard to tell, really. There was a chance that the reason he didn't have any creases in his forehead was because he'd been to see the plastic surgeon. He had light brown hair that he had to have blow-dried, because the only men she knew with hair as perfect as Kevin were either gay or looked like Kevin did — a wannabe Rico Sauvay. That was Michaela's name for men who thought they had "it," but didn't.

This Mr. Sauvay had "dressed" for the occasion in a western-style maroon shirt with a small navy flower print and oyster-colored snap buttons, tight Wrangler jeans, and what Michaela figured had to be real alligator boots stained the same maroon as his shirt. Yep, if there ever was a cowboy pimp, she was looking right at him. He even had a gigantic silver belt buckle attached to his belt. John Wayne had to be rolling over in his grave. Tonight might actually turn out to be fun. If they did wind up going to Boots and Boogie, the real good old boys there might not welcome Kevin with open arms. In fact, it was quite possible that the contractor would be out on his painted-on Wrangler ass before the night was through.

That thought made Michaela smile. "Yes, exactly, Kevin. When in Rome."

"I knew this was going to be fun!" Camden squealed.

Kevin shifted in his seat, looking uncomfortable. Probably wishing he were in his suit slacks rather than a pair of jeans that appeared to be cutting off any circulation from the waist down. Goodness, what was Camden thinking?

Uh-oh, was Michaela doing it again? Were her reasons for not liking the partners her closest friends chose more about herself than Kevin or Summer? Then she watched as Kevin put his arm around Camden, gold rings with ruby jewels on two of his fingers and a diamond one on his pinky. Hmmm, in this case, she was pretty sure it had nothing to do with her wanting to control her friend and who she dated, but instead wanting to protect her friend, who actually didn't look like she wanted any protecting from the lech.

It didn't take long before they made it to the restaurant.

"I hear this place is great," Camden said as they pulled into the parking lot. "It got five stars in the paper. The chef comes from Guadalajara so it's not like real Mexican food."

"Excuse me?" Michaela said. "Last time I looked at an atlas Guadalajara was still located in Mexico."

Kevin patted Camden's knee. "That's why I love this woman. She says the cutest things."

He had to be kidding. Camden looked at him with these goo-goo eyes that stirred the stomach almost to the point of retching.

"Oh, you two. You know what I mean. It's not the typical taco and burrito menu. The food is gourmet Mexican. For example, I read that they have a dish where the pork is cooked in banana leaves. Pibil style or something like that. And, it is supposed to be the new hot spot. After we eat we can hang out at the bar and then there are two dance floors. One with pop and that rap stuff, the other a bit more down to earth with a live band. We don't even need to go over to Boots and Boogie, because this place has it all and is supposed to be all the rage."

"Fun," Michaela said, trying to keep the sarcasm out of her voice.

"Now, come on. We *will* have a good time tonight. I know there is a fun master inside of you just waiting to come out and play. It'll be like Mr. Rogers' Neighborhood for grown-ups."

"You're a disturbed woman."

"Yes, I am. But I have to tell you, it's a blast. Try it for a night, Michaela. Let down that guard of yours and kick up your heels. You just never know what destiny has in store for you."

"I didn't know destiny had anything to do with tonight."

"Destiny has everything to do with every-thing. Now let's go have some of that pibil pork or whatever and a Cadillac Margarita."

For someone who was such a maneater and who always tried to come off as a sophisticate, listening to Camden at that

195

moment reminded her why they were friends. When it came down to it, Camden's dinginess *was* endearing and laughable, and she was able to laugh at herself.

"Okay, señoritas. Let's make it fiesta time." Kevin laughed. Michaela stepped out of the car. He was still laughing. "Get it? Like Miller Time, only fiesta time."

"I get it," Michaela replied, and walked ahead of the couple while she was sure they busied themselves with a game of grab-ass.

Once seated with margaritas at the table, which Michaela planned to nurse through the dinner, she reminded herself of her mission, and talk turned to Uncle Lou.

"Hey, Michaela I am so sorry about your uncle. He was a really good man. I liked him a lot."

Michaela had just taken a sip of her drink and nearly shot it back out as the lie poured from Kevin's mouth. She put on her game face. "Yes he was. It's horrible."

"Do they have any leads at all as to who murdered him?" Kevin asked.

Camden glanced at him. What kind of look was that? A warning? What was going on between these two that concerned Michaela's uncle? Or was she being paranoid? "No. At least they haven't said anything to me about a lead. I don't know. It's a bit strange, though, how one of the detectives has been behaving toward me."

"Really? How is that?" Kevin motioned for another round from the waiter.

Michaela hadn't taken but two sips. "Well, he was really nice to me right after I found my uncle."

"He better have been," Camden cut in.

"Then he came over that evening to question me further, and again he was gracious, understanding, and he listened without what I assumed was any judgment."

"Is this that cute detective?" Camden asked and smacked her lips together. "Sooo divine." Kevin shot her a nasty look. "Oh, but so not you."

That was true. Kevin Tanner was certainly no Detective Jude Davis. Not by a long shot. No doubt, the detective had never even received a traffic fine. Kevin on the other hand . . . well, she was sure he'd dabbled in his share of dirty secrets.

"Let her finish," Kevin said.

Michaela noted the agitation in his voice. She had him right where she wanted him. She was tossing out the bait. "Yes, it is the same detective. Anyway, earlier today I was working one of the horses and he came by. But he was no longer Mr. Congenial. He'd obviously done his share of interviewing and someone on his list apparently made a suggestion that I was unhappy my ex left me, and I could have blamed my uncle for it."

Kevin took a long pull from his drink. "That's ridiculous!" Camden exclaimed.

"That's what I told him. He made some further insinuations about it until I asked him to leave. I was pretty uncomfortable with the direction in which things were going."

"No doubt," Kevin said. "You don't think someone is setting you up to take the fall? I mean, God knows you would have never harmed your uncle."

"That's a good question, *Kev.* What do you think? I do suppose it's entirely possible. I heard or read somewhere that the first twenty-four hours of a murder investigation are the ones that yield the most important facts. So, maybe someone decided to divert the detective's attention by exaggerating my circumstances and embellishing quite a bit."

Kevin nodded. "That's too bad. It could be that. But I am sure the police will find out who did this and justice will be served for Lou."

Michaela took a sip from her margarita as the waiter set down their food. She wasn't terribly hungry. The talk had dulled any hunger she might have felt earlier. It still felt wrong to take pleasure in anything, even simple pleasures like good food. Setting her drink down and thanking the waiter, she turned back to Kevin. "I didn't realize you knew my uncle so well. I was under the impression that the two of you had a rather tense relationship. Isn't it true that you'd recently made an attempt to purchase his property and even after he told you no, you remained persistent? Apparently you don't like to take no for an answer."

Camden set her fork down, her mouth full of pork pibil. She did not appear especially happy. She glared at Michaela, who attempted to smile sweetly. Camden's eyes narrowed, making her look like a Cheshire cat who'd just shoved a canary in her mouth only to discover that she'd really bitten into a snake. Oh yeah, she was pissed off, but Michaela knew she'd get over it, especially if she didn't have anything to do with killing her uncle, which she hoped was true. But this Kevin jerk, she had a feeling in her gut, was responsible in some way for her uncle Lou's murder.

Kevin let out a halfhearted laugh. "Don't be silly. That is crazy talk."

"Is it?" Michaela asked.

"Of course. I had nothing but respect for

your uncle. Sure, I would have loved to acquire his land. After all, he owned some prime property. A resort hotel and golf course would be great and do a lot to help boost the local economy. But I understood Lou's position. He'd owned that land for years and loved it. I don't think he needed it all, but that was not my business."

"No, it wasn't, but you still persisted, didn't you? And, now that my uncle is gone, it might be easier for you to buy property from a grieving widow."

"Michaela, that is enough," Camden said. "Kevin is a businessman. He wouldn't harm anyone. Please stop. We came out to have a good time. Okay?"

Kevin shook his head. "No. It's okay. I understand. I do. You're sad and probably feel miserable, and I can't blame you for lashing out. You've been through hell. I'm sorry if I ever made Lou uncomfortable, or you for that matter. He was a good man. I'm sorry for your loss. I did respect him, and I don't take no easily. I wish I had. Please accept my apologies."

Michaela studied him. He did seem sincere. Strange. Really strange turn of events. How to handle this one? "Then you don't plan on pressuring his wife Cynthia to see if she has an interest in selling to you?"

He shook his head. "Uh, no. I've come across some other property that will work as well, if not better."

Oh yes, he had, hadn't he? Suddenly that act of sincerity he'd expressed became just that — *an act.* "You have, haven't you? The old dairy farm, right behind my place."

Kevin didn't reply right away. He took another drink. Camden looked at him. "That's correct. I did acquire that piece of property recently."

"I can't wait to have condos or a golf course right behind my property."

"Maybe you won't have to. I'm willing to make you a very nice offer for your place and that way any condos I might build behind your land won't offend you."

Michaela pressed her back into the booth. How did Camden not see this guy's transparency? "You want to purchase my property?" she asked, amused.

Kevin nodded. "I'm willing to pay you full market value for it, and it's my understanding that you could use the cash."

Michaela shot Camden a dirty look. Was Camden telling this jerk that Michaela was having financial problems? Camden tried to smile, looking like a deer caught in the headlights.

"Excuse me?" Michaela raised a brow.

"I'm fine, and I'm not interested in selling."

"Fair enough. Can't hurt to ask," Kevin replied.

Michaela knew that this was far from over. Her gut nagged her. Kevin was like a fox that would lie in wait. She'd been married to one, and she'd learned to recognize the traits. What really disturbed her was that she couldn't help wondering if this guy hadn't been using Camden all along to get to her.

"It never hurts to ask. And, you did, and she said, 'No,' so, let's see if we can't lighten the subject around here. Please," Camden said, fidgeting nervously with her hands.

"Sure," Michaela said. For the remainder of their dinner, she tried to stay as involved as she could about topics as simple as the weather to as complicated as politics in the Middle East, but her mind kept wandering back to Kevin Tanner's proposition and the fact that the man had a horse on his newly acquired property hours ago. She wanted to question him further and see if he could answer her question as to where the horse had disappeared to, but decided for now to wait for another opening. She also couldn't forget the conversation she'd overheard between Camden and Kevin just the night before. Were they two simply fantastic liars with a huge secret to hide?

As they finished dinner and moved over to the bar and club, Michaela had a thought. "So, Kevin, have you ever ridden or owned a horse before?"

He nodded. "Sure. My first wife owned Arabians. Pretty horses to look at, but gawd, what a pain in the ass. High strung."

"Maybe. I'm not completely convinced. Sure they can be a bit more squirrelly than some of the other breeds, but I was out at the Scottsdale Arabian Show a few years ago to watch the stock horses and I was impressed. They're beautiful and agile. I actually wouldn't mind having one of my own. So, you don't have a horse now?"

"No. I like to look at them, but riding is not for me."

"Huh. Did you know that there's a horse been taking up house in your old dairy barn?"

"What?"

Camden shifted in the booth. "Yeah. My stud, Rocky, got loose today and he charged right over to your place. He apparently found himself a girlfriend. There was a mare there. In a stall, flirting with him."

Kevin shook his head. "That's impossible. I was over there two days ago and there was nothing there. Nothing but a bunch of cobwebs and rotted wood. I don't know if you're playing a game with me, but it's making you look a bit foolish."

"Me? Playing a game? Tell him, Camden: There was a mare there earlier today and then when I went back, she was gone." Camden didn't say anything. "Camden, are you going to back me up on this?"

"Technically, I didn't see a horse. You told me there was a horse there."

"I don't believe this." Michaela stood and put her hands on her hips. "Someone *is* playing games here, but it isn't me." She started to leave.

Camden caught up to her as Michaela walked toward the bar. "I'm sorry, hon, but I didn't see a horse." Michaela kept walking. "I think you're tired and angry and —"

"And what? You think I'm losing it? That I didn't see a horse in *Kevin's* barn?"

"No. That's not what I'm saying."

Michaela stopped and faced her. "Really? Then, why didn't you defend me back there?"

"I'm sorry. I'll go tell him right now that I believe you. I *do* believe you."

"You can tell him whatever you want, but I know what I saw and I also think Kevin Tanner is hiding something. And, I think he's making a fool of you."

Camden looked like she'd been punched. "What?"

"I think the man is playing you to get to me so he can buy me out."

"I don't . . . think that's true." Camden stuttered on her words. "I think he . . . really likes me. Men do like me."

"Yes they do. They certainly do. But not always for the right reasons. I think that men tend to play you, Camden." Michaela walked away from her friend, leaving Camden stunned and hurt — her own stomach sank as despair blanketed her heart.

Nineteen

Michaela sat down at the bar, shoving down her emotion, trying hard to keep from crying. Had Camden's greed for the good life come before loyalty and friendship? Could money and Kevin's love be *that* important to her? Enough to betray? Enough to . . . kill?

"A Coke, please. Can you make sure no one takes my seat? I have to go to the restroom."

He winked at her. "You got it."

When she came back there was a glass of white wine waiting for her, not a Coke. She called the bartender back over and pointed at the wine. "I didn't order wine. I asked for a Coke."

"Yeah." He tossed a dish towel over his shoulder, and leaned against the bar, his dirty blonde, longish hair falling down in front of his eyes.

"Yeah. Can you take it back?"

The bartender lifted his head, tossed back the hair, and gazed past her. "That would be rude, don't you think," a voice from behind her said.

Her stomach dropped as she recognized the voice and turned to face her ex-husband. "Brad."

He looked at her with his light brown eyes, the kind that made you wonder if they were green, hazel, or brown. They were brown. Poop brown. He ran a hand through his hair, which she was glad to see was thinning. The hair was the same color as the poop-brown eyes. His other hand was wrapped around a drink. Surely a gin and tonic: a mean man's drink, as far as she was concerned.

"I can stand." He squeezed himself in between the chair, the bar and her.

She pulled as far from him as she could and crossed her arms. "What do you want?"

"I wanted to say hi. Is that a crime?"

She laughed. "It's all a crime when it comes to you."

"Now, now, sweetie, you know that's not true . . . or fair."

Michaela eyed the wine. Suddenly it looked good. She took a long sip from it. "I am not your sweetie." She poked him in the chest. "And, I would appreciate it if you would leave now. Don't you have your Barbie doll to keep you company? What's she doing? Making sure her lipstick is just so?"

"My, you have gotten nasty. I'm having a drink with Bean." He nodded at a table in the corner where Michaela spotted Bean, who looked shell-shocked while drinking what appeared to be a Shirley Temple.

"What are you doing with that poor man?"

"We're friends."

"Friends, my butt! You used Bean while you worked for my uncle and you're up to something now with him, aren't you?"

"God, Michaela, always so suspicious."

"Of you. Uh, yeah. With good reason, I might add."

"Bean called me. He said that he wanted someone to talk to about Lou. He's sad."

"I don't believe you."

He shrugged. "It's the truth. Guy needs a friend right now. He's all distraught and so I told him that I'd take him out for some dinner and we could talk. Honest."

"Great, now leave."

"Don't be like that. I wanted to come by and say hello, buy you a drink. We used to sleep together, after all."

"Don't remind me."

"Look Mick, I really just came over to tell you I was sorry to hear about Lou. I figured you're having a hard time. I know how close you were with the guy and Bean says that you've been pretty upset. So, I'm sorry. I am."

If she could have crawled inside the barstool she was seated on, she would have. She eyed him. Frankly she was getting sick and tired of people saying things she doubted they meant. "Sure. I bet you are."

"Why would you say that? Of course I'm sorry."

"Please, Brad. It's no secret that you weren't exactly pleased you got caught all tangled up with Miss Do-Si-Do. I think you had a plan from the get-go. You wanted to have your cake and eat it, too, but you choked on it, and it was my uncle who saw to it that you choked."

Brad rolled his eyes. "Is that what you told that cop who came around asking both me and Kirsten a ton of questions? Were you the one to tell him that I have some vendetta toward you? You know that's not true. I don't appreciate having police at my back door looking into my personal life."

"Oh, and like you didn't tell the detective that I was so in love with you and wanted a baby so much that I was happier being in the dark about your affair. That I was angry with my uncle for showing me the truth.

209

I'm sure you don't appreciate the police having a peek at your personal life. It hasn't exactly been stellar. But, I'm also sure that you have *nothing* to hide either. God knows you've never kept any dirty little secrets from me."

"You will not let it go, will you?"

"Excuse me?"

"Me, you, this bitterness you feel over me and Kirsten. I know you pulled that little horseshit stunt on me the other night. I'm not too happy about it, but I'll let it go. See that's the kind of guy I am. I'm a good guy. You need to let it all go, too, sweetheart."

"Brad, trust me when I say that I have let it go, but it doesn't mean I have to associate with you at all . . . and why in the world would I ever believe anything you say is sincere and truthful?"

"Dammit, Michaela, it was one mistake. One little mistake. So, I fooled around. She came on to me, and damn . . . well, she threw herself at me, and most men I know would have done exactly the same thing that I did. I didn't mean for it to get out of hand. I didn't want to carry on with her. It just sort of happened. And yes, I was not happy that Lou got involved in it. He should have stayed out of it, but he didn't. I know he thought of you like his own daughter and that he was trying to protect you, but I would have come around and we could have worked it out, if he hadn't sent you those pictures. I don't love her. I never have and never will, not like I love you. Come on Mick, I *do,* I still love you. Give me another chance. Let's work it out. We can keep trying to have a baby and I'll be there this time for you. I know how bad I messed up. I miss you a lot." He touched her shoulder; she swatted his hand away.

Michaela could hardly find words. "How dare you!"

"What?"

"How in the hell did I ever marry someone like you? I must've been drugged or insane. I can't believe my ears. One *little* mistake? No, it was a giant mistake and not just one time either. She came on to you? Hmm, well I don't remember anywhere in the vows we took, it stating that it was okay to be unfaithful if the other party instigates it. Or that just because you can get it up when a hot girl struts by doesn't mean you have to say yes. And, as far as my uncle doing the right thing? You *bet* he did. I'm so grateful every day for what he did. Work it out? Now you want to come back to me? And, you even have the audacity to mention trying to have a child with me, when you damn well know that we, and let me state it again — *we* — owe thousands in medical bills to an infertility specialist, which you won't cough up. You have to send your girlfriend over to hound me to sign divorce papers and you won't even meet your obligations? My guess is the only reason you're even suggesting any kind of reconciliation is that Kirsten threw you out on your ass tonight for some reason and you need a place to go. I suspect that right about now, tucking your tail and trying to convince me to take you back is rather appealing. And as far as love . . . Well, I believe you don't love Kirsten, and know what, I believe you don't love me, because the only thing a selfish prick like you can love is *yourself*."

"Why, you little —"

"Everything okay here?" Michaela turned to see Joey Pellegrino, beer in one hand, the other clenched. "Is he bothering you?"

"I am not bothering her," Brad spat back. "We're having a private conversation."

"Actually, he is bothering me."

"The lady says you are. It looks like your 'private conversation' is over. I think that if you want to wake up in the morning looking as you do tonight — uh, in one piece, that is — then I suggest you leave." Joey stared at him.

That stare alone would have done the job, but the words . . . oh they were great, too.

Brad started to say something, then walked away mumbling under his breath.

"Thank you," Michaela said. Her hands were shaking and she decided to finish off the wine in one fell swoop.

"Easy there. He really got to you, didn't he?"

"I guess. He knows how to get under my skin."

Joey sat down next to her. "My offer still stands. I know some people, a few friends of some of my cousins who could make his life fairly miserable."

"No. I'm fine. Don't do anything foolish. I appreciate the thought, though. Hey, where is Marianne?"

"She and the kids are in the restaurant. I came in here for a beer. She doesn't like me to drink in front of the kids."

"Oh, the boss, huh?"

"Yeah, you know, I gotta do the right thing for the kids, and honestly I had to get away from them for five minutes. Joey Jr. is a handful. Kid is practically climbing the walls, screaming in my ear. And, then the baby on top of it, I tell you, it's enough to make me crazy sometimes. Anyway, I don't have a lot of time, and it's good you're here.

I found something out about who your dad owes, and how much."

"Who?"

"Danny Amalfi, my aunt Luisa's godmother's brother's son."

"Huh?"

"It don't matter. He's a lowlife bookie and low man on the totem pole in the family. But your pop is into him for a hundred grand and keeps coming back. Danny don't say no, he just keeps racking up the debt knowing that your pop has some land and his credit probably ain't so great, that's why he doesn't borrow on it to gamble with. Danny's thinking he can get himself a nice little ranch out of this deal, if he plays his cards right."

"My mother would have to sign any papers having to do with their home and property."

"Right. She's the boss, too. Women. But she may have no choice, if your pop keeps sinking the ship. Anyway, Danny tells my cousin Pauly that he can force your pop to give up his land if he hooks him for a few more grand."

"Oh, God, no. This is bad. Do you think Danny had anything to do with my uncle's murder?"

"No. Danny might be one to break a kneecap or two, but he's a wuss, and like I told you, it's code that you don't go after a guy's family."

"Okay. I suppose that's a positive," Michaela replied. "But what am I going to do about my dad?"

"You gotta talk to him."

"I know."

"Listen, you get your dad to stop this nonsense. I think I can handle Danny. He owes me a favor, a big one. I think I can maybe make this thing go away for your dad, or at least get it reduced."

Michaela was stunned. "You would do that?"

"We're friends. You're a good lady. You've had it rough lately, so let me see if I can help."

She threw her arms around him. "Thank you so much. Oh God, I'll pay you back when I can. I will."

He pulled away and was definitely blushing now. "It's nothing. You talk to your pop."

"I will, I promise. Thank you again. I won't forget it."

"I better head out. You got a ride home?"

"Don't worry about me. I'll get home."

"I don't think Mr. Shifty will bother you again."

They said goodbye. She decided it was time to get a cab home. She'd had just about enough, and tracking down Camden and Kevin wasn't an option. She was still pretty angry and she was sure Camden's feelings were mutual.

She headed out of the restaurant, careful not to be followed be Brad or Camden. She didn't see either of them. Good. It was brisk outside and she buttoned up her jacket.

"Michaela." Dwayne and Sam walked toward her. "What you doing?" Dwayne asked.

"I'm waiting for a cab."

"You have a bit of the drink, huh?" Sam asked. She nodded, not wanting to get into all of it. "Well, how far you live?"

"Ten minutes."

"Ah, ten minutes, cuz, let's give her a ride home," Sam said.

"Yeah, definitely. Come on."

Michaela shook her head. "No guys, that's okay. Looks like you just got here. Go on in. I'll be fine."

"Ah, c'mon." Dwayne put an arm around her. "Sam don't need to eat nuthin', anyway."

Sam rolled his eyes. "Why you always gotta do that?"

"What?"

"Insult me? Ever since we been kids, you talking about my eating and how big I am.

Just 'cause you scrawny."

Dwayne laughed. At first Michaela wasn't sure Sam was kidding, but then he started laughing, too, and as the breeze picked up, and exhaustion began wearing on her mind and body, she agreed to a ride home.

Dwayne drove an older Bronco. The car smelled of horses and saddle soap, which was perfect as far as she was concerned. "You doing okay?" Dwayne asked.

"I guess. And you?"

"Me too. Sam and I been talking about it."

"Yeah, still can't believe it," Sam said. "But, let's talk about something else. We been through a lot."

Michaela nodded.

"How's Rocky?" Dwayne asked. "You still wanting to show him?"

"I don't know. I'm actually thinking that I need to geld him." She told him about Rocky's field day.

"He figure out that pastures *are* greener on the other side," Sam said.

Michaela laughed. "I guess so. But that old place isn't exactly next door. I mean, he really had to follow his nose."

"Acting like he had some loving before, by doing that," Sam replied.

"Nah, like Michaela said, he just following his nose," Dwayne said.

"Yeah, I s'pose. Stud horse been bred or not still got the instinct."

"Oh my God," Michaela blurted.

"What?" Dwayne asked.

"That's it. Oh, my God. How come I didn't think of it until now? That's it." Her mind reeled.

"What she talking about, cuz? What you talking about, girl — *shit. Goddammit! What the hell!*" Sam yelled. He kicked the back of Michaela's seat.

Michaela turned around to face Sam. His body stiffened, and his eyes rolled back into their sockets. "Dwayne? Dwayne!" Michaela cried.

Dwayne turned. "Oh no!" He pulled the Bronco off the road and braked.

"What is it? What's going on?" Michaela yelled.

"In the back. Lift the hatch, get his duffel out. Get it!" Dwayne ordered.

Michaela complied as Dwayne climbed into the back seat with Sam. She handed it to him. Dwayne opened the bag, pulled out a bottle of pills and shoved one down Sam's throat. He held his mouth shut. "Swallow. Swallow. Juice. There's juice in the front. In the glove compartment."

Michaela suddenly realized that Sam was

having a diabetic seizure. She found the juice and gave it to Dwayne. A few minutes later, Sam seemed to be doing much better.

"Are you okay, Sam?" she asked. "I didn't know you're a diabetic."

"Oh yeah."

"That's why I tell him not to eat so much," Dwayne said, pulling back out onto the highway.

"That's why I tell you I needed to eat." Sam laughed, trying to make light of the situation. "Sorry about my cussin'. Happens sometimes when the blood sugar drops."

"Don't worry about it. I understand." They pulled into her place. "Do you want me to make you something to eat?"

"No. I think I should get him home. I'll take care of him," Dwayne replied. "You okay?"

"Sure. I'm fine."

"I walk her to the door," Dwayne told Sam.

Sam nodded and said goodnight. It was nice, especially after everything that had been happening, to have Dwayne make sure she got inside the house okay. When they reached her door, Dwayne turned to her. "You started to say something about you had it figured out, or something like that, right 'fore Sam had his seizure."

She waved a hand at him. "It's nothing. It's crazy, really."

"What?"

She didn't know if she could trust Dwayne, but he *had* been in Vegas the morning Uncle Lou was killed, so he hadn't killed him. That she was sure of; but could he be the one who'd been scamming breeders by selling off sperm that was not Loco's? Sure, he said that he didn't have any affiliation to the program, and he was a really nice guy, but she bit her tongue anyway. "Oh, I just figured out why Brad was hassling me back at the restaurant. You weren't there, but my ex was giving me a bad time."

"You need me to talk to him?"

She shook her head. "No. But thanks for the lift home. I really appreciate it." She got inside the door, locked it, and leaned against it. What she didn't want to tell Dwayne was her theory about who was the father to those foals — her very own Rocky.

TWENTY

Michaela woke up the next morning knowing that before she could prove her theory about Rocky being the father to those foals, she would have to get his DNA sent over to the AQHA. As she headed out to the barn, she couldn't help thinking that by doing this she could be implicating herself in a crime that she didn't commit. Maybe she should speak to an attorney before going ahead with it. Maybe she should go to Ethan with this. She wished Uncle Lou were there. He'd know what to do.

She tossed in a flake of hay for each one of the horses, and when she came to Rocky's stall, she opened it up. "Hey big guy." He turned and looked at her. "This won't hurt." He bobbed his head up and down and then turned back to his breakfast. It was almost as if he knew what she'd said. She loved that horses, like dogs, are social and love to communicate. They like to be around other animals and people for the most part.

She pulled out several strands of Rocky's mane and placed them in a plastic baggie. Back at the house, she typed up a letter to the AQHA. It wasn't an easy letter because who in the world would believe it? God, she prayed that it wasn't true. But she made the decision to take a chance and send it in, along with Rocky's hair samples.

What had alerted her to the possibility that Rocky could be the father to the foals in Ohio was something Dwayne — or maybe it had been Sam? — had said last night, that the horse had followed his nose. The dairy farm was close by, but not so close that Rocky would have caught a whiff of the mare in season. Yet, he'd beelined it straight to her — as if he'd been there before.

It might seem crazy, but Michaela was inclined to believe that someone was bringing in a mare to the dairy farm while in season, then taking a back trail in to get Rocky out. The barn was far enough away from the house that someone could do this. Leading him to the barn, using him to "breed," and then returning him. If this were the case, there was quite a bit of nasty business going on. Not the least of which was that someone was stealing her animal time and again. Boy, if she got her hands on that person, she'd . . . well, she'd kill him! How dare someone do that to poor Rocky! Okay, so Rocky probably didn't mind too much. But, still, it was wrong. Very, very wrong!

Horse owners were being scammed into thinking that they were going to be getting foals with Loco's pedigree, not Rocky's. Now, Rocky was no dumpy animal. He boasted those great breeding lines, too. However, Loco had won several championships and earned a wad of cash, and the titles helped to drive his stud fees up.

The question was, if this were true, it had been going on for some time now. She would first have to find out if her theory was correct. Rocky had never been typed with the AQHA because he wasn't being used to stand stud. She took the letter and the hair specimen down to the Postal Annex and sent it via overnight mail. She'd gone online last night to find out who she should send it to, and she planned to make a follow-up call either later that afternoon or early tomorrow morning. She'd probably sound like a loon, but it made sense to her. Michaela's gut told her that this was a possibility, and she had to pursue it. Her gut also told her that Brad could very well be the one who had been working the scam. He would have still been living in the house when the initial contracts were signed with the breeders. He could have gotten Rocky in and out of the dairy farm in about two hours' time. But she would have woken up if he'd gotten out of bed. Maybe it all took place after she'd kicked him out. She'd have to go back and look at the dates. Plus, she wanted to go over the contracts and lawsuits to see if she could learn anything from them. She had a full plate waiting for her after working the horses.

By the time she returned from the Postal Annex, Rocky was finished with breakfast. She got him out and readied him for his morning workout.

The beauty of being in the arena with her horse during those forty minutes was that she forgot all her worries . . . everything. She only focused on what she and her horse were doing. They became one together.

"Poetry in motion."

She brought Rocky to a stop and looked up to see none other than Detective Jude Davis. Oh, no. What now? Why did this guy have the knack for showing up at the worst possible time? "Hello, Detective. What can I do for you? I believe we discussed all we needed to yesterday."

"Yeah, we did." He shoved his hands into his pockets and looked down at the ground, then back up at her. "I don't believe you had anything to do with your uncle's murder."

She patted Rocky's neck. "You don't?"

"No. And, well . . ." he paused, "I'm sorry about bringing up that you and your ex were trying to have a baby. I'm sure that hurt and it was why you were so resentful and defensive."

She stared at him, not knowing what to say. He did look apologetic, but he'd fooled her before when he'd been all nicey-nice while questioning her in her home and then "coming to the rescue," the other night. Then, he'd turned around and showed up at her folks' place asking all sorts of questions about her marriage. And yesterday? Well, that had blown her initial impression of him. Was he really sorry?

"Look, I'm going to do something way out of line here. So if you say no, it's fine, but . . . I was wondering if we could have coffee sometime."

She almost started laughing. "Coffee?"

"Uh-huh." He waved his arms in front of him. "I know I was tough on you yesterday. I was, but I'm a good judge of character and the way you reacted, in all honesty, put any doubts I had about you and what happened with your uncle to rest. Not that I ever really thought you might have murdered him, but I have to look at all the possibilities."

"So now you want to have coffee with me?"

"Okay and a muffin, too, or you know, a croissant."

Wait a minute. Was he asking her out? Wasn't there some policy within the police force that made that against the rules? He shouldn't be asking her out. Should he? Could he? Well, he did preface it by saying that he was out of line. And, he was. Wasn't he? Heat rose to her cheeks. "Detective, can you do that?"

"Do what?"

"Ask me for coffee?"

He smiled. "It's not like a date. It's more of an apology coffee meeting kind of thing. I told you that I feel badly that I was a bit rough on you yesterday. Granted I was doing my job."

She couldn't help but smile back at him. She sure did want him to be sorry. She'd been fooled before, but there was also a part of her that wanted to stay angry at him. "An apology coffee meeting thing? Hmmm. And, so what, we go out for coffee and you say that you're sorry, which you already did anyway, and there you go."

"Kind of."

"Kind of. Okay, Detective Davis, you know your apology, the one you just gave me is pretty sufficient. But I have to ask you, you seemed, uh, fairly suspect of me. Why the change of heart?"

"I told you, I can read people. Gut feeling. You know what I'm thinking, let's forget it. I'll be in touch about the case." He pulled a pair of sunglasses out of his front jacket pocket and all of a sudden looked very TV coplike. And, it made him even more attractive.

"Coffee is good. When? Where?"

"Do you know the bakery on Third? The Honey Bear Cottage?"

"Know it well. Best lattes in town."

He pointed a finger at her. "Good. Then that's where, and why don't we say day after tomorrow? I know that tomorrow will be a rough one for you, so if you want to wait until next week, I understand." His voice turned far more serious than it had been.

"Tomorrow? What are you talking about? What's going on tomorrow?"

"Didn't your uncle's wife tell you? The coroner's office released his body and she's decided to have his services as soon as possible."

Michaela shook her head, totally confused. "No she didn't tell me. I assumed it would be the end of the week. Thank you for letting me know. I'll give her a call."

"I'm sure she's planning on letting everyone know today."

Michaela nodded.

"Would four o'clock work, then, on Thursday?"

"Four it is."

"Also, if you need anything tomorrow, please don't hesitate to let me know."

"Thanks."

She watched as he walked down the hill. Why was she feeling so weird about him? Okay, one minute he was nice, the next he was not, and then he was again. Did he really believe that she had nothing to do with her uncle's murder, or was this some ploy he used to get people "to talk?" Not like she had much to say. Okay, so she did have some interesting theories at this juncture, like someone had killed Uncle Lou because he discovered who was substituting Loco's sperm with another stud's — possibly Rocky's. And why, even with all this horrible business going on, did Michaela hope that his desire to meet her for coffee meant more than some simple apology or the need to drag further information from her? Men!

And, what was going on with Cynthia? Why hadn't she called to let her know about Uncle Lou's services, and why the rush? Sure, she could understand wanting to get it over with, let him rest in peace . . . but why hadn't she asked Michaela to help her with the plans?

She dismounted and led Rocky out of the arena and down to the crossties, where she was reminded of yesterday's incidents. Should she have told Davis about the mare and the dairy farm, and what she thought was going on? Probably. But he might think she was losing it, and she'd been so caught up in the moment when he'd been there. He had that knack about him. Mesmerizing. Sort of. Also, she needed confirmation from the AQHA before she went further with her hunch. She had a feeling the contracts, the AI program, and the missing money had something to do with her uncle's murder. She decided she would tell Davis over coffee.

After sponging Rocky down, she put him away. She worked two more horses and then headed to the house. Camden was out. She'd never come home last night. God, she hated distrusting her friend. It was so damn uncomfortable. But she couldn't help it.

She showered quickly and headed out. Since Joey ruled out the possibility of the mob putting a hit on Lou because of her dad, there were others she needed to talk to. People who may have had a reason to want her uncle gone. She needed to start by looking into the lawsuits filed against her uncle, and as much as she didn't want to, she needed to go see her father and call him on the floor about his gambling. She also had to go see Cynthia. Her uncle's wife owed her some answers. She would find out why Cynthia was in such a rush to bury Uncle Lou. Michaela also planned to tell Cynthia that she knew Cynthia was pregnant.

TWENTY-ONE

Michaela called Cynthia's house a couple of times, with no luck. She didn't answer her cell phone either. Michaela had a sinking feeling in her gut, because the last time no one answered a phone at Lou's . . . well, she couldn't even think about it.

She decided to take care of her next item for the day and then find Cynthia. Calling her parents' house, she learned from her mom that her dad wasn't there.

After dropping by a few local spots where she thought he might be, she found her dad at Roger's Sports Bar. He wasn't there to drink. That wasn't his vice. In fact, she'd put money on it that he was drinking a seltzer with lime. He'd come to watch the football game he'd bet on; he'd done it for years. Old habits die hard.

She sat down across from him. He didn't even look at her, his eyes remaining on the screen. "I'm only watching, Mickey.

That's all."

"Dad, you've never been able to lie well. Besides, I already know. I know how much you're in for, and to who."

"Oh." He still didn't look at her. "You going to tell your mom?"

"She also has a pretty good idea, Dad. She just doesn't know the amount."

Benjamin Bancroft finally gazed at his daughter. His eyes were the same hazel color as hers. But, she recognized the look of shame suddenly covering his. "How did you find out?"

"Does it matter? I did, and I know you're in trouble. Quite a bit."

"Did someone come to you? Were you threatened by anyone?" He reached for her hand.

"No, Dad, nothing like that." She noticed he wore a fresh bandage on his right hand.

"I'm sorry." He looked back at her, his eyes watering.

She squeezed his good hand. "Oh, Daddy." He nodded, reminding her of a scared child, not the disciplinarian she'd grown up with. "How long have you been into this again?"

"I don't know, a few months, maybe."

"A few months? And, you've gone through a *hundred thousand dollars?*"

He nodded. "I couldn't say anything. I don't know how it started. The way it always does. I get down about something, obsess about it, and then I make one small bet and that leads to another then another and it gets out of control before I know it. I kept thinking I can make it back. I can make it work."

Michaela could never really understand that thinking. To her it was insane. How do you *not* know when you're out of control? How does one bet lead to another and another? Her stomach churned. She wanted to scream these questions at him. But she'd done that years ago while home on spring break and exhausted from working and going to school — resentful that she had to go above and beyond most of the other kids at Cal Poly, where she studied animal husbandry. He'd just kept apologizing until *she* finally felt guilty for her own anger.

What she'd read and learned over the years did at least convince her that gambling was an addiction, like drugs or alcohol, and it wasn't about the gambling itself, *or* even the money. It was the momentary thrill, the possibilities. It took gamblers out of the realities of their world and placed them into a fantasy. Gambling gave them a high similar to drugs or alcohol and fed them tons of endorphins while in the process. But the crashes were huge, as harsh realities set in when these people lost their homes, their livelihoods, and ultimately their families.

"Okay, well, Dad, what's done is done. I'm going to help you, but you are going to have kick this thing for good. I know I'm enabling you by taking care of this debt, but I can't stand to see Mom hurt by this. It'll tear her up. And, you can't lose your place."

"I know. I need help."

"Fine."

"How are you dealing with the money? You don't have that kind of money."

"I know a relative of your bookie. He's looking into what he can do for me . . . I mean for you."

"Oh honey. No. I can't let you do that. I don't want you getting hurt because of me."

She squeezed his hand again. "You have to let me do it. And, I promise I won't get hurt, but here's the deal: You find a daily meeting with Gambler's Anonymous, get a sponsor again, and stay straight. In fact, for the next month or however long it takes, I am going to personally escort you to those meetings. I also will have my friend report in regularly to see if you've gone to borrow money from anyone, because this guy knows all the shady characters around. You're a good man, you're a great dad and husband; you can beat this thing. You are bigger than it is. Do it for me, for Mom, but really Dad, do it for yourself. Because I am certain you do not want to die a lonely old man. And, I can almost guarantee that if this continues, that is exactly what will happen. Mom will leave you, and I don't think I could stand by and watch you destroy yourself any more. It's too painful."

The tears were coming down his face now. God, she hated talking to him like that. But she had no choice. She had to have some kind of leverage over him, and when it came down to it, she knew that family meant everything to him.

"What do I tell your mom, about the meetings?"

"I think you have to tell her the truth. I know it's going to hurt her. I've got to leave that up to you. Tell her that you're going back to GA and you're turning the books over to either me or a bookkeeper. We both know that Mom doesn't like to handle the finances, but it's obviously not a good idea for you to run them. Not at this point."

He nodded. "I don't know what to say. I love you. That's pretty much all I can say, kid. And, I am sorry for putting you through this, especially now. I'm weak."

"No you're not."

He shook his head. "I feel rotten over this, over Lou. I didn't mean for any of it to happen."

She watched his face twist into anguish. "Dad, what do you mean?" She got the feeling by the way he was talking that it was more than the gambling, and more than her uncle dying.

"The police have been talking to me."

"Yeah, they've been talking to me, too."

"Honey, I think they have me listed as a suspect."

She squirmed in her chair. "Why?"

He held up his hand. "I went to see Lou the morning he was killed. My fingerprints . . . are on the pitchfork."

"What?"

He nodded.

"Dad, what are you saying?"

He sighed. "That morning, early, I went to Lou and Cynthia's place. I hadn't slept the night before because we'd talked and it didn't go well. I'd told him what was going on with me and the gambling, and he said that he'd think about helping me out. He said that I needed to talk with your mother, and I told him that I couldn't do that. He hung up on me." He took a sip of seltzer. "I couldn't sleep that night and I knew he'd be up by six, so I headed over to see him. I found him in Loco's stall. We . . . had words. He said that he wasn't going to bail me out. That he had his own problems to deal with and that I needed to come clean with you and your mother. He was right. But I reacted badly and I grabbed the pitchfork and threw it, then punched the wall. That's how I hurt my hand. Stupid, I know."

"Yes it was, Dad. What were you thinking? Don't you see how this addiction eats you up? You could have hurt Uncle Lou, and you did hurt yourself! Now, the police think you could have done this?" She paused and choked back emotion. "Your addiction turns you into someone you're not. Someone I don't know and don't want to know."

Where was the dad she grew up with? The one who'd take her on trail rides and play cowboys and cowgirls with her and her friends? Sometimes they'd pretend to be the posse after the bad guys, or sometimes they were the horse thieves trying to outrun the posse. Those were great days and good fun. *That* was the father she remembered. Not this man, reduced to heated arguments with a brother he adored — someone who hid from the world through an addiction that caused nothing but pain.

"You're right. I don't want to be this man any longer. I don't. I'll do whatever it takes. I'll tell your mom everything. I'll be honest and we'll get through it. But you should know that I think the police might arrest me. I think they're already looking into the gambling and they know I was at Lou's place the morning he died. You know, that was the last time I saw him. That morning." He choked on a sob and broke down.

She scooted her chair up and put an arm around him. She let her father cry for several minutes. She noticed a few people glancing over at them, but it didn't matter. He needed her and she would be there for him. "It's going to be all right, Daddy. It is. And, I know Uncle Lou is watching us, and he loves you. You have to forgive yourself. You *have* to. He would have. I'm sure he did. Do this for him. And, as far as the police go, I know you didn't kill him. I know it.

"And, Dad, I'm going to find out who did."

TWENTY-TWO

Michaela saw her dad to his car and followed him home. They walked into the house together. Her mom was in the kitchen. "Hi, you two. Oh, Michaela, I didn't know you were coming by. Good, good. I'm making a lasagna for tomorrow's service. You want to help?'

That was Mom, always doing, always one step ahead. "I would, Mom, but there's some things I need to take care of. I ran into Dad and thought I'd stop by and say hi."

"Oh, nice. Ben? Are you okay?" Her mom looked from Michaela to her dad and back again.

Michaela cut in before her dad could answer. "I think he's tired, right, Dad?" She knew he needed time to think about what he would say to her mother.

He nodded. "I'm going to lie down for a bit." He kissed her on the cheek and walked into the kitchen, where he gave his wife a hug.

Janie frowned. "Benjamin Bancroft, do you feel okay?" It wasn't often that he was outwardly affectionate.

"I'm fine. I love you." He headed back toward their bedroom.

Michaela's mom looked at her. "What was that all about?"

"I think you should let him rest right now. He's got quite a bit on his mind, but don't worry, Mom. Everything is going to be fine."

"Michaela?"

"Mom, please. It's not my place. Daddy will talk to you when he's ready. Trust me."

"I don't like the sound of this, but fine. It appears I don't have a choice."

Wanting to change the subject and needing to find out about Uncle Lou's funeral, Michaela asked, "Mom, when did Cynthia inform you about the services?"

"Last night."

"She didn't tell me. I was out for a bit anyway."

"I'm sure she's tried to call you. It's at one. Why don't you meet us here and we can all go together."

"Sure." She kissed her mom on the cheek. "See you tomorrow. I love you. Oh, what should I bring?"

"How about that pear tart you do so well?"

"You got it." She knew that she left her mother feeling a bit confused. For now, she had to not only see what she could find out in order to seek justice for her uncle, she also had to keep her dad from going to jail. Once her mom found out about the gambling it would be heartbreaking, but her father going to jail would be devastating.

On the drive to Cynthia's she recapped in her mind everything she'd learned over the past few days. First: Ethan had fought with her uncle and never explained why. She would get to the bottom of that, because she hated suspecting that he had anything at all to do with this. Then there was Camden and her boyfriend. Their phone conversation still had Michaela reeling. Not to mention that Kevin now owned the dairy farm and had a mare housed there that he claimed to know nothing about. There was the issue with the contracts and the breeding and her suspicions around that. She had a feeling Brad was responsible for that mess. But a killer? She wasn't sure.

Bean had been acting strangely toward her, but she didn't think he had the ability to pull off a breeding scam and she certainly didn't think he could become angry enough to kill. Anything was possible, though. Plus, what was his continuing friendship with Brad all about? Sam and Dwayne had been off to Vegas with the horses. Summer had worked for Uncle Lou and handled a lot of the paperwork in the past. Could she have killed Lou for some reason?

She'd pretty much ruled out the mob, but there were still those lawsuits against Lou that she had to get to the bottom of, which led her to ponder Cynthia. She was pregnant, and she was hiding something — like a lover, or possibly something more sinister.

After getting out of her truck at Uncle Lou's ranch, she walked through the breezeway and over to Loco's stall. He came to her, his hot breath pouring through his nostrils onto her hand as she rubbed his face. Neither Dwayne nor Sam looked to be around either. Dwayne's truck was gone and she wondered where they might have gone. "Too bad you can't talk," she said to Loco, who pulled his head away and shoved it in his feeder.

She called out for Bean. He should at least be around. Deciding to see if anyone was up at the house, she knocked on the back door. No one answered. She turned the knob; it turned easily. "Cynthia? You here?"

She walked in through the laundry room. Cynthia wouldn't get upset if Michaela waited for her in the house. She headed into the kitchen. From down the hall, she thought she heard someone crying. No, it was more than crying and as she got closer, she realized it was Cynthia and she was sobbing.

"Cynthia?"

Michaela saw her as she rounded the corner of the hall, slumped down against the wall, her face in her hands. "Cynthia? What is it? What's wrong?"

Cynthia didn't say anything. She didn't lift her head as she held out a note. It was stained. With what? Oh God, it looked like droplets of blood. Michaela took it from Cynthia's shaking hand. It read, I AM SORY I KILL MR. LOU.

"What? What is this?"

Cynthia looked up at Michaela. She uttered, "Kitchen."

Michaela stomach tightened as she entered the kitchen. Bean lay on the floor next to the table, a gun in his right hand, blood seeping from his temple.

TWENTY-THREE

Something was wrong here. So very wrong. Bean had killed Uncle Lou? Then, he'd committed suicide? Michaela's head filled with confusion as she struggled to wrap her brain around this.

The police showed up within minutes. Cynthia had called 911 immediately after finding Bean, and it was apparent that Michaela had come in right after that.

Detective Davis was there along with a team of other cops. He'd asked Michaela and Cynthia to wait for him in Uncle Lou's office, where they now sat on the couch. Michaela held Cynthia's ice-cold hand. "I don't understand why," Cynthia said.

"I don't know either."

"Bean loved Lou. He loved me. We helped take care of him. He was here because we had been meeting at this time of day for a few weeks now. I was teaching him to read." She choked back a sob. "He's come every day at the same time even the last few days, since Lou . . ." She shook her head. "I told him that he would have to wait a bit before I felt like teaching him again." A nervous laugh escaped her lips. "But, Bean didn't understand that. Obviously. That's why he's been showing up in the kitchen every day, waiting for me to teach him. Today I went out for a walk knowing he would show up here; I didn't want to face him. I didn't want to tell him to leave me alone. I knew it hurt his feelings, but I haven't been able to do anything like I used to." Cynthia couldn't speak anymore. She buried her head in her hands and sobbed.

Michaela rubbed her back, shoving down her own sorrow and disillusionment the best that she could. "I'm sorry, Cyn. I really am."

Davis entered the room, then stopped. He looked at both women with sympathy. Cynthia wiped her face. "Why did he do this?"

"Mrs. Bancroft, we don't know."

"Did he really kill himself?" Michaela asked.

"From what we can assess so far from the scene, I would have to say that he did."

Michaela nodded. "Do you think he killed my uncle?"

Davis sat down in the chair across from the women. "I don't know of any other reason for him to write that note and do what he did."

"I don't believe it." Michaela shook her head. "I'm sorry, but I don't. You met Bean. The man was like a six-year-old child. He couldn't have done this. He didn't have the wherewithal."

"Ms. Bancroft, I hear you, and we will investigate this situation completely. I did meet Bean and yes, he was very childlike. However, I have heard of some children gone very wrong who have done horrendous things to siblings, friends, even parents. There is not a lot of sense to be made out of a situation like this."

Michaela had had a similar reaction to Bean and his behavior just the other day. She'd even wondered if he somehow feigned much of who and what he really was. Had his behavior all been an act? But why? And for all those years? Or, was he like a child who had become angry at something Uncle Lou did and reacted in the heat of the moment before he'd realized what he'd done? If that were the case, then the morning that she'd discovered Lou's body, Bean likely would have reacted differently than he had. She couldn't help wondering if he would have even shown up. That is, if he truly had the mentality of a six-year-old, wouldn't it have been more likely that, after doing something so terrible, he'd run and hide? He'd seemed genuinely shocked over her uncle's death. She brought this up to Davis.

"Because of Bean's emotional immaturity and low IQ, it is possible that after killing your uncle, he blocked the memory due to the trauma it caused him. Then something might have sparked his memory, which upset him, causing him guilt, and he couldn't take it. I don't think he murdered Mr. Bancroft intentionally if he in fact did. I'm not a psychiatrist, so I can't say for certain. But believe me, we will continue to try and find out exactly what happened."

Michaela sighed. None of it sat well with her.

"I am going to need to take statements from both of you. Separately, of course. It's procedure."

"I need to use the bathroom," Cynthia said. "Is that okay, Michaela? Do you mind going first?"

"No. Go ahead."

Cynthia tried to smile, but it was forced and came out looking more like a frown.

After she left the room, Davis said, "I realize that this seems incomprehensible to you, but from everything I've seen so far, it appears that Bean committed your uncle's murder and killed himself."

"Yes, it's difficult to believe, but I guess so. I don't know what else to think. If the police are sure that's what happened . . ." She shrugged.

"The evidence points in that direction."

She nodded and looked down.

"I don't want to sound crass. You and your family have been through a rough time, but at least now you can bury your uncle with some sense of peace."

Her head jerked up. "Sense of *peace?* I'm not sure about that, Detective. I don't know how much peace can be found when you learn that a man with the mentality of a child has murdered someone you love dearly, then kills himself. There's no peace in that."

"I'm sorry."

Neither one said anything for several seconds. She felt like she was suffocating in that room with Davis, who stared at her. She needed to get out of there and think . . . or not even think, but just *be.*

"Why don't we go over what happened here today and how you found Mrs. Bancroft and Bean?" Davis finally asked.

Michaela told him everything from the time she arrived at the ranch. She didn't recognize her own voice as she relayed the story to him. It sounded far off, as if someone else was explaining to Davis what she'd encountered. But it was her. It had been her. Her neck and shoulders tightened with each word she spoke, and she knew that if she didn't get out of there soon, she would crack. Right there, in front of Davis, she would break down. Thankfully he finished his questions. He stood and held a hand out to help her up from the couch. His hand was warm. He squeezed hers and then let go. "I am sorry for all you've been through."

"Thank you." She saw Cynthia briefly and told her that she had to go. Cynthia seemed to understand.

Walking past the kitchen, she saw that Bean's body had already been covered with a tarp. She couldn't help but look. Was it morbid curiosity that made her do it? Or the fact that she still couldn't accept any of this? She heard herself say out loud, "Why?"

A police officer approached her. "Ms. Bancroft, you really shouldn't be here."

She turned to leave. Her eye caught the corner of the kitchen counter. On top of it sat a book. She walked over, ignoring the cop. She looked down at the book — *Peter Pan*. The same book that she had found yesterday in the stall at the old dairy farm.

Twenty-Four

Michaela felt in her gut that Bean hadn't killed himself, and she doubted that he'd murdered Uncle Lou. He just didn't seem capable. How wrong could she have been about Bean? Had he really done it and fooled everyone? She needed a sounding board.

She walked into Joey Pellegrino's shop fueled by confusion and this strange twist of events, one that she didn't want to believe. "Hey, Mick. How's it . . . wait a minute, what is it? What's wrong?" Joey came out from behind his shop counter.

She tried hard to keep her emotions in check. "I need someone to talk to."

"Yeah, sure. Wait a sec, will ya? I gotta take care of a customer first." Joe walked over to help out some guy in the paint department. Once he'd finished, he locked the door behind him and turned the OPEN sign around to CLOSED. "Figure by the way you look and sound, you'z don't want no one buggin' us."

"Thanks. I appreciate it."

"C'mon. Follow me to my office."

They walked past aisles of nuts, bolts, and nails. He pushed away a pale blue curtain to reveal boxes upon boxes. He pointed to one of them. "My office. Take a seat. It ain't fancy, but it'll do." She smiled and was glad she'd come to see him as she sat down on the box. Joey sat down opposite her. "So, tell Joe what's goin' on." Oddly enough — or considering that it was Joe, maybe not so odd — opera music played from the radio in Joe's *office*. "Wait a minute." He got up and turned the radio down, then grinned and blushed as he turned around. Obviously he hadn't wanted her to see his *softer* side.

She started with how she'd found Lou dead in Loco's stall, how Ethan was keeping something from her that was related to an argument he'd had with her uncle; how Camden and Kevin Tanner had joined forces and their intentions appeared dishonorable. Then, she told him about the cancelled checks and contracts and how Uncle Lou's memory was apparently fading on him, and how Dwayne and Sam both thought he could use a vacation. She filled him in on Cynthia's pregnancy, the horse at the dairy farm and what she figured had been going on there, and how she thought Brad was somehow connected. Finally she told him about Bean's apparent suicide and the doubts she'd had about him — whether or not he was just a really good actor, or someone who enjoyed playing the victim card.

"I mean, doesn't it seem odd to you?" she asked Joe. "Here's a guy with the emotional and probably the intellectual equivalent of a six- or seven-year-old and supposedly *he* did this? Why?"

"Maybe he got pissed at your uncle. You know, like you said, even the cop told you that he's seen it all. That there are some mean kids out there. And, this Bean guy was no kid, even if he acted like it."

"Yeah. But what about him sleeping at the old dairy farm with that mare? It had to be him taking care of the mare. I don't think he could have come up with some type of breeding scheme on his own."

He shook a finger at her. "You said so yourself that maybe you had some doubts about Bean, like maybe he was faking some of it. You know he's obviously been around horses, watched your uncle's operation. Maybe he saw a good thing as far as money and he thought he could get some of it. But once he realized that he wouldn't be able to get away with it . . . well, then it all soured on him. Then, maybe he figured, you know, like your uncle was gonna connect it all, or maybe your uncle *did* put the pieces together, and voilà! The guy goes all looney and stabs him with the pitchfork." Michaela winced. "Sorry."

"It's okay. No, Joe, it still doesn't ring true. Yes, it *does* look like Bean was involved in this somehow, at least the breeding scheme, which I'm still sure was going on."

"What about these two guys — Sam and Dwayne — who worked for your uncle? Bean worked with them, too."

"Yeah. Maybe." She shrugged. "They just don't seem like bad guys."

Joe laughed. "Oh my friend, things are never what they seem."

"The morning my uncle was killed though, they were in Vegas."

"Can you confirm that one?"

"Pretty sure. They were taking out a few horses. I'm certain there are hotel and restaurant receipts that can confirm their whereabouts. As soon as Dwayne heard about what happened he was on his way back."

Joey rubbed his chin. "I don't know. Sounds like one mess. I gotta tell you, Mick, why don't you let the police take care of it? They think they've got it all figured out, right?"

"I don't think they do. It's a gut feeling, but I really don't think they *do* have it figured out."

"But you ain't no detective, and I'm afraid you're gonna get hurt mixin' yourself up in this thing."

"All I'm doing here is talking with you, bouncing off ideas. I trust you, and you've got good instincts."

He smiled. "I do, don't I? Okay, since we're *just* bouncing out ideas here, you telling me about this wife of your uncle's gives me an idea. The lady is preggers, and you're thinking you heard somewhere in your family rumor mill that Uncle Lou didn't have the goods. You ever think that maybe she got knocked up by another dude, and then knocked off her hubby?"

"I did think of that, and I keep telling myself that maybe the pregnancy test I saw was wrong, or maybe Uncle Lou never *had* the vasectomy."

Joey shook his head. "You gotta tell the cops this. They need to know she's expectin', and you gotta find out if Lou was able to make that happen for her. Pretty big motive for murder, don't you think? And, if

Lou's wifey was doing the deed with some other guy, well . . ." He shrugged, his large palms face up. "You know the guy bangin' her . . . oops sorry, sometimes I don't use the nicest language."

"No problem."

"Anyway, the guy sleeping with Lou's wife could have taken him out on account of her. Man gets all funny when he knows his seed's been planted. He might've gotten all possessive over Cynthia, with the kid comin' into the world. Or, it could have been a planned thing between them. They wanna get rid of Lou, so they can crawl off somewhere, start a new life as a family. Plus, your uncle wasn't exactly poor. Leave the money for the wife and she and her new family might be lookin' to have a *real* nice life together."

"True. I hate to think that, but of course, it *could* be true. You're right, I need to give the police this information, because I don't know who she might have been cheating on my uncle with. If she was, you're exactly right: it does make a motive for murder, doesn't it?"

"You bet. But don't you go looking into it. If Cynthia and her boyfriend — if she had one — took your uncle out, and you sniff around, it's possible you could be in

255

danger too. You remember, we're just throwin' out ideas here."

"I got one more thing." She opened her purse and took out the cancelled checks and the contracts from the breedings. "Can you take a look at these?" She handed them to him.

"The contracts you was talkin' about?" She nodded. "What am I lookin' for?"

She started to tear up. This was all getting to her. "I wish I knew. Maybe where the checks were deposited? Maybe see if somehow Cynthia is connected, although if she is, I don't know why she'd ask me to look into it for her."

"Cover her tracks. Criminals know how to manipulate. I'll check into it. I got a second cousin who I think has a nephew in banking, maybe he can find something out."

"Thanks. I don't see Cynthia as a criminal, though."

"Maybe not her, but if she was cheating on your uncle, her lover might be *real* trouble, and people do insane things for love."

Michaela *could* buy that. Love did seem to make people crazy. That's why she was determined to tread carefully when it came to the romance department, especially after the way Brad had screwed her over. "Possible. I don't know. Look, I've got one more thing." As if he wasn't already doing enough for her.

"Name it."

"Can you see what you can find out about a Dr. Verconti? See when my uncle might have gone to see this guy. I always thought his doc was Dr. Sherman. The same doc my family has seen for years. Anyway, I found a prescription for Lou from this Dr. Verconti and I don't know if there's any way to find out why he prescribed Ativan for him, but if you could, I'd be grateful."

"Ativan, huh? For anxiety. Yeah, well, I gotta tell you, gettin' medical record info is tough, but I'll see what I can do. You say Verconti, huh? Italian. That might work in my favor. Who knows, I might have a cousin who knows somebody who knows someone who could get the lowdown from this doc." Michaela nodded and sniffled, tears again welling in her eyes. Joey was being so good to her with all of this, but talking about it, she couldn't stop the emotion rising in her again. "Hey, hey. C'mon now. It's gonna be okay. No more cryin'! Sure, I'll see what I can do for you. I told you I would."

"I know. It's hard, that's all. And you're being awfully kind to me, Joe. Whenever you want to bring your daughter by, I'll get her started on those riding lessons, and we'll see what we can do about finding her a horse. In fact, I've got one I can start her on," she said, thinking about Booger. He'd make a perfect kid's horse. If he could put up with Camden on his back flopping all around, he'd handle having a kid on him just fine.

"Maybe over Christmas break. That's in a coupla weeks, and by then the dust should have settled some for you. Look, why don't you go on home and get some rest. I'll check things out, see if there's more to any of this. Try not to worry your pretty head any longer."

She stood. "Thanks, Joe."

"Sure. I'll call you if I find somethin' out. And, well, anytime you need someone to talk to, I'm here for you." He thumped his chest and stood. "I'm glad you came to me."

"You're okay, Joe Pellegrino."

"You ain't too bad yourself. Be careful."

She was glad she'd gone to see Joe. The man was true blue. But she couldn't help feeling even more confused than ever. She knew what it was like to really want a child. There were times in the past when she thought she'd die if she didn't get pregnant, and as difficult as it was, she'd had to come to terms with it. Knowing that ache, she couldn't help wondering now if Cynthia could have wanted a baby and a life with a new man badly enough to kill for.

TWENTY-FIVE

Michaela left Joe's hardware store and suddenly felt famished. She knew there was nothing at home to eat. When was the last time she had eaten, anyway? The day had gone by in another blur — fast and furious and more confusing than ever. Joe was right: She needed to tell Davis that she thought Cynthia was pregnant and not likely by her uncle. Right now though, she had to eat, and she wasn't too sure what to say to the detective. She'd have to select her words carefully, especially since Davis seemed certain the case had been solved with Bean's *suicide.* And, what if that were all there was to it? She doubted it, but still, what if her theories were just her imagination gone wild? Michaela knew she'd wind up sounding like a complete lunatic to Davis, and she really didn't want that. Nah; she'd hold off calling him until maybe later, and if she didn't reach him, she'd leave a message. For all she knew he'd already packed it up for the day and gone home. He'd likely be out with some cop buddies having a beer . . . or maybe home with his daughter. The thought of Davis having a kid made her smile. She'd bet he was a great dad. Let calling him go until later. Plus, she promised her mom that she'd bake a pear tart for the reception. Couldn't let Mom down.

Michaela picked up the ingredients she needed for the tart at the grocery store and thought about grabbing something to make for dinner, but didn't have the energy to cook for herself. And a microwave dinner didn't sound appealing. Before loading her groceries in the truck she called over to the China Lion down the street. She ordered some Kung pao chicken and an egg roll. That would do.

When she walked into the restaurant the smells of ginger, garlic, and red pepper spice assailed her senses. Her stomach growled. Mmm. Good choice. The place didn't look to be too busy, which meant her order probably wouldn't take long. She walked up to the hostess booth and gave her name. The petite Chinese woman said, "One minute, please. I see if food ready." She nodded politely and disappeared behind a red drape.

Michaela heard someone call her name

and saw Sam sitting alone in one of the booths. He motioned her over. "Hi," she said. "How are you?"

He motioned at the spread of food in front of him. "Not too good. I eat even more when I'm upset. You know . . ." He shook his head. "Can't believe Bean would do this. Good man. A little slow, you know, but good. Just snapped in the head. Dunno. Don't understand, but it's terrible. Found out when we got back from the feed store, me and Dwayne. Bad dream, I tell you."

"More like a nightmare. I can't believe it. Do you really think Bean had the capacity to kill my uncle and then himself?"

"Dunno. Looks that way. That's what Mrs. Bancroft tell us. Who knows what goes on in the mind of a man? Maybe Bean be more of a thinker than we all figure. Maybe he have some anger stuff going on and Lou make him angry."

"Maybe." But it sure didn't sit well with Michaela. Bean might have been slow and even a bit odd . . . but angry? No. He was too kidlike to be *that* angry. However, she *had* been wrong about people before. Hell, look at what she'd been married to. "Where's Dwayne?"

"He back home. I eat. He don't eat when he upset. It be that way since we were kids.

I can't help myself though. He real tore about all of this with Bean and Lou. Real sad and like all of us, mixed up 'bout it. Sit down." He sipped his beer. "Want one?"

"No. I ordered takeout. It should be ready in a minute. Uh, I hate to sound like a mother, but Sam, should you be drinking beer and eating like that with your diabetes?"

"Probably not. But I can handle it. Know how to take care of myself since I was a kid."

"You've been a diabetic since then?"

"Nah, been taking care of myself since I was a kid."

"Didn't you live with Dwayne's family growing up?"

"You got that one backward. He come to live with us when he was like fourteen, I think. Can't remember. My *makuakane* and *makuahine* — my dad and mom — always love him, you know. His parents drown in a boating accident off Oahu. Sad story. Dwayne come to live with us, but he fit right in. My family always love him."

"I thought you said that you've been taking care of yourself since you were a kid." She was starting to think that Sam had had too much to drink. "Sounds to me like you had a very loving family."

"Oh you know, all us kids grow up on the

islands take care of ourselves. We learn from Mother Nature, you know. Just a figure of speech is all. Me taking care of myself, just the way it was, and Dwayne, too. We have a lot of fun together back on the island."

"That's really sad about Dwayne's parents. I had no idea." It did explain why she noticed that sad, faraway look in Dwayne's eyes at times.

"Yeah, bad stuff. Tough."

"But both of you are close with your parents?"

"Sure. Yeah. I want to go back home now, open a restaurant. Or go *somewhere.* Need to get off the mainland. Too crazy here."

"It does feel crazy right now, that's for sure. I had no idea that you wanted to own a restaurant."

"Oh sure. Been my dream for a long time now." He rubbed his thumb and middle finger together. "Need cash though, you know. I want more than a restaurant. Want to run a luau, or hotel, you know, think big. I almost went back a few years ago, had a buddy with an opportunity to open a place on Maui and we was gonna have us the best luau around."

"Sounds nice."

"Yeah well, didn't work out. Maybe now, I go home and find a job in a restaurant and try and work my way up. Being here for a while make me think I could go back and open a Mexican place. I make good tacos. I like them, too. Maybe Chinese." He smiled. "Like I say, I love food." He laughed and ordered another beer.

Sam was a talker, and since he was rambling on, she decided to do some more fishing. He might have answers to some of her questions related to the deaths, or on her theories about the breeding program and the lawsuits. "Hey Sam, did you know my ex-husband, Brad, very well when he worked for my uncle?"

He took a swig of his beer. "That guy? What a jerk."

"I know."

"Not just to you. He boss everyone around the ranch when he can, when Lou not around. He make Dwayne so pissed. Only one who like him was Bean, but that guy like everyone. Too bad he didn't take out your ex instead, huh?"

Michaela nodded, not exactly knowing how to respond to that. "Did Brad do a decent job at the ranch? I mean, when he was working."

"What? Handling the breeding?" He shrugged. "S'pose so. What's so hard? He gotta help the stud do his thing to collect the . . ."

She held up a hand. Might as well go for the jugular and see what Sam thought of her theory. "I know. He collected the semen. I guess what I'm getting at is, do you think Brad could have been involved in selling breedings to horse owners for a cheaper stud fees than Loco's, and substituting another horse's DNA in place of Loco's?"

"Semen? Sure. Don't think it would be too hard. Get into where the containers were and make a switch, yeah, not too hard. You know I even tol' Lou and Dwayne that with an animal like Loco on the place, we need better security. Horse worth $125,000, and his stud fees alone are $3,500, who knows someone figure out a way to work it? Charge what, even half that and supplement the sperm, well, you send out say even one sample a day during breeding season and you could make some nice cash. I know Lou had a security company out not long ago after I talk to him, make him see he got a lot of money tied up in those animals. I know he planned to get some cameras set up around the place and some alarms real soon. Lou be too old-fashioned for too long. He still livin', well, *was* livin' in the dark ages. Bad people out there. Take your money. Steal your horse. You don't know.

Just don't know."

She leaned into the table. "So, you *do* think it could have been possible for someone to be running this type of scam, and now the owners of these mares have caught on, and they've started suing the ranch." She sighed.

"It could have happened. Like I say, bad people out there. I don't know." He moved the food around on his plate. "You know, Dwayne mention to me something about Lou being sued by some people in Ohio. Dwayne think Lou just having memory trouble and accidentally shipped the wrong stuff out."

Michaela nodded as the hostess set her takeout down. "But you don't?"

"Like I say, don't know what to think. Crazy stuff."

"Wow, this could just be the beginning, then. If this were really happening, there could be hundreds of foals out there that aren't really Loco's, and owners will find out when they go to register them with the AQHA. This might only be the first batch of lawsuits. Not good." She shook her head as the reality of how severe this situation could be dawned on her. "We haven't even come into this year's foaling season. Oh, God. Wait until this batch of folks want to register their foals, if there is another group that was duped like the people who already filed lawsuits. It could be *a lot* of money."

"Anything possible." Sam took a bite of his egg roll.

"The AQHA has not found a match for those foals and all of Lou's studs are DNA typed and on file with AQHA."

"Yeah, tough. I *do* think there something fishy, too. Don't know what, but it don't smell right to me."

"Can I ask you something else?"

"Shoot."

"Do you think my ex could have been involved with this kind of a scam?"

"Your ex is one strange duck. He don't have the full deck, you know." He tapped the side of his head. "He know a lot about the animal and he a good lyin' man."

"I know. Thanks. Look, I better let you get back to your dinner."

"Anytime I can help." He downed the rest of his beer.

"Be careful, Sam. Go easy on the beers. Do you need a ride home? I owe you."

"Nah. I'm fine. I don't live far. I walked over and if I have to, I can call Dwayne."

She left Sam to eat and drink his sorrows away. So, Sam thought that Brad was more than capable of deceit. Duh! But was the man she was once married to also capable of stealing money, then murdering her uncle and now killing Bean and making it look like a suicide? She was beginning to think that Brad was capable of anything.

Twenty-Six

Michaela made a quick stop at the barn to feed the horses. Even though she had food on the brain she tried to give each horse down the aisle some special attention with love pats. Most of them nudged her hand away and tossed their heads. Even Leo had no interest in making nice. She was late, so she couldn't blame them in the least. "I see how it is," she sang out, tossing flakes of hay onto her wheelbarrow to make her rounds. "All you guys want is your chow. What am I? Chopped liver?"

Finished, she went on up to the house to reheat her dinner. While she nuked it she played her messages. One was from her mom just checking up on her, another from Ethan with basically the same message. The last caught her interest: "Hello. This is a message for Michaela Bancroft. My name is Henry Stein and I'm an attorney with Gold-bloom, Richards, and Stein. Please call me at your earliest convenience. It's in regard to your uncle's estate." Michaela jotted down the number. She tried to call, but no one was there. It was after hours. She'd try back tomorrow. Wonder what the attorney wanted?

The microwave buzzed. Ah yes. Food! She pretty much shoveled the Chinese food into her mouth, except for half the egg roll, which she shared with Cocoa, who was acting a bit neglected. She tossed the ball for her a few times and watched as her old dog jiggled across the family room to retrieve it, until finally deciding she'd had her fill. Game over, Michaela knew it was time to get to baking. As much as she didn't want to get up and make the tart, she'd promised her mom, so after cleaning up she went to work. She'd forgotten how therapeutic baking could be. No wonder when Mom was stressed-out she cooked and baked everything from one of Julia Child's cookbooks.

Putting the finishing touches on the pear tart, she wondered what was going on with Camden and if she'd show up back at the house. They needed to talk. Michaela was setting the tart in the oven just as the phone rang. It was Joe. "Hey, Mick, I got something for you."

"So soon?"

"What can I say? I got a cousin who's got a friend whose sister works as a nurse for that Dr. Verconti."

"You sure do have a lot of cousins."

"I know. Lots of aunts and uncles, too. You know, we're a good Catholic family. So, anyway, word is this Verconti is a pill pusher, you know. Hands out the Xanax, Prozac, Vicodin, and your uncle's Ativan like candy. Your uncle never did come in to see him."

"What?"

"According to the nurse, he called saying he was feeling all jittery and stuff, having panic attacks. The doc prescribed Ativan with a few refills."

"Was there anything she said about how he heard about the doctor?"

"I thought of that, too. Nuthin'."

"Weird."

"I got something else for you, too. This one is bigger."

"What do you mean?"

"You're right that there is some type of breeding scheme that's been going on and I think I found out who's behind it." Michaela sat down at the kitchen counter, knowing Joe was about to tell him that he found out it was Brad. She sighed. "Well, I called up the owners of the mares and played like I was an investigator for the AQHA, and asked if they remembered if it was Lou Bancroft they spoke to and who sold them the breedings."

"Yeah?" she asked with baited breath.

"They mostly said that he was the one, except two of them gave me a different name."

"Whose name did they give?"

"That horse trainer of your uncle's — Dwayne Yamiguchi."

Michaela about dropped the phone. "No."

"Yep. That's what they said. Told me that Dwayne was the one who sold them the breeding for a discount. They sent the check to Lou rather than making it out to the ranch, which they thought was odd, but Dwayne apparently told them that was because Lou was changing the name of his business."

"Wow, I hadn't even thought about the fact that the checks were made out to my uncle personally."

"Yeah. If you want my opinion, this guy Dwayne's been the one takin' your uncle for a ride and somehow wirin' money from an account he likely opened maybe via the Internet. Still checking on all that, though. Anyway, I think this guy was pretending to be Lou on the phone when he talked to these folks, but it looks like he wasn't as careful as he thought, and a couple of times he accidentally slipped his real name into the conversation. He probably got Lou's social security number and private information and opened the checking account I'm still tryin' to track for you, too. It ain't hard to get people's private info, and that guy was probably pretty tight with Lou, makin' it easy for him. Also ain't too hard to sign the checks and contracts in Lou's name. Maybe the guy been planning on making a run for it with the dough. Whether or not he killed your uncle . . . I don't know. Maybe he put Bean up to it and knew Bean wouldn't do too well taking the fall. You got me." Michaela didn't say anything. "You okay, Mick?"

"I guess. Thanks, Joey. I appreciate it."

"No problem."

Michaela hung up the phone, stunned. It took her a minute to decide how to tell Detective Davis, but she had to call him *now* and tell him what she'd learned — of course, keeping Joe's name out of it. To her dismay, she couldn't reach Davis and instead left him a message to call her back.

Dwayne, of all people? Why? But she didn't have time to think about it as Camden stormed into the house. She walked up to Michaela and waved a file folder in her face. "You were right. Okay? I give in. You were freaking right — again!"

"Whoa. Wait. What the hell is going on, Camden? What are you talking about?"

"Kevin Tanner. Look at this. Look at what I found on his desk." She tossed the file down onto the counter.

Michaela picked it up and thumbed through it. She had to sit down again. It was a set of plans. Her uncle's name written across the top: LOU BANCROFT. Flipping through it, she saw that Tanner had detailed *every* dealing, *every* phone call, all conversations with her uncle, and *then* all conversations and correspondence with anyone he was working with in trying to take over Uncle Lou's property. He included dates, too. The most disturbing date in the file was the day that her uncle was killed: four days earlier. Her uncle's name was written next to the date with a red line drawn through it. Below that was scrawled, *Deal is closed.* Right below that note was another that read, *Call Cynthia Bancroft to see about negotiations.*

Michaela's stomach twisted as she found sketches and drawings with plans as to what was to be done with the property. It included an eighteen-hole golf course, along with a spa and boutique hotel resort. She couldn't believe any of this. "Oh my God."

"You were right, and I feel like such an ass. The guy totally used me, and the worst part is, he plans to knock you off your property and spread his corporate crap everywhere. He bought that dairy farm with the intention of taking over this entire area."

Michaela put an arm around Camden, who had changed her hair color yet again — now it was chocolate brown. "I have to ask you something."

"What?" Camden looked at her, her lip quivering.

"I overheard a conversation you had the other night with Kevin about him being a 'killer,' and how easy it would be for him to take over the land since whoever it was you two were talking about was now gone."

Camden shrunk back from her. "Wait a minute, you don't think we were talking about Lou?"

"I hope not. But try and look at it from my perspective."

Camden sighed. "When I referred to a piece of property Kevin had his eye on I was talking about a chunk of land owned by a competitor of his. Some guy who was just arrested for embezzling and making illegal real estate agreements. Anyway, both Kevin and this man bid on the same property recently, and Kevin lost. I was telling him that it would be easier to acquire that property now. I'm such a jerk for falling for that moron!"

"But, I also heard you tell Kevin that he didn't have to worry about being a suspect."

"Kevin was the one who squealed on the guy. He was trying to involve Kevin in his illegal deals. He wouldn't do it, but that doesn't make him a nice guy. He's still a bastard."

"You don't think Kevin could have murdered my uncle since he wanted his property so badly? These plans indicate he had motive."

Camden laughed. "The guy is afraid of his shadow. He's an ass and made a fool out of me . . . but no, I don't think he killed Lou. I think he sees an opportunity now to try and go after Cynthia, though."

Michaela frowned. "I'm sorry I listened in on your phone conversation and that I ever doubted you."

"Yeah well, I'm sorry I didn't listen to *you,* and now we have the guy I was supposed to be in love with and vice versa trying to take over everyone's land."

"We'll figure it out." The timer went off on the oven. She took out the tart.

"Thanks for being a good friend."

"You, too."

"Listen, I need to go back over to Kevin's and get some of my stuff. I'm also going to tell him that we're onto him, and he doesn't have a prayer of getting Lou's land or yours!"

"Can't it wait?"

"No. I don't want anything left there."

"I'll come with you."

Camden shook her head. "No, hon. You look tired."

"But what if he tries to hurt you?"

Camden smiled. "You don't know me as well as I thought you did. Tanner should be afraid I might hurt him."

Before Michaela could further protest her phone rang again. Davis was on the other end. She explained what she'd discovered about the breeding scheme, including what she'd found at the dairy farm — the same *Peter Pan* book that Bean had been reading right before he *supposedly* offed himself.

"How did you get this information about Mr. Yamiguchi?" Davis asked warily.

"I can't tell you that. But trust me, it's the truth. Will you at least look into it?"

"All right."

"I think that you should also know I suspect that my uncle's wife is pregnant, and . . . well, I don't think he was able to

278

father children."

"Why do you think she's pregnant?"

"I saw a test in her wastebasket." She knew how that sounded, but it was the truth and Davis needed to know. "I think that there's more to my uncle's murder and Bean's suicide."

"You're a regular Miss Marple. Younger and uh, more attractive, but you certainly have done your share of detecting over the last few days, haven't you?"

"I guess you could say that."

"Maybe you should join the force. I have to tell you that I'm not pleased about your detecting. Murder is serious business. I don't want you getting hurt and I think I can do my job without you putting yourself in danger."

"I'm not in any danger."

She heard him sigh on the other end of the phone. "I have to tell you that you're making my job more difficult."

"Don't mean to, but I thought you should know all this."

"Thank you for the information."

"That's it? 'Thank you for the information?' " Michaela started pacing her kitchen floor.

"What do you want me to say?"

"I want you to go and question Cynthia

Bancroft. I don't know, maybe ask her if she killed my uncle or if her *lover* did. I also want you to see what was going on at my uncle's ranch with the AI program. Also, there's a big-time developer who wanted to buy my uncle out. Kevin Tanner. Have you talked to that creep?"

"You *have* been busy."

Was he mocking her? Ooh, this guy knew how to get under her skin! "Obviously busier than you. You just want to sew this thing up, and I hate to tell you, Detective, I don't think it's as simple as it looks."

"Why don't you let me and my people decide that? I will look into everything you're telling me. I'm not discounting anything you've said. It's my job to try and take this type of information and sort through it. See where it all might fit. I am not putting you on the back burner. I promise."

"I sure hope not."

"I also have some news for you. About fingerprints on your pitchfork."

Michaela calmed herself. She wanted to hear this. "You do?"

"Yes. It seems a Ms. Kirsten Redmond's prints showed up along with yours."

"Kirsten?"

"Yes."

"Well, have you asked her about it?"

"I plan to. I can't arrest her on anything. Not yet, anyway."

"Not even for harassment?"

"She may have an explanation."

"What kind of explanation?"

"We'll have to wait and see. I haven't reached her yet, but I will keep trying until I do. And, I'll see what I can find out about Mr. Yamiguchi, as well as Mrs. Bancroft."

"Thanks," Michaela replied and hung up the phone.

Damn! Just when she thought she might have it all figured out, Davis sideswiped her with the news about Kirsten. None of it made any sense to her. None of it at all.

Twenty-Seven

After performing her morning rituals, Michaela got ready for Uncle Lou's funeral and put on a simple black dress. After today, she'd likely burn it. The stupid dress would hold too much pain. Strange thing to think about, but it was a reminder, and reminders carried plenty of weight with them.

She slipped into a pair of classic black pumps. Her hands shook slightly as she tried to apply a little makeup. She pulled her hair back into a sleek, low ponytail and tied it up into a chignon. Today would be rough.

Ethan had offered to give her a ride, but she'd already planned on going to the service with her mom and dad. Camden didn't feel right about going with her family. "I'll be there," she said. "This day needs to be about your family and your uncle. I'm always running late, as you know, and I don't want to hold you back or be a pain.

Not today anyway." She smiled, and Michaela was grateful that her friend knew how to act when the occasion called for it.

Michaela's parents were waiting out front when she drove up to get them. Good. She wanted to get through this day as quickly as possible. Their mood was solemn. She smiled at her mom, who looked as if she'd already been crying.

"Hi," her dad said. "You doing okay?"

She nodded her lie. "How about you?"

"Oh, you know. It isn't easy."

She believed there was a double entendre in his words. She knew that once they got past this, she would have to help her dad through what she figured would in some ways be more difficult for him to recover from than losing his brother. His addiction had been shrouded in secrets and lies. It was his vice, and allowing it to die and be buried would be something that he couldn't accomplish in a day. Every day of his life, her dad would have to bury his gambling addiction. Michaela was determined to help him through it.

They shared small talk on the way to the funeral home, and her mom went over the day's schedule. After the services there would be the gathering at her parents' place.

A handful of people had already arrived at

the funeral home. The director seated the family up front and off to the left, where they could look out and see others inside the home, and the guests could view them. It was almost like a separate room, but still open.

Her dad grabbed her hand and squeezed. She had the feeling he needed her more today than she needed him, and that was okay. Her mom took tissues from her purse and handed a couple to Michaela. She whispered, "Just in case."

Soon Cynthia came in, escorted by Dwayne. Sam waddled in behind them. Dwayne nodded toward them. Cynthia offered a weak smile. Then she looked right at Michaela, and her eyes, filled with anger, bore straight into her. Davis must've talked to her, because Michaela had never seen that look before. And, Cynthia had to have put two and two together. How? She wasn't sure, but that could be the only explanation as to why Cyn was looking at her that way. Interesting that she was on Dwayne's arm . . .

Oh, God. It struck Michaela like a horse kick in the face. Dwayne and Cynthia! Maybe he was her lover and he was the father of her baby and together they'd killed her uncle! But Dwayne had been in Vegas that morning. Still, Cynthia wasn't. Could she have taken Uncle Lou out before going off to the gym? And . . . oh, wow. Maybe Joey was right. Cyn had asked Michaela to look into the breeding scheme. Could it be to cover her own tracks? She didn't have time to let her mind run away with her. The room was filling up and she saw the pastor head toward the pulpit.

Out of the corner of her eye she caught another familiar face: Davis. He gave her a slight wave. She nodded and tried to smile in spite of everything. Why was he there? Out of respect? Doubtful. She'd heard somewhere before that killers often showed up at the funerals of their victims. Yes. That had to be why he was there. Watching people. Seeing their reactions. That meant he'd taken seriously what she'd told him the night before. Cynthia's anger toward her proved that. He wasn't blowing her off like she'd feared. Good man, she thought.

With her parents on either side of her, she almost felt like a child again. And on this surreal day that security flooded through her, as her six-year-old self returned momentarily, and she reveled in the comfort.

Once the pastor took the pulpit all was calm, actually peaceful. Michaela listened to his words of faith and an eternal afterlife.

The scent from the roses covering the casket wafted throughout the room. She'd been raised Catholic, so she understood the meaning of the pastor's words. Lou had not been much of a churchgoer, but she knew that when he did attend, it was at the Presbyterian Church. She noticed that there were far less rituals than in the church she was accustomed to. The pastor spoke freely of Lou's love for his animals, his wife, and his family. *His wife. Traitor!* Her mind conjured up worse words, but she pushed them aside, as they felt blasphemous, considering. When the pastor ended with an invitation to accept Christ, he asked if anyone wanted to share a story or talk about Lou.

Ethan approached the pulpit first. With tears running down his face he said, "Lou Bancroft was the only father I ever really knew. He was my friend and an excellent man. I will miss him dearly as I know you all will, too." He started to choke on his words. After a pause, Ethan went on to tell a funny story about when he was a kid and Lou thought the best way to teach him to ride was to put him on an ornery pony that enjoyed bucking him off regularly. "Lou would tell me that I'd better get back up on that pony and ride him, or I'd never learn. So, I'd get back on him, and to this day I think it was the best thing anyone ever taught me. I learned to persist. Granted, Lou did give me a hard hat, so I wouldn't bash my head in." Quiet laughter sounded throughout the room. Ethan wiped away his tears. "Goodbye, my friend."

Michaela wanted to run to him, wrap her arms around him, and hug him tight — let him cry on her shoulder, like when they were kids, although it was usually her crying on *his* shoulder. He always teased her about being a big crybaby. She watched as he slid in next to Summer, who put her head on his shoulder. Talk about irony. She tried not to watch.

There were more stories from friends and people Lou had dealt with over the years about his honesty, his gentle touch with horses, his humor, and his love for life.

Finally, Michaela mustered the courage to go up. She shifted her weight back and forth, looking out at the sea of faces, not sure if she could go on. Then, she looked at her dad, who winked at her.

"My uncle Lou was the most decent person I have ever known. When I was a little kid he taught me the meaning of compassion by showing me an injured mare and how to take care of her. He taught me how to ride, and in many ways he is the reason that I train horses today. When I was a teenager I could go to him and tell him pretty much anything, and that lasted until only a few days ago.

"He knew what it meant to laugh and enjoy life. He wasn't a risk taker, but when he wanted something he went for it. He was the type of person who knew how to find balance, and stay balanced. We will miss his warm, easy smile and all that he had to give. For me, the one thing that seems to help the most is the idea that he is still close by. He remains in our hearts, our souls, and memories, and no one can take that from us. Thank you."

She spotted Camden in the back, who smiled at her. Thank God she had her friend back. She also spotted Joey. True blue, that man. As she stepped down she glanced over at Davis again. He nodded and smiled at her, a look of sympathy in his eyes.

Michaela took her seat as the pastor announced the gathering that would take place at Ben and Janie Bancroft's place.

Moments later everyone filed out of the home, and because Lou had chosen to be cremated, there was no actual burial. Cynthia stood at the front and greeted guests. "I'm sorry for everything," Michaela told Cynthia.

Cynthia nodded. "Thank you," she replied coolly.

Dwayne stood next to Cynthia. It took everything she had not to say anything to the two of them. She wanted to scream at them both: "I know what you've done!" But soon enough Davis would solve this case. And, maybe that was why he was really there. Waiting for the services to be over. Shadowing Dwayne and Cynthia, preparing to arrest them. Had he found out something new? Something that revealed they were more than just lovers, that they were also killers?

Michaela's parents chose to stand with Cynthia at the front. Why wouldn't they? They had no idea what Michaela knew. She decided to head for the truck, not feeling like talking to anyone. She had to get out of there.

Davis grabbed her arm as she was walking out. "That was a beautiful eulogy you gave. Touching. I really thought you did a nice job."

"Thanks. I get the feeling you've spoken with my uncle's wife?"

He nodded. "Early this morning. You're right, she is pregnant."

"I knew it."

"But she wasn't keeping a lover. At least,

I'm fairly satisfied with that."

Michaela put her hands on her hips. "What do you mean?"

"Mrs. Bancroft showed me appointment cards with a Dr. Collins."

"Dr. Collins?" Michaela knew him quite well. He'd been her doctor when she'd tried to conceive.

Davis nodded. "Yes, and it seems as though Mrs. Bancroft and your uncle were in to see him several times for consultation. They wanted to have a baby. I followed up with the doctor before heading over here. Mrs. Bancroft used a sperm donor. Her story checks out."

"Oh my God. I thought for sure . . . I thought she'd been unfaithful. I thought Dwayne and her had somehow planned this. No wonder she looked as if she hated me."

"It was an easy mistake to make, Michaela. I can see how you assumed what you did."

She was stunned. Wow. She'd really been off base there, now hadn't she? "Well, what about Dwayne, and what I told you about the breeding scheme?"

"We only spoke last night. I'm following up."

"Is that why you're here?"

"Among other things. I wanted to make

sure you were all right."

"You did? I'm fine. Really. That was nice of you."

"Coffee tomorrow, right? The Honey Bear? Four?"

"I'll be there."

Davis's pager went off. "I've got to go."

"Everything okay?"

"Police work." He started to walk away quickly. That page must've been important.

TWENTY-EIGHT

Michaela walked to her truck and leaned against it, looking out at the green rolling hills of the cemetery and the flowers that adorned various graves. The little chapel and funeral home were connected on one of the hills to the left of her. It was a crisp December day — typical Southern California weather — not overcast, but rather a blue sky filled the air with a handful of billowing clouds. Normally, she would have considered it a beautiful day — definitely a good day to get out and ride . . .

"Nice speech."

Michaela turned to see none other than Kirsten standing there, decked out in a black v-neck tight-fitting dress that left nothing to the imagination. "What are you doing here?"

"I came to pay my respects. Your uncle was a respected horseman and I felt I owed it to him to come by."

"God, can't you go crawl under a rock or something? You're not welcome here."

"I didn't know I needed to be invited. It was in the paper, and like I said, I'm only doing the right thing by paying respect to the consummate cowboy."

Oh brother. Michaela didn't have the strength for a go-around with her. "Thank you. That was kind of you." She figured if she stayed the course that Miss Rodeo America would be on her way. Kirsten was another one she'd like to question. She owed Michaela some answers, like why in the hell were her fingerprints on Michaela's pitchfork? And, hadn't Davis seen her in the funeral home? She knew he was trying to locate Kirsten. Come to think of it, Michaela hadn't spotted her either, and Kirsten was definitely one who made sure she was seen. That was strange in itself. But she had to have been in the home to have heard Michaela's eulogy.

"I know you ran into Brad the other night."

"I did." Nope. The bitch wasn't going to exit nicely.

"I would really like it if you could back off of him. I don't know when you're going to accept that he is gone out of your life. He ain't coming back." Michaela shook her head and sighed. "Oh, he told me all about how you bought him a drink and tried coming on to him, how you wanted him back and how you would forgive him."

Michaela didn't think her neck and shoulders could grow any tighter, but she was wrong. "Honestly, Kirsten, I don't know why we're having this conversation."

"Because you can't keep your hands off of *my* man."

Michaela laughed. She didn't want to go here, but she had no choice. "The last thing I want back in my life is Brad. Okay? Let me explain to you and hopefully you'll understand this, but Brad was the one who came on to *me* the other night. He begged me to forgive him and take him back. Once I told him, unequivocally, no, he had to be chased off by a friend of mine. He apparently crawled back home to you; I don't know why he fed you this ridiculous story. You two get off on the drama. You deserve each other, but the facts are, he's a creep and always will be. And, you, like me, will probably find out the hard way when he dumps your ass for a new model in a couple of years."

Kirsten pulled her arm back to swing. "Why, you bitch!" Her arm was caught in midair by none other than Summer.

"I don't think you want to do that, Kirsten. Why don't you try and show some class for once in your life and go home? Leave this family alone, especially Michaela."

Kirsten's face twisted in rage, but being outnumbered she did as she was told, and like the snake she was, slithered off.

Michaela faced Summer. "Thank you." Summer was the last person Michaela would have expected to do what she'd just done, but today was turning out to have quite a few surprises to it.

"Don't worry about it. I saw her accosting you and I figured she was the last person you needed today. For that matter I'm sure that I'm a close second, especially after our talk the other day."

Michaela smiled. "Normally I would say yes, but funny as it may seem, I don't feel that way. I'm glad you were there to stop her. I wasn't prepared for that at all."

"I'm sure you weren't." She shrugged. "I want to tell you again that I know I've made my share of mistakes in the past. I really want to make up for them now. I'm sorry if I came on strong the other day. I'd really like it if we could be friends."

Michaela bit her lip. "Friends." She reached her hand out and Summer shook it. That was a tall order, but why not? She could try, especially *if* Summer was having Ethan's child.

TWENTY-NINE

The afternoon wore on at Ben and Janie Bancroft's house. Michaela tried to talk to Cynthia, but Cynthia was always engulfed by waves of people. Also, Michaela's mom kept her busy bringing food out to the table. Cynthia left early, before Michaela had a chance to speak with her. Her mom said that Cyn was tired and wanted to go home, so Dwayne and Sam drove her back to the ranch.

Camden lightened the mood with her crazy antics. She even got Michaela's mom to laugh. By the time the last guest left and Michaela and Camden finished helping with the dishes, all Michaela wanted to do was go home and climb in bed.

As she finished drying the dishes, her mom said, "Thank you girls for all your help today, and Michaela, for what you said about Lou. It was lovely." Her mother brushed a hand through her hair, which had recently begun to pale with age, going from golden blonde to blonde with some silver woven into it. She was still a beautiful woman and Michaela thought of her as someone who embodied the word *grace,* like Audrey Hepburn.

"You're welcome, Mom. It's how I felt, and as far as helping out, there's no question about it."

"Me, too, Mrs. Bancroft. I'm glad I could do it." Camden folded a dishtowel and set it down on the kitchen counter. She hugged Michaela and her mom. "Well, I hate to bug out on you, but I'm tired. Do you mind?"

"No. Go on home. I'll see you there. Thanks for your help."

Michaela went into the family room with her mom. Her dad sat in his easy chair. "Hi, pumpkin. You did good today. Lou would be proud of you." He looked at his wife. "You should know that I told your mom about my gambling."

Her mom shook a finger at her. "Don't you ever keep secrets from me again. I know you think I'm weak and that my heart is easily broken. But you're wrong. I'm tougher than the two of you put together."

"Mom, I didn't think it was my place."

"Oh horse pucky." Michaela stifled her laughter. "We're a family and when we have a problem, whether big or small, I'd better be told up front. Got it?"

Her dad winked at her. "Got it," Michaela said.

"Both of you got it?"

"Yes ma'am," her dad replied.

She turned back to her daughter. "I'm not going to leave your father. But I *am* dragging his rear to church from now on. I won't take no for an answer. And, I'm going with him to those Gamblers Anonymous meetings and watch him walk in, sit down, and I will take a book with me and wait for him in the car while he works out whatever it is he needs to work out."

Her dad turned red. "See why I love your mother?"

"Yes."

"I didn't take vows to break them. I knew when I married you, Benjamin Bancroft, that you were far from perfect. We'll get through this the way we do everything. *Together.* Now we'll let our daughter go home. She looks tired."

Michaela stood and hugged her mom, who whispered, "Thank you," in her ear.

Her drive home seemed longer than usual. She cranked up the radio and tried to sing along to Keith Urban's latest. Glancing in her rearview mirror, she noticed a set of high beams approaching . . . fast. What the . . . The truck was right on her tail, horn blaring at her. "Geez, buddy, back off." Michaela stepped on the gas; the truck stayed with her. Panic rose inside her. She went to reach for her phone, but it was in her purse on the floorboard and she needed both hands on the wheel to deal with this idiot behind her. Again she sped up, but the other vehicle hung on her bumper, then passed her, cutting her off so close that she had to slam on her brakes, which sent her truck into a spin. Dizziness swirled in her brain. *Is this what it's like to have your life pass before your eyes?* she thought. Visions of her parents, Uncle Lou, Ethan, Camden, raced in front of her at gut-wrenching speed. She couldn't think or feel anything, other than her heart racing.

Then her world went black.

THIRTY

When Michaela opened her eyes, her truck was on the side of the road. She must have hit her head on the steering wheel, because it sure did hurt. She rubbed it and felt a knot. She couldn't have been out for too long, though, because no one had discovered her as yet. She leaned back against her seat. What in the world just happened? That certainly felt intentional, as if whoever drove that truck was *trying* to run her off the road. Still dizzy, she couldn't think straight, but didn't want to just sit there. What if the asshole came back? Her hands shaking, she used her cell phone to call Davis, who told her that he'd be there soon.

Waiting for him, she tried to make sense of what had occurred. Maybe it was high-school kids goofing around. She didn't *really* believe that. And why had she called Davis? Damn, she definitely was *not* thinking clearly.

When Davis pulled up next to her and got out she could see the look of concern on his face. "What happened?"

Yep, maybe she shouldn't have called him. Playing the damsel in distress wasn't her style. "I don't know, some kids or someone was driving on my tail and then raced around me and cut me off. I slammed on the brakes and maybe I hit something slick because I lost control and spun out."

He took out a small flashlight. "Did you hit your head?"

"Uh, yeah, but I'm okay."

He shone the light on her forehead. "That's quite a knot. Did you lose consciousness?"

Hmmm. How to answer this one? She knew he'd likely make her go to the hospital if she said yes, and okay, she probably should tell him the truth. But damn, she *was* okay, and all she wanted to do was go home and climb in bed. After some aspirin and a good night's rest, she'd feel a whole lot better. "No."

"You're lying." He pointed at her.

"What?"

"I said, you're lying. I didn't get to be a detective by not being able to spot liars and right now you're not telling me the truth. Come on, let's go see a doctor."

She sighed. "I don't want to. I'm so tired after today."

"No whining. You're going to the hospital."

"Hey, I'm not whiny. That's not nice. Can't I just go home? Please?"

"Nope. And, now you *are* whining." He reached his hand out. "Come on."

She decided to quit arguing, able to tell it was a battle she wouldn't win. She took his hand. He put his arm around her waist and led her to his car. "I just banged my head a little. I can walk."

"You certainly are hardheaded. No pun intended."

He opened the door and helped her in, then went back to lock up her truck. It was nice . . . well okay, maybe even more than nice. It felt good to have a man's arms around her, wanting to take care of her. There she was — doing it again. Fantasizing. Stupid. Is that why she'd called Davis, so she could continue to live out some bizarre romantic fantasy? He was only doing his job, what every police officer would've done in this situation. She didn't need a man. She was doing fine on her own. His arm around her still felt nice, though.

He stayed by her side as they walked into the hospital. Rubbing alcohol and cleaning agents smelled as offensive to Michaela as the gloomy interior of the aging facility. Ugh. She hated hospitals. Then again, who didn't? She waited to be seen by an ER doctor.

Davis was still concerned. "Did you get a good look at the truck? License plate? Make? Anything?"

She shook her head. "It was dark and it all happened so fast. The truck might have been blue or black, I don't know. It definitely wasn't white. I honestly don't know." Something flashed through her mind: the moment when her truck was nearly clipped. Wait. There was something. "You know what, I don't think there was a plate on the back."

"Are you sure?"

"No. Like I said, it all happened so quickly. Do you think it was intentional?"

"Do you?"

She didn't answer right away. She had when it happened, but this week had been so filled with drama and trauma that her mind immediately assumed the worst. "Honestly, it felt that way, but again, it could have been kids being stupid."

"I don't like it."

"What are you thinking?"

"I probably shouldn't say anything to you,

but I have to wonder, since we found Kirsten Redmond's fingerprints on your pitchfork, if she might not have anything to do with this."

Michaela recalled what had occurred between her and Kirsten earlier that day after her uncle's funeral. She told Davis about it.

"I didn't see her at the funeral. She must've been hiding in the back. I had to rush off."

"Kirsten drives a Mustang, but Brad drives a truck, and it's a *new* truck. Maybe that's why I didn't see plates."

"Maybe. I definitely plan to visit Ms. Redmond and your ex again."

"By the way, how were you able to match Kirsten's fingerprints on the pitchfork? DMV records?"

He laughed. "I wish. Believe it or not, the DMV won't let us use their records to track criminals. We found her prints because she worked for the county rec center some time back. Government agencies are required to take prints and they are managed by the State Department of Justice, who actually keeps track of arrest records and other sources in what's called AFIS or Automated Fingerprint Identification System."

"Oh." She didn't expect this lengthy

answer, but something about him talking shop was endearing.

"I know that Ms. Redmond and your ex have given you a bad time. They both might be involved, or at least Ms. Redmond may be, in trying to scare or possibly harm you. If she caused this accident and I can prove it, this could be considered vehicular assault."

"Kirsten could go to jail?"

"If we can find enough evidence to arrest her, you bet."

Kirsten wearing an orange jumpsuit. That did sound appealing.

After another hour of being checked out, monitored, given some ice and Motrin for the pain, Michaela was finally released. Davis had her home in less than twenty minutes. They pulled up to her house. He stopped the car and turned to her.

"I need you to do me a favor and let me be the cop, okay? No more of this snooping around. You could get hurt. In fact, you did get hurt tonight."

"You think the accident is connected to my uncle's murder?"

"I'm not sure. I still have plenty of questions for some people. The evidence points to Bean, but I'm not willing to close this case yet. We're still waiting for handwriting analysis to come back on Bean's note, too. Now, let this go, and let me do my job."

"Fine."

He helped her inside. "I can stay the night — on the couch, you know — make sure that you're okay."

"No need. My roommate is home."

He brushed her bangs out of the way of her bump. "That looks pretty nasty to me. I know the doctor said that it would be fine, but I can hang out here, at least for a while."

"I'm okay."

"I know. I'm doing my job. That's all. I think it would be a good idea if I stayed."

Was he pushing so hard to stay simply out of concern? "Don't they have officers who do that? You know, to babysit those who may be in harm's way?" she joked.

"Sure, but look, I won't bother you, and I can do some work here and then take you to your truck in the morning."

"Suit yourself." She went to get him some blankets and a pillow. He *was* just doing his job after all.

Wasn't he?

THIRTY-ONE

The next morning Michaela woke to the sound of voices and remembered that Jude Davis had stayed the night. But wait. Who was he talking to? Camden surely wasn't up this early.

Rounding the corner into the kitchen, she could smell fresh coffee. She stopped short when she saw Ethan there with Davis. They each held a cup of coffee and looked to be hanging like good ol' boys together. Cocoa spotted her and began wagging her tail. Michaela started to back up, hoping they wouldn't see her. But she was spotted. "Mick?" Ethan said.

"Hi guys," she said meekly. Dammit, here she was looking like the damsel in distress again. And why did Ethan insist on taking it upon himself to drop in whenever he damn well felt like it? Not that she hadn't appreciated it in the past, but what must it look like? Oh no. Prickly heat rose on the back of her neck. *What must it look like!* Davis was here before Ethan arrived. In fact, the guy had stayed the night. And what was Davis thinking, with Ethan barging in as the sun came up! Oh why did she care what either one thought anyway!

"Good morning," Davis said and went to pour her a cup of coffee.

Ethan wiggled his eyebrows at her, his expression reminding her of a Cheshire cat, confirming her worst fear: He assumed Davis spent the night because the two of them had slept together. The heat on her neck turned to perspiration. "I came by to check on you and Leo. From the looks of it though, you're doing a-okay."

She couldn't resist giving him a dirty look. "Thank you." What had Davis told him? Or *not* told him?

"I need to use your restroom," Davis said.

As he left, Ethan smiled at her. "You and the detective, huh?"

"No, Ethan, it's not like that. I can explain."

He held up a hand. "No need to explain. I don't care what you do. Actually I think it's good you're moving on with your life, and Davis seems like a nice guy."

She walked over to where Ethan was standing and put another scoop of sugar in her coffee. Her stomach tightened. "Yes, he is."

His eyes narrowed. "Mick? What's that bruise on your forehead from?"

Oh-oh. Well, she got her answer about what Davis had told Ethan: nothing. Good. Knowing Ethan, he'd be all up in arms about the accident and make a big deal, feeling the need to hover over her. And, Davis was doing that duty. She should never have called him last night. She would've been just fine. She touched her forehead. "Oh that. It's nothing. I banged it."

"I'll say you did. What do you mean it's nothing? How did you do it?"

She really did not want to go into it. "I . . . uh, I opened this cupboard here" — she pointed to the cupboard above her, where she kept her plates — "last night, and I guess I wasn't paying attention." She had actually hit her head on that damn cupboard quite a few times in the past. Lying to Ethan did not come easy, and she despised herself for doing it, but having him worried would make it worse, in her opinion.

"Okay. You better be more careful. You always have been a klutz." She smiled and sipped her coffee, silently thankful he'd believed her. "There's something I came by to tell you, and I need you to hear me out."

Oh brother. She definitely did not like the sound of this. She sipped her coffee and nodded.

"This weekend, while I'm on the vet staff in Vegas . . . well, I thought timingwise it would be a good thing because Summer isn't quite showing yet, and it really is the right thing to do. I know that it is."

"What are you trying to tell me?"

"We're . . . getting married this weekend, and I want you there."

Michaela about spit her coffee across the room. "What?"

"Y-yeah," Ethan stammered. "It's uh, really why I came here to see you."

"I think that's great," Jude Davis replied, walking back into the kitchen. "Sorry, I couldn't help overhearing. Congratulations."

"Thank you. Hey, why don't you join us? It's not a long drive over and we'd love to have you. I'm sure Michaela would want you there, too." He looked at her and winked.

She was going to kill him.

"I'd like to. But I'm working until five tomorrow, and then I have plans."

"Well it's not a long flight, in case you change your mind or your plans fall through —"

"No! He said that he had plans," Michaela interrupted. Both men looked at her. If looks could kill, she was doing her best to take Ethan out at that moment.

"Why don't I go out and take care of the horses for you? Relax for a change. Enjoy the morning," Ethan said.

Michaela wanted to make a smart-ass remark back, because he'd really done it to her this time. It would have felt good to say something about his being sure that his bride would show up this time, but she decided against it. It wouldn't do any good. How could he marry Summer? What the hell was he thinking! Why did he have to race to the altar? And after what Summer had put him through before. *"The best thing for everyone."* Stupid. That's what he was being — stupid. She had a good mind to go drag Camden's skinny ass out of bed and have her whip up several pitchers of her killer concoction. And what about Davis? Surely he'd picked up on Ethan's not-so-subtle hints that he thought they'd slept together. Men!

As Ethan left for the barn, Davis asked, "How's your head feel?"

"Fine. I guess we better go and get my truck." She looked out the window and watched Ethan heading out to the barn to

312

feed the horses. She was done chasing fantasies.

On the way to her truck Davis said that he didn't mention to *Dr. Slater* about what had happened the night before. "I didn't feel it was my place. I know you two are close and I figured I'd let you be the one to tell him."

"We're not that close." Now, why did she say that?

"Really?"

"We grew up together, sure, and he's my vet and yeah, he's a friend, but that's it. He's getting married this weekend."

Davis glanced at her. She needed to change the subject. "When do you get to see your little girl?" That was safe.

"Katie. This weekend. I can't wait. Those are the plans I have. I promised her dinner and we're going to see *The Nutcracker* in L.A."

Michaela sighed. Funny — she was relieved. She'd thought Davis's plans surely involved a woman. "That sounds fun."

"The kid is great. We have a great time together." He beamed, and his love for his daughter was almost infectious as Michaela felt herself smiling while he talked about her. "She's a bright kid. You know, she's doing sixth-grade math in fourth grade. Whoever said girls aren't good at math doesn't know what they're talking about. And she loves ballet. She started taking lessons a couple of years ago."

"Wow. I envy you. A daughter." Listening to him talk about her started a bit of that yearning again inside her. What it must be like to love someone so much. A child. She could only imagine.

"She's the best. Hey, do you give riding lessons?"

She thought about Joey and her promise to teach his daughter Genevieve how to ride. "Yes, I do."

"I bet you're wonderful with kids. My daughter would love to ride. Do you think maybe you could give her some lessons?"

Teaching Davis's kid to ride would mean that she would see him, maybe quite a bit. How did she feel about that? She flashed back to Ethan and his words about her moving on. "Sure. That sounds good."

"I can't wait to tell her. Of course, you probably want to wait until after the holidays. I know things aren't easy right now. And between you and me, I don't know how this case is going to go."

"You have doubts, don't you, about Bean?"

"I think you know that I do. Technically

I'm not supposed to talk to you about it, but since you're the one who opened some of these new doors, Miss Detective . . ." He pointed a finger at her. "There will be no more police work on your end. Agreed?"

"Agreed." She would try to let it all go and allow Davis to do his job, but it would be tough, because her uncle's murder and the surrounding circumstances troubled her. "I guess you'll be talking to Dwayne Yamiguchi today? And Kirsten? *And* Brad."

Davis didn't reply as he pulled up next to her truck. "Take care of that head, Miss Marple. See you this afternoon. The Honey Bear Cottage."

"Best lattes in town. Until then, Sherlock Holmes."

"Ah, but I have a license to investigate, *and* the training. You need to go train horses."

"I get it."

He waited until she drove off. What a gentleman Davis was. And, Ethan . . . well, he was one royal pain in the ass, and she'd had it up to there with his antics. First keeping secrets about what was going on between him and Uncle Lou, and now marrying Summer. Okay, so they were *supposedly* friends now, but Michaela still had reservations about the woman. She simply was not

Ethan's type. Or, maybe she was. Who was she to determine Ethan's type when it came to women?

When she arrived home, Ethan was still there. "Just finished feeding everybody."

"Thanks."

"No problem."

"Ethan?"

"Yes?"

"What the hell are you thinking? I need to know. And I also need to know what happened between you and Lou."

He looked away for a second then back at her, his eyes filled with an intensity she didn't often see in him. But when she did, he meant business. Good, because so did she. "I suppose I owe you."

"You do."

He went around to the cab of his truck and opened the glove compartment. He handed her a photo, one of her uncle and another man, circa the late 1960s, she figured. "What's this?"

"That's Lou and . . . my dad."

"Your dad?"

He smiled sadly. "All my life, I wanted a dad. Right? Sure, I never verbalized those exact words to anyone, but you even once said to me when we were kids that if you could, you'd get me a dad for my birthday."

He laughed. "I think we were like five or something. I don't know, but I never forgot you telling me that. And I knew that you would be my best friend for life, because anyone who wanted what I wanted so badly for myself without me having to say it was someone I would always be close to."

Where was he going with this? She *did* remember telling him that when they were kids, and he'd replied that it was impossible to give him a dad. That a dad wasn't someone you could go buy at a store. Ethan had told her that dads were men who *wanted* to be dads, that there was no one who wanted to be his. Michaela had always wished she could have changed that for him.

"Growing up, your family was like my family. Our mothers were like sisters. I know they still talk all the time, even though my mom is so far away." Ethan's mother had moved to Florida a few years back to be with a man she'd met on a cruise. The relationship hadn't worked out, but Ethan's mother found she liked living on the Florida coast. "Your father wasn't exactly like a dad to me, just because he keeps to himself, but Lou treated me like a son. Remember how he used to take us trail riding? And, he'd come watch my football games when we were in high school? He was even the one

317

who advised me to become a vet. I looked up to him. I loved him, always wished he were my dad. Then, when Summer cancelled our wedding, he let me stay at the guest house and didn't expect a dime from me. Of course, I paid him. But my bank statements show he never cashed the checks."

He sighed. "Lou obviously knew my dad." He pointed to the photo. "He knew my dad and he knew he wasn't dead, like I'd been told by my mother. He'd known all these years, even knew where he lived. He *knew*."

"I'm sorry. I am so confused."

"Summer was the one who discovered it. While doing his books she saw checks for significant amounts written to a Tom Beckenhour. She asked Lou who the guy was. He told her that it was a buddy he'd bought some horses from. She asked him which horses so she'd know how to organize it on the books. He got a bit gruff with her. She mentioned something about looking at some of the previous years on the books and that this Tom received these checks on a regular basis. Lou told her to mind her own business. But it still bothered Summer because of the way Lou was acting. He even told her that he'd handle those transactions, and for her not to worry about it. Then, she found this photo while looking for some transactions from a few years back that the IRS asked for during that audit they did of the ranch last year."

Michaela remembered that well. Uncle Lou was angry about being audited, but Summer had done a decent job preparing for it, and the government found that all the deductions he'd taken on his taxes a few years back were legit.

"She noticed the resemblance to me." Michaela studied the picture, and it was true. The man in the photo with Uncle Lou did bear a striking resemblance to Ethan. "Well, she started looking into it, and she found out that Tom Beckenhour is some washed-up rodeo cowboy that Lou knew back in the '60s. They'd been buddies on the circuit. He introduced this guy to my mom one night and . . . well, *I'm* the product of that one night."

She shook her head. "Whoa."

"Right. It gets worse, though. Tom Beckenhour knew about me through Lou, who tried to get him to do the right thing. But this loser was a drunk and ran away from my mom and me."

"So, your mom and Lou *did* do the right thing not telling you about him. Did you ever think of that?"

Ethan shrugged. "No. I didn't, because I guess the guy did sober up when I was around ten years old and wanted to be a part of my life, but Lou has spent the last twenty years sending him cash to keep him away from me. That's why we had the falling-out. That's why I took off and was so angry and didn't tell you why I left to go rafting. I didn't say anything to you until now, because I had to make sure it was all the truth. Then on top of it, Summer tells me she's pregnant. I had to process it all, but now I feel like I have to tell you. I know you've been having doubts about me and my loyalty to Lou. I'm sure you've even wondered if I could have killed him."

"It'd be a waste of time to deny it."

"I loved Lou and I was hurt by the lies, but knowing him and knowing the extremes he went to, to shine the light on the *real* Brad for your sake, I understand why he did what he did for me. Lou wanted to protect the people he loved from being hurt. So he kept secrets, buried lies, and held on tight to all of us. Maybe too tight, and secrets and lies always catch up with you. The thing I don't get is why he continued to pay this guy off even when I got older. Why he didn't let me make my own judgments. Again, I've come to the conclusion that was him holding on as tight as he could, afraid of losing those close to him."

Michaela nodded. She took Ethan's hand and held it for a moment before saying anything. "Funny how you can love someone so much, you'll do almost anything to keep them from walking away, even if it means hiding behind a lie. Don't you wonder though, just what kind of man this guy who's supposedly your dad is? To continue to take money from Lou after all these years, and agree to stay away, does not bode well in my mind as to what your father would be like. I mean, if he really wanted to know you he would have told Lou to go to hell."

Ethan looked hurt by the words as he pulled his hand away from her. "I suppose that's true."

Why did she have to be so blunt? "What about your mother? Have you spoken with her about it?"

"No. I can't. Not yet anyway. I need to go and see her about this. I've been so angry though."

"She may be able to shed more light on it. I think you need to get to the bottom of it, Ethan, or you'll never be able to move on."

He nodded. "I did contact him. Tom. My father."

"You did?"

"Yep. He's married and has two kids. Weird, huh? I have two brothers."

"Are you going to meet him? Are you going to ask him why he did what he did?"

"I don't know if I want to or care to. But I want you to know that I forgive Lou. You know that the man was a father to me. Someone who loved me so much and wanted to protect me because he felt it was the right thing to do, even though it may not have been, proves to me that I *was* wrong to ever be angry with him. All he did was love me like a dad should, and now I feel horrible. The guilt is almost unbearable." He teared up.

Ethan rarely ever cried and her heart ached for him. "You and I both know that Lou would have understood. He loved you a lot. That's obvious. So please, don't do this to yourself. Promise me? Don't keep going down this road. Talk to your mother, maybe meet this man, but most of all forgive yourself. Lou did not take your anger to his grave."

Tears streamed down his face. "I hope not."

"He didn't."

"Yeah, well, I've done a lot of thinking about Lou, and you, and what you said about Summer over the past few days, and loving someone . . . and family. All of it. What I needed and *wanted* growing up was a dad. Sure, I had Lou, but there's a difference between someone who treats you like you're their kid and someone who *is* your dad. There just is. I can't explain it. Maybe I'm old school and believe that blood is thicker than water, though my heart knows it's ridiculous. You get love where you're supposed to. Right?" He wiped his face with the back of his hand. "Look at me, crying like a baby. Stupid."

"No. It's not."

"You're a good friend. I love you for that and more. Like I said, I've been doing a ton of thinking and through it all I've come to the conclusion that I have to be a father to this baby Summer and I are having. That's why I have to marry her, Michaela. I told you earlier, it's the right thing to do."

Michaela nodded. "Well, you have always been good about doing the right thing. But do you have to rush into it? It all seems so sudden."

"I know. I guess I'm just old-fashioned. I don't want Summer to have to walk down the aisle while seven or eight months pregnant, or after we have the baby."

"If you were so old-fashioned, you wouldn't have jumped in bed with her. Oops. That one kind of slipped out. I'm sorry, but it's how I feel. And another thing, how do you know this is your child?"

He looked wounded by the suggestion. "The timing is right. Of course it's my child." Oh God. Typical man. As if after sleeping with him a woman would never go to bed with another man. "Mick, it's my life. It's my child's life. I'm going to do this. With or without your support."

"So, it's this weekend, huh?" He wasn't going to listen to reason.

"Might as well be." He smiled.

"I guess there's nothing more that I can say, if this is what you want."

"Will you be there for me?"

"Oh Ethan. I don't know. I have tickets for the rodeo, but I don't think I can go. With Lou and everything . . . well, I don't think so."

"I need you there. You're my best friend. I can't imagine you not being there. Please."

She finally nodded, still not believing that she could agree to hand Ethan over to a woman who likely could never really love him. Not in the way he deserved.

THIRTY-TWO

After Ethan left, Michaela needed to get out and work the horses. She felt bad that none of them had received the attention they should have been getting over the past few days. A workout here and there simply was not enough; it was time to get back in the saddle, so to speak. She needed to. The revelation about Ethan and Summer's impending nuptials had her in a tailspin, not to mention last night's near-miss on her life, which she still was freaked about. Her head ached a bit, but she didn't know if it was from hitting it, or from everything else that filled her mind.

After lacing up her Ariat boots, she again called the attorney who'd left her the message the day before. His secretary said that he was in court and that she'd have him return her call. As she put Leo out on a hot walker to give him some exercise, she couldn't help wondering what the lawyer wanted with her. It didn't take long for her to get involved in her work and thoughts of Ethan, Summer, attorneys, and even Jude Davis went away for the time being.

She worked Rocky and three more horses in the arena, finally winding up on a trail ride with Booger, giving him a chance to stretch his muscles. In between she gave the horses a quick rinse and let them stand in the sun to dry before putting them back in their stalls. She worked right through lunch, and damn, it felt good. Something about getting up on her animals and working them through their paces helped to heal her.

By the time she finished it was almost five. Where had the day gone? It almost felt like normal again. As difficult as it was, life did go on. She wondered if Davis had gotten anywhere with the information she'd given him about Dwayne. She still couldn't believe that Uncle Lou's right-hand man would have anything to do with this mess, but according to Joey, Dwayne had everything to do with it.

She got her answer when she made it back to the house and played her messages. Jude Davis had called. "Hi Michaela. It's Davis here." Oh no! She'd forgotten their coffee date. "Sorry I couldn't make it to The Honey Bear Cottage for our coffee. I tried to reach you on your cell." She sighed. Thank God. "But I was in the middle of an interrogation. I wanted to let you know that we arrested Dwayne Yamiguchi today on charges of fraud. I don't know if they'll stick, but I made calls to the owners of the mares you mentioned, and a couple of them gave me Dwayne's name as their contact. We don't know what he did with the money yet, and of course, he's denying everything. I've also called The American Quarter Horse Association and they received your letter and DNA samples. The results should be back tomorrow. Dwayne will be arraigned in the morning and the judge will set bail. You *do* make a fine detective."

So, Dwayne was behind bars for fraud. But it still didn't resolve who could have murdered her uncle. Dwayne might be a crook, but a killer? Plus, he wasn't even in town the morning Uncle Lou had been killed. Her mind wandered back to Cynthia: the anger in her eyes at the funeral service. But Davis said that her story checked out. Still, couldn't she have also had someone on the side that she was cheating with? Wasn't that a possibility?

She didn't have time to ponder these thoughts because her doorbell rang several times, insistently. "I'm coming. I'm coming." Patience. Whoever it was certainly had none. She flung the door open. "What in the world?"

There stood Brad, suitcase in hand. "Hi honey. I'm home."

"Like hell you are!"

He frowned and leaned against the doorjamb, preventing her from slamming it in his face. "Now, honey, let's get past all the bull between us. I'm here because I know we belong together. In fact, I found out that Kirsten was causing you some trouble and I told her exactly what I thought of her and that you were the best thing that ever happened to me."

"Get off my property."

He stuck his lower lip out. She thought about ripping it off his face. "Can't we just talk?"

She crossed her arms. "We have nothing to talk about. If you don't get off my property, I'll call the police."

He waved his hands in the air. "Women. Fine. Have it your way. I did a good thing for you, and you kick me like a dog." He pulled out a chewing tobacco tin and unwrapped it.

"You *are* a dog. No, actually you're a cretin. I would never put you in the same category as a dog. They're far better than you could even aspire to be. You are dog shit. That's what you are."

"You'll see what I did for you. I called the police about Kirsten. I think they'll be having a long talk with her and she's gonna be in some big trouble. And I did it for you."

"Okay, Brad, what the hell are you babbling about?"

"Let me in the house. We'll have a beer and talk about it."

"Bullshit! Tell me what you're talking about and then go away. Far away. Wait a minute: When did you start chewing?"

"Oh, that. I can stop that. Kirsten liked me to do it. Told me it was a man thing to do. Woman used to buy it for me."

"Really?" Now wasn't *that* interesting, considering that Davis had found the tobacco wrapper on the ground the other night after finding the pitchfork? "What are you up to?"

"You'll see the light after I tell you what I did. See that we belong together. That I still love you, and I know you still love me." She wanted to puke. "Kirsten knew it, and it's been killing her. She got pissed because she says I talk about you too much. But she's right. I can't stop thinking about you."

"You seemed to have no problem not

thinking about me while you were screwing her."

"Dumb, I know. But I needed to sow my oats, stretch my wings a little." He tapped his chest. "But it's always been you, honey. Always."

"Right." She had to ask herself again: How in the hell had she ever wound up with this idiot?

"Anyway, I found a big-ass scratch on my new truck, and I asked Kirsten about it because she drove it to the store last night. First she tried to play all innocent. But she snapped and told me that she ran you off the road last night. That she was tired of you coming between us." *It was Kirsten last night.* "But, baby, I am back and I see the error of my ways, and I will never treat you badly again."

What an ass. "I appreciate that, Brad. And, thanks for doing the right thing by turning your bimbo in to the police. She could have killed me last night. But as far as you and me —"

"Yeah. You ready to make that baby we want so much?"

She shook her head. "Leave!"

"What did I say? I thought we were good."

"Leave."

Camden drove up and got out of her car.

330

"What's the shithead doing here?" she asked as she approached the front door.

"You still friends with this dumb chick? Man." He shook his head.

"Dumb? Did you call me *dumb?*" Camden walked over and punched him in the nose. Hard. Nice right hook, too. "Don't *ever* call me dumb. I might be shallow. I might be a bitch. But I'm not dumb."

"Ouch. What the hell? You're freaking crazy. You're both crazy bitches!" He held his bloodied nose.

"I'll take crazy, but dumb? No," Camden replied. "Get out of here. I think you've already been asked nicely, and my left jab is even better than the right hook."

They both cracked up watching Brad hightail it off the property. "That was amazing," Michaela exclaimed. "Where did you learn to hit like that?"

"Kickboxing. You should come with me some time."

"You are full of surprises. How come you punched him, though? I could've taken care of him. He would've left. I don't think I've ever seen you so angry before."

"What can I say? I ran into Kevin earlier, and he called me dumb, too. I guess it got under my skin."

"I guess!"

Michaela told Camden about her day: Dwayne, Kirsten, and finally Ethan.

"He's really going to marry her? Why the rush? She couldn't even be showing yet."

"I know. I asked him about that. But you know Ethan, always the good guy, always wanting to do the right thing."

"The *stupid* thing this time. How are you?"

"What do you mean? I'm okay, I guess. Sure, I know he's making a mistake, but I'm not living his life."

"Look, it's no secret you love him. He loves you, too."

"He's my friend."

"Talk to him and tell him how you feel."

"I know you mean well, and want the best for me, but I am not in love with Ethan. And even if I was, he's having a baby with another woman. Who needs that kind of complication in their life? Ethan made his bed, he can lie in it."

"Yeah, well, I know you'd like to lie in it with him, and I only want that for you because I love you, too."

Michaela hugged her. "I know you do. But it wouldn't work between us. It just wouldn't."

Camden pulled away and looked at her, obviously deciding not to push the issue any further. "Well you can't go to that wedding alone. I'm coming with you."

"That would be great."

"Yeah. We can stay at the Bellagio. I've got an old boyfriend who works there as one of the managers. He likes me, and can get us a real good deal. Oh, shoot. Wait a minute. I have a job interview in the morning."

"A job interview?"

"Yes. Believe it or not, I think it's time I get off my ass and do something for a change."

"You're settlement isn't going to come through, is it?"

Camden shrugged. "That obvious?"

"Well, first off, I would never buy that you actually want to get off your butt and work."

She laughed. "Ah, you know me so well."

"Where's the interview?"

"Get this, the Chanel makeup counter at Nordstrom. Free samples. Huh? Beautiful, right? And, I know I'll get it. I can do it. I can sell makeup, girl."

"It's perfect for you. It really is." She gave Camden about a month . . . *if* she landed the job.

"But it's not a problem. I can book a flight and make it over there in time for the wedding. I'll call my pal and have him hook us up. Meet me there when you get to Vegas, or if you beat me, I'll make sure you have a key to the room. In fact, I'll see if I can't get a room for Ethan and the princess there, too."

"You'd do that?"

"Of course. I would do anything for you, and so would Ethan. Think about it, before you let him go and marry Summer. Think about talking to him."

"There's nothing more to say," Michaela said.

THIRTY-THREE

The next day after working the horses, Michaela finally received a call from the attorney who'd been trying to get a hold of her — Henry Stein. "What's this all about?" she asked him.

"Ms. Bancroft, I have some news for you. Your uncle, Lou Bancroft, has left you the bulk of his estate." Michaela nearly dropped the phone. She couldn't say anything at first. "Ms. Bancroft?"

"Yes, I'm here. What do you mean, my uncle left me most of his estate?"

"Exactly that. According to his will, you receive his ranch, his home, three million dollars from various investment accounts, and his horses." Michaela was speechless. "I'll connect you back to my receptionist and you can make an appointment with her for next week to come in and work out all of the details."

She believed that she thanked him before

speaking to the receptionist. After hanging up she just sat there, trying to let what she'd been told sink in. Uncle Lou had left almost all of it to her. Why? Why not Cynthia? She had to clear her mind. A trail ride. Yes. She'd take Booger out for a ride.

She went through the motions of taking her old gelding out, brushing him, throwing a pad and saddle up on him, sliding a bit into his mouth, and putting his ears through the headstall — trying only to focus on the task at hand. She got up on Booger and rode out to one of the back trails. Why would Uncle Lou leave all of his possessions to her? And then another thought — an ugly one. The lawsuits. Did this mean that the lawsuits were also hers to deal with? And if so, could Uncle Lou's ranch be lost? No. She couldn't allow that to happen.

Cynthia. She had to speak to her. Doubts or not about her, she had to find out if she knew that Lou had planned to do this. She put Booger into a lope. He reluctantly did as she asked, especially when she gave him a slap on the rear with the ends of her reins. That woke him up a bit.

She rode to Lou's ranch. What the hell? There was Dwayne. She saw him blanketing one of the horses. Unbelievable. He had to have made bail. She may have made a deal with Davis about no more detective work, but she certainly didn't agree *not* to confront people about their crimes. Although Booger wasn't off the track by any stretch of the imagination, being atop the horse strengthened her resolve while she rode on over to where Dwayne worked. She *could* get away quickly if he made a move.

Dwayne looked up at her and something about his expression caught her off guard. She saw sadness there. Despair. "I see you know," he said.

"Yes, I know. I know exactly what you've been doing for God knows how long to my uncle, and I want to know why. Why in the hell would you scam owners out of money and breed them to Rocky instead of Loco? I realize that hasn't been proven yet. But you and I both know that it will be."

He crossed the mare's blanket straps under her belly, fastened them, and stood up slowly, staring at her for long seconds before saying anything. Why was he looking at her like that? Booger lifted his back leg onto the front tip of his hoof, going into resting mode. She gave him a squeeze with her calf — enough to wake him. She wanted Booger on alert and ready to run if needed.

"I did not do what the police have accused me of."

"Really? How do you explain that your name came up when the owners of those mares were questioned?"

"I . . . don't know."

"That's a great defense, now isn't it? You don't know?" She shook her head. "You better hope you have a good lawyer, because I think the police also believe that you may have killed my uncle and Bean. And I think so, too. I'm not sure how you did it, but the police will figure it out. I believe that." As the words escaped her mouth, she again realized that she was possibly confronting a killer. Alone. What the devil was she thinking? She started to back Booger away.

Tears sprang to Dwayne's eyes. "Wait. I did not kill Lou. I did not kill Bean. I loved both of those men. I loved them like they were my own brothers! And I did not steal money from Lou or frame him, or steal money from anyone. I never posed as a breeder. If you look at all of this, I am the one who is being framed."

"Oh come on!"

"How is this not obvious? You think if I put together a con that the police say I did, that when I talk to horse owners, I give out my name? How dumb do you think I be?"

Michaela couldn't respond. Dwayne had never struck her as stupid, and the point he was making was a decent one. If he was trying to steal money, why *would* he give out his name? No. She wasn't going to buy into this. He was a liar. He had to be. It was the only thing that made sense.

"You have to believe me. I did not do this."

Now the tears flowed freely down Dwayne's face, and something inside of Michaela softened. Could he be telling the truth? Should she at least listen? "Then who? Who would have done this, and why?" She still made a point of keeping her distance. He didn't approach her, but instead put the mare back in her stall and returned with another one for the nightly ritual.

"I think a lot about this when the police ask questions, fingerprint me, and put me in the cell until I make bail."

Ha! "Yeah, how did you make bail? It had to have been at least a few thousand dollars. I've never known you to be loaded. What did you do, use the stolen cash?"

He shook his head. "I tell you, I did not do this. I have a little savings. A little from my auntie who passed away a couple of years ago."

"Sam's mom? I didn't know she died."

He nodded. "Yeah. He don't talk about it much. Too hard for him. But it was that money I use."

She still didn't know what to think, but if he was lying, he sure was smooth. She sighed. "So who, Dwayne? Who do you think could have done this?"

He looked at her, his face taut. "Brad."

A flashback flooded her about Brad having dinner with Bean the other night, and how she'd wondered they were still so tight. Then, another thought came to her: Kirsten and the prints on the pitchfork. The fight with her at the funeral, and getting run off the road. And, Brad showing up at her place, trying to worm his way back into her life, pretending to be Mr. Nice Guy by tattling on his girlfriend. "Why do you say that?"

"You know what I think?"

"No, but I'm all ears."

"I think Brad find out that I be the one who Lou had follow him and his girl around to get pictures to prove to you he no good."

"*You* took the photos? *You* followed Brad?"

He nodded. "I agree with Lou, the man no good. He no good with the horses and he no good to you, so I follow him and take the photos and give them to Lou. Sam help me, too. I think when Brad find out I did that, he got mad, and he been planning on getting even ever since."

"Why?"

Dwayne laughed. "Why? 'Cause Brad know that this place going to you."

"What? How did you know?"

"Lou talk to me about it. Tell me that if something happen to him, he gonna leave it to you because you good with the animals and he didn't want Cynthia to have to worry about it. He afraid it be too much for her. He ask me to stay on with you. Help you out, if he passed on."

"He did?"

"Yes."

"Okay, how about Brad? How did he know?"

"He know because he used to get the mail sometimes for the ranch and give it to Lou. Envelope came back from his attorney and Lou asked me who got the mail, 'cause it looked like someone had opened it and tried to reseal it. I knew it was Brad." He shrugged. "I got no proof. But my gut say so. The man already been cheatin' on you, and I had the pictures. Brad realize he lose out on big cash if something ever happen to your uncle."

Michaela thought back to the conversation at the bar with Brad — his pitiful apology and excuses — and his appearance at her house. Was that because he knew she was about to inherit her uncle's ranch? Had that also been a part of his plan? Kill Lou, and get back into her good graces? But why the breeding scam? Suddenly, it hit her. The scam was to set Dwayne up and get him out of the way. That bastard! But was Dwayne telling the truth? Again, she had to wonder. And the money? How did Brad gain access to the bank accounts? Did he have the breeders sending checks to another address — one he had set up just for this purpose? Could he have forged the checks? Shit, Brad could hardly write his name legibly, and Uncle Lou had fairly neat handwriting. Damn if she wasn't terribly confused.

"I know he's the one who do this to me, Michaela. I told the police. But I don't think that detective believed me. I tell you Brad hated me. Hated Lou, and Brad a bad man. He did this. I can prove I didn't kill anyone. For one thing, I was in Vegas. That I can prove. I can also prove that I . . ." He blushed. "I spent that night before and morning with a woman I met in the bar at the hotel. I still have her number. I gave it to the police. I didn't steal anything and I didn't kill no one. You have to believe me. You have to."

Michaela closed her eyes and uttered, "I believe you."

THIRTY-FOUR

Michaela *did* believe Dwayne, but it was hard to swallow that Brad had put this thing together. Still, the man had lied to her more than once, cheated on her, manipulated her . . . and yes, she was starting to believe he was capable of stealing, and even murder, especially if he thought he might get some real money out of it. He must have figured that the owners of the mares would eventually be asked about their contact for the AI breedings. Brad had made sure he slipped both Lou's and Dwayne's names in, figuring that they'd both be caught. But why murder her uncle? Revenge? Or had Uncle Lou discovered the truth? Is that what he'd wanted to talk to her about the morning he was killed? Had he been about to blow the whistle on Brad? Her ex probably hadn't thought far enough ahead to take into account that, eventually, Lou would be able to put two and two together. The timing worked as far as Brad being one of the breeding handlers at the time the mares in the lawsuits were being bred. Brad never did think things through all the way, and this was case in point, assuming he was behind all of these events. Unless killing Lou was part of his evil plot.

Before she left Dwayne, he'd told her that the police were not allowing him to leave the state. Therefore he couldn't compete in the calf roping events at the NFR. "I can't believe it. First year in five I haven't competed. Me and Hobbit was gonna win, too. Just feel it in my blood, you know. Just know it." He wiped tears from his face. "Sam's driving there tomorrow to get the horses for me. But I worry about him with the seizures. Something happen to him on that drive, well . . ."

Michaela immediately volunteered to go with him. "I was heading there anyway. Ethan's getting married and wants me to come."

"What? Oh no. Not to that dipshit Summer?" She nodded. "Girl be trouble. I promise. That man have nuthin' but trouble for years to come with that one."

"I know. What can I do?"

"Tell him no piece of ass that good. None."

She couldn't help but laugh, and Dwayne smiled, too. She was going to help Dwayne out of this mess. She'd been partly responsible for getting him in trouble. Now, she'd do what she could to make sure Brad didn't get away with this. "So, I'll drive to Vegas with Sam. He can go to the wedding with me, and then we'll bring the horses home. We'll stay the night. Camden's flying over, later in the afternoon. She's getting us rooms at the Bellagio."

"Your crazy friend. I like her. She fun." He laughed. "But don't let Sam be staying there. He spend too much dough in a place like that. He need a cheap Motel Six. That work better for him. Not so good with money, my cousin."

"Not a problem. He can drop me and head to the other side of town."

"He good with food, though, so you watch him. Tell him to take his medicine."

"I will."

"Thanks for doing this. You a good friend. You didn't have to believe me, but you see people in the heart and that is good. You have a good faith. I like you for that and am grateful you trust me. If I can get that cop to believe me, then we all be good again."

They arranged for Sam to swing by her place in the morning. She asked Dwayne to take care of Cocoa and her horses while she was gone, and he said that he would.

She wanted to give Davis a call and meet with him. She needed to tell him that she believed what Dwayne was telling her about Brad, but first she needed to talk to Cynthia. She also couldn't help wondering if Kirsten was behind bars yet. She put Booger in one of the open stalls and asked Dwayne to feed him just a little, because she'd still have to ride him home.

"He can stay the night. It's getting dark and I can drive you home."

"No. A night ride won't be too bad and God knows he could use the exercise. Thanks anyway."

The house smelled like spaghetti and garlic bread. She walked into the kitchen and saw Cynthia standing over the stove. Cynthia turned, looking startled to see Michaela. "Hi. I didn't know you were coming by. I'm glad you did."

Something about her demeanor had changed. She didn't appear angry any longer with Michaela. Almost the opposite — happy to see her. "I came by to talk to Dwayne."

"He's had a bad couple of days. He told me everything."

"Do you believe him?"

Cynthia nodded. "The man wouldn't hurt Lou. Not in a million years."

"Then what do you think happened?"

"I think that Brad was involved."

'That's what Dwayne thinks," Michaela replied.

"And you? What do you think?"

"I don't think that Dwayne had anything to do with the scam. I have my doubts about Brad." She paused. "But I didn't come here to talk about that."

Cynthia turned back to stirring the spaghetti. "Finished. Will you join me? I couldn't eat all of it."

"I don't have a lot of time. I rode over here and I'm losing daylight."

"You sure?"

Michaela nodded. "Cynthia, I know you were upset with me the other day, at the funeral. Why?"

Cynthia sighed. "Sit down." Michaela joined her at the table. "You've spoken with the attorney? The wills and trusts guy?"

"Today."

"Well, I spoke with him the day before the funeral and he told me how Lou had adjusted his will."

She hadn't been angry over her telling Davis about the pregnancy.

"I had no idea that he'd changed it, and

at first I was angry. Very angry."

"Understandable."

"I was angry at you. Him. If it had been up to me and I'd inherited this place, I would have probably sold it off in the future. It's a lot of a ranch for me, and that Kevin Tanner has already tried to call me to discuss the possibility of buying the ranch."

Bastard! "You wouldn't sell this place."

"I've got to think about me now, but you're right, I won't be selling the ranch, because it's all yours. I've had time to think about that. Lou did the right thing. He left me plenty of money. No, not the ranch, but I know and he knew that I can't handle this place and would likely sell. I don't love horses the way you do."

"You're really okay with all of this?" She couldn't help but feel a bit angry at the thought that Cynthia would even consider selling this ranch that her uncle had loved and devoted his life to.

She shrugged. "I have to be. I don't have a choice, and what good would it do me to be mad at you, or at Lou? He was only doing what he felt was right. Granted, I wish we could have discussed it, but maybe this place was never mine."

"What do you mean?"

"Your parents and Lou raised you to take

on a ranch. I need to go home. My parents are in Seattle and I need to start over. I'm having a baby."

Michaela couldn't act surprised. "I know."

"You *know?*" Her eyes widened.

"I saw the pregnancy test in your trash the other day. I threw a tissue away and missed and . . . well, anyway, I saw it."

"And, you assumed the worst, didn't you?"

"Yes."

"That cop. Davis. You're the one who told him I was pregnant?"

There was no sense in denying it. "Yes."

"That explains it. He's a thorough detective. He's even gotten a court order that the baby have a DNA test when he or she is born to compare it with the donor we used. But I assure you, as I did him, that I don't have a problem with it. I never cheated on your uncle, and he wanted this baby as much as I did. We didn't tell anyone I was trying to conceive because we didn't know if I'd even get pregnant, and besides, we didn't want the criticism we thought we might receive. With Lou being sixty-one, it was a risky thing for us, but I knew he'd make a great father, and I knew that he would live to be a hundred. At least, I believe he would have."

"Cyn, I'm sorry."

"Don't be," she said. "It's better this way. Makes it easier to leave. You loved your uncle and he loved you. Why wouldn't you assume the worst of me?" Michaela tried to apologize again, but Cynthia shrugged her off. "I'll be fine. We'll be fine. I'm leaving next week."

Michaela nodded and left her uncle's home — *her* home, feeling like a real jerk and knowing she'd lost a friend.

THIRTY-FIVE

Sam showed up at Michaela's place right at seven a.m. She'd had enough time to feed and pack after getting up early. She hadn't slept well; the confrontation with Cynthia still weighed on her. She was just finishing out at the barn when Sam got out of his truck and asked to use her restroom. "I figure long ride, better go."

"No problem. It's the first left down the hall. Use the kitchen door. It's unlocked. In fact, do you mind grabbing my stuff? It's right there next to the door, and then lock the bottom lock? Camden might be up, but I doubt it, and I don't want to leave it unlocked."

She thought about Brad, and about Camden punching him. If he was the scumbag Michaela thought he was, then locking the door for her friend was prudent. After riding Booger home last night, she'd called Davis to tell him about her talk with Dwayne and what she thought Brad had done. She had to leave a message. Then, when she checked her messages on the house phone, he'd left her one saying that his daughter had broken her ankle at ballet class and that he was in the emergency room with her. She tried his cell, but it went to voicemail. She'd call again during the drive to Vegas and tell him about Brad, as well as check up on his daughter. Poor kid. What a bummer.

While Sam used the bathroom, Michaela locked up her office and then walked around the back of the trailer to make sure all the latches were securely locked down. She was sure Sam had already done so, but it was a habit. When she'd been a kid, her dad had forgotten to lock the latch on the trailer and it flew open while they were on the highway, nearly causing an accident. Thank God there weren't any horses on board. They were on their way to pick up a few, just as she and Sam were today. It turned out to be a good thing that she checked the latch, because she could see that one of them wasn't down all the way. She retrieved a hammer from her office and locked up again. Then she pounded the latch down. Once done, she climbed into the truck as Sam appeared. She put the hammer in the side pocket of the truck, figuring it would be good to have once they loaded the horses. The damn latch was tough to get down even with the hammer.

Sam handed her the overnight bag. "Thanks," she said.

"No problem. This is good of you to come out with me like this. I feel so bad for Dwayne, you know. Guy is heartbroken. Tol' me to go watch some of the events tonight. Gave me rodeo tickets. He's a good man. Don't deserve this. He did not do anything wrong."

"I'm glad and I can go with you and help out."

Michaela knew Sam was a talker. But goodness, who knew he could carry on for hours! He talked about the rodeo, horses, Hawaii, girls he'd loved, and of course good food. He was still talking over halfway into their six-hour ride.

"Man, tough week, huh? Losing Lou and then Bean. It's hard to lose loved ones."

"It sure is. Dwayne mentioned that you lost your mother a couple years ago. The other night at the Chinese restaurant when you mentioned your folks, I guess I thought they were both still living."

"Nah. My mom died, but you know, I still sometimes think she's around. Too bad. She a good woman. She didn't have much love for me though."

His words caught her by surprise. "Why?"

"Oh you know, I be a big disappointment to my folks. Say I got no motivation. I got to follow my cousin and not be my own man."

"Ouch."

"Yeah. But I'm good. It's not true. I got plenty motivation. Like I say, I want to start my own luau now. I could have done it already, if my mom left me some money."

"She didn't leave you anything?"

"Nah. All go to Dwayne. But I get it. He a good guy and helps me out. He could have helped me out to get my restaurant back on Maui, but you know he believe my folks saying I no good with the green stuff. That's fine. I find a way. I think we gonna have to get some gas."

Sam pulled off at the next exit and filled the truck. "You need to go to the bathroom?"

"No. I'm good."

"Want a Coke or something?"

"Water. Thanks."

"Yep. You mind getting my meds out of the glove compartment? I gotta take some now."

"Sure."

She watched as Sam entered the convenience store. That must have been tough growing up in Dwayne's shadow. But Sam seemed to have a good attitude about it. Still, she could sense there was some pain. Maybe he'd stuffed it all down — literally. She was aware that eating the way Sam did could sometimes be due to painful emotions. Maybe she could get him to talk some more. It might make him feel better.

She opened the glove box and took out the pill container. "Topomax?" She'd never heard of the medication but then, she didn't have diabetes and didn't know anyone else who did. She read the label, which contained an alcohol warning, and she noticed that the prescription was from a Dr. Verconti. Wait. That was the same doctor who'd prescribed the Ativan for Uncle Lou. The pill pusher. Sam must have recommended him. She'd definitely be asking him what he knew about her uncle's anxiety issues again. Sam had told her that Lou needed a vacation, but it looked to her like he knew more, especially if he'd told Uncle Lou to call this doc.

Sam was walking back to the truck when her cell rang. Joey said, "I got some info for you. And you ain't gonna like it."

Sam climbed into the truck and she

handed him the pills. He swallowed one and pulled back onto the highway. She smiled at him and pointed to the phone. He nodded. "What do you mean, I'm not going to like it?" she asked.

"Get this. The checks were all being transferred from a Washington Mutual account in your uncle's name into an account with The Los Angeles Grand Cayman Trust company. And, let me tell you, that place is hush-hush. All transfers were made online. But I got a cousin who has a friend who's married to the sister of one of the bigwigs at that trust company. That's how I got this info." Thank God for Joey and the million cousins. "The account at WAMU was set up online, like I suspected, but you can't do that with the trust company. They do banking in large sums. They have the L.A. branch, but all deposits wind up in the Caymans and it's under Cayman law once the money is out of the United States, which means no taxes and very difficult to trace."

"You say you can't open an account online with them?"

"Nope. You got to go in and do it. Your friend Dwayne may not be the one who put this thing together. Everything I've been able to find says his hands are clean on this. But his cousin, Sam, he's one bad dude.

He's the one who opened the account. And get this: The guy did time a while back on the islands for forging bad checks and for identity theft. He knows what he's doing."

Michaela gasped. "Are you sure about this?" Sam glanced at her. She mustered a smile. Oh no, what if he could hear their conversation? She tried to adjust the volume on the phone.

"Positive. That guy has stolen over half a million dollars from your uncle. You better call the police and tell them, 'cause I'm betting he's planning to get the hell out of Dodge soon. Looks like he made another transfer yesterday, and he bought a ticket from Vegas to the Caymans. Know what else? That dude caught a flight from Vegas at 11:30 the night before your uncle was murdered. Got him into John Wayne Airport a little after midnight. Then he caught a flight back to Vegas the next morning. Early. At seven. He was back in Vegas before eight that morning."

"Oh my God."

"Yep. You better find that guy."

"Already have, Mom. Thanks for telling me. I'll take care of it when I get back. I'm actually on my way to Vegas to pick up some horses. You know Sam Yamiguchi, right?"

"Mick? Did you hear what I just said.

What the hell is wrong with you?" Joey asked.

"Yeah, *that* Sam. Anyway, I'm with him and I'll be back in town tomorrow, so maybe I can stop by and see you and Dad then."

"Oh, shit. You're with Sam right now?"

"I am. Yep. Like I said, be back tomorrow and I'll stop by. Maybe you can make some of those cookies I like. You know, the ones you gave to Detective Davis the other day."

"You want me to call this Davis?"

"That would be good. Well, I better go. We're traveling through the Mojave now."

"Got it. Be careful. I'm on it."

"Love you, too, Mom." She flipped the phone shut and sat back in the chair. Sam eyed her again and smiled. She smiled back, knowing she was stuck in a truck in the middle of the Mojave Desert with a killer.

THIRTY-SIX

Keep him talking. Think. Got to think and act normal. Okay.

"Your ma, huh?"

"Yeah." She tried hard to sound light, but she could hear the strain in her voice. Did Sam wonder about it? Had he overheard Joey on the other end of the phone? "She's been trying to learn financial stuff, you know. With Uncle Lou dying, she figured it was time for her to get a grip, in case something happened to my dad. She doesn't know how to open an account, if you can believe that." *Keep it light.* "My dad and I told her she should learn how to do those things. Funny she had no clue that you can open bank accounts online."

Was he buying this? She sure hoped so. All she had to do was make it to Vegas. She didn't think he planned to kill her. Why do that? He only wanted to get out of town, and she probably made a good cover for him. Dwayne obviously had no clue what his cousin was capable of. Man, she was scared, because if Sam found out that she was on to him, all bets would be off. She eyed the hammer in the side pocket next to her seat.

"Oh, yeah? Huh."

"So, your luau idea sounds great. I was wondering why you didn't ask my uncle for a loan when the opportunity came about. He might have given it to you."

"I think that, too. But you know, I ask him and he tell me no. Say he like me and all, but Dwayne tell him I better off training horses than running a business. Lou tol' me that he not in the restaurant biz, but in the horse biz and a man got to make his own way."

"Yes, my uncle was a practical man." She was pretty sure now that she understood Sam's motive for killing her uncle and for setting up the breeding scheme — all in the name of revenge. The money didn't hurt either, especially since it looked as though Sam figured he was going to make his way to the Caymans or wherever and enjoy it. The guy did more than stuff his anger away. He'd let it stew, and he'd carefully planned this all out until the timing was right. "That was what, a couple of years ago, you could have bought into the luau?"

"Sure was. But like I said, no worries. I'll have my place."

She changed the subject. "My friend Camden is flying out today. Good thing it's a short flight to Vegas. She wanted to go to Ethan's wedding."

He shook his head. "Big mistake. Big one on Ethan's part."

She couldn't argue with that. Her stomach hurt badly, and she could feel her shirt sticking to her back from perspiration. *Keep him talking.* "You see Dr. Verconti? I saw it on the pills. I think my uncle was seeing him for his memory problems."

"I told him he was a good doc. His old doc say there was nuthin' wrong with his mind."

"What did you think?"

"I think you full of shit."

Her back stiffened. "What?"

He pressed down on the automatic locks. "Your mom got a deep voice."

So, her cell phone wasn't as good as she'd hoped. "My . . . dad got on the phone for a minute."

Sam pressed down on the gas. "You a poor liar. I notice the way you talk to whoever on the phone; it wasn't your mom. I listen, and I know I hear a man's voice. Then you try to turn down the volume. I'm not stupid."

"Sam, I have no idea what you're carrying on about." She shifted uncomfortably against the leather seats.

Sam took the next exit off the freeway. He barely slowed down on the exit ramp. She thought about trying to jump out. When he did slow down to turn the corner, heading south, he grabbed her arm, holding tight. His grip burned. He was strong. *Really strong.* Michaela's adrenaline pumped. She had to do something. "Sam? We're friends. We've been friends for a long time."

"We not friends. I don't have friends. I look out for me. It always be that way. I tried to make friends. Dwayne, Lou, Bean, even your jackass ex-husband. But no. No friends. People screw you. All the time."

"That's why you did it then, huh? Killed my uncle? Because you thought he screwed you out of having your own restaurant?" There was no use in faking it any longer. He knew and she knew that the truth had been exposed. How she'd missed it that Sam was the one all this time, she didn't know.

"Yeah. Your uncle, even Dwayne could've helped me out. But no. They like my parents: tight. Don't believe in me. I been planning this for some time. Ever since they both say no. I figure, fine. I get the money and start my place somehow. Then I learn how to do it. The breedings. I was in Ohio with Dwayne at the Quarter Horse Congress when I met some people looking for a good stud. I got their numbers. Told them I'd have Lou call. There's others, too." He paused. "Lot of money in good horses. I didn't want to kill Lou. I made more money stealing from him. I only want to frame him and Dwayne for fraud. Get them in trouble. Let them see how it feels to have people look at you with distrust. Lou would have lost his license. Dwayne would have never been able to show his face in the quarter-horse world again, or Lou either."

"So why? Why did you kill him, then? If all you planned to do was frame him for stealing?"

He made another turn and drove down a narrow dirt road, heading straight into the desert. "Because Lou figure it out. When we got to Vegas with the horses, me and Dwayne, we unloaded them. We went to our hotel and the bar downstairs, had a few drinks. Some hooker came onto Dwayne and he left with her. Good friend, huh? Good cousin! But he also forgot his cell phone, and it rang. I saw it was Lou. I answered and pretended I was Dwayne."

"How did my uncle not know that it was you?"

Sam suddenly changed dialect and voice. "I did not get to be who I am today, sweet pea, without studying." Oh my God. He sounded exactly like her uncle! Lou had always called her sweet pea. She closed her eyes tightly for a second, not wanting to believe any of this. He smiled wickedly at her. "I study people, voices, actions. I listen to everyone and everything. I am much smarter than anyone ever gives me credit for, and ambitious. I told you my parents were wrong about me."

"Where are you taking me?"

He didn't answer. "On the phone with your uncle, he told *Dwayne* that he knew who was running the breeding scam and that he thought he could prove it. He knew it was me. I was glad Dwayne went with the woman. I flew home that night, rented a car, killed Lou in the morning, got back to the airport, and made it back in time to meet my cousin for breakfast."

"You're really disturbed."

"No. I'm smart. You know what though, your uncle was a smart man, too. He also told me that he had found out the medication he was taking for headaches — the medicine I suggested and called in for him, and asked my doctor for — was for panic attacks and agitation, not so good for headaches. Old fool. I could've pulled anything over on him. What he didn't know was that I changed out his pills when I picked them up from the drugstore for him. I put my meds in his."

"Topomax?"

"Yes. You *know* what Topomax is for?"

"For diabetes, I assume."

He shook a finger at her. "No. Topomax is a drug for seizures, all right. But not diabetic seizures. I have what the doctors call a bipolar disorder."

No kidding.

"But give that medicine to someone who don't need it and it can cause memory loss and confusion."

Oh my God. Talk about twisted! "But what about Bean? Why did you kill him?"

"Bean not as retarded as we all thought. Yeah, he took care of that mare for me near your place. Good place to keep her. She get your stud, Rocky, all riled up when I needed him."

"You bastard!"

"Worked for me for a while. I tell Bean that the mare be his and he can live there at that dairy farm with her. But then Rocky get out the other day. Bean tol' me that he saw him there. He call me up right away, like I tell him he had to. I tell him that if he ever saw anyone or anything go on there without me knowing, that I'd take the mare away from him. I also say he couldn't tell no one about the mare. But after I got that mare out of there and had the horse killers come meet me with her. Bean learned what I did, and he said he was gonna tell on me. Ha! The retard was gonna tell on me!

"So, I know every day he go and read with Mrs. Bancroft. I saw her out walking before Dwayne and I went to get some feed the other day. I knew Bean was in the house. I thought, good timing. Tol' Dwayne I needed to check on one of the mares in the pasture I didn't put away. I went in, killed Bean, wrote the note, wiped it all clean, met Dwayne back out at the barn, and we take off for the feed store."

He stopped the truck. "Get out."

"What?"

He reached down into his boot, pulled out a gun, and unlocked the doors. "Get out!"

"You'll never get away with this. People know I'm traveling with you. They're looking for us right now. You can't kill me. The police know you have a ticket to the Caymans from Vegas tonight. Don't delude yourself." Michaela was sweating like crazy, her gut twisted in fear, her mind trying to grasp for words that might reach him. Maybe she could still reason with him.

"I didn't steal a half a million dollars to *not* get away with murder. I *will* get away with it. Now get out of the damn truck!"

She didn't move. He yanked her arm and started to pull her out of the truck on his side. Her hand folded around the hammer in the side pocket and as he started to pull her out of his door, she swung the hammer as hard as she could, hitting him on the side of his face. He yelled in pain. She opened up her door, jumped out, and started running. The sand slowed her down and she tripped. Sam was on her fast. She hadn't hurt him enough. She reached out and tried to poke him in the eyes. His breath was hot on her. He held her to the ground. She tried to knee him in the privates, but instead aimed too high and got his massive gut. He groaned. She won a little leverage as he gasped. He was wavering. What was going on? She squirmed out from underneath him, got to her feet, and started to run again. She was running as fast as she could when she heard the humming of what sounded like a helicopter overhead. Yes! She slowed and watched as the chopper flew lower. Emblazoned on the side of it were the words LAS VEGAS POLICE.

Michaela looked back to see Sam on the ground, convulsing in one of his seizures.

Thirty-Seven

Thank God Joey's cousin's best friend's uncle's daughter-in-law worked as a dispatcher for the Las Vegas Police Department. Between her and Davis, who didn't ask Joe how he'd gotten his information, they were able to get a chopper in the air and locate Michaela rather quickly, before she either died at the hands of Sam or was blown away by the Santa Ana winds out in the Mojave.

The police arrested Sam and took him under watch to a hospital in Vegas, where once released he would await trial for two murders and a whole lot more. Michaela was also taken to the hospital and released after being checked out. A police officer kindly drove her to the Bellagio, where she called Camden from the lobby of the hotel.

"You're late," Camden said.

"I have a good excuse."

"Come on up. I got us a suite."

"I take it you got the job."

"Nope. My lawyer called and my ex coughed up the money I was asking for. Suppose he figured I'd be a stiletto heel in his side forever. Now get your ass on up here. I've got something for you."

Michaela laughed and it felt *so* good. In the suite, Camden handed her a bag from Dolce & Gabbana. "What is this for?"

"Look, if I'm going to let you make the biggest mistake of your life along with Ethan, you might as well look damn good doing it . . . Oh my God! What in the hell happened to you? You look terrible. You already been out with the horses you were picking up? What, did one go crazy and throw you? I've warned you about those horses. And where's Sam? Thought he was coming with you. Wasn't that what you wrote in the note you left me in the kitchen?"

"Long story. Tell you over margaritas."

"You're on, sister. Now you better get your ass in gear if we're going to do this."

Michaela cleaned up and put on more makeup than usual with Camden's help to cover up the bruise on her forehead, as well as the scratches she'd suffered during the fight with Sam. She relayed as much of the story to Camden as she could while she did her face.

"I can't believe what you've been through," Camden said. "Murder — twice — buried your uncle, figured out the scam of the century, run off the road by a psycho bitch from hell, two trips to the hospital, about killed by the murderer, and now you're about to lose the love of your life. You're amazing."

"No. Now I'm depressed."

Camden laughed. "At least that detective was a positive, right? That man is *divine.* And, from what you've told me, he is into you."

"Davis, yeah. He is a great guy. I should call him." Michaela turned her cell on. There were a half a dozen messages from a worried and concerned Davis. He answered on the first ring.

"Are you okay? I just got off the phone with the Vegas PD. My God! I've been worried sick."

"You have?"

"Yes!"

"I'm sorry. It's just that with all that happened, I didn't really get much of a chance to call. I've kind of been . . . tied up. But I'm fine."

"You are?"

"Really, I am."

"I wish I could come on out there, but my little girl . . ."

"That's right, her ankle. How is she?"

"In a cast, but she'll be fine. But between the two of you, I think I've developed an ulcer."

Michaela laughed. This guy really cared. "I'll be back in a couple of days. I think I'll try and get some R&R. Then, I have to figure out how to get Dwayne's horses home. The police impounded the truck and trailer. But that's the last of my worries."

"I'm working on getting Dwayne cleared of the charges. It doesn't look as if he had anything to do with his cousin's crimes."

She sighed. "Thank God."

"You *should* take some time out. See that rodeo you were talking about."

'The NFR isn't just some rodeo. It is *the* ultimate rodeo. You'd love it. Too bad you couldn't come."

"Yeah. How long you think you might stay?"

"I'll get things figured out by Sunday and leave here Monday morning."

"What are you doing on Tuesday?" he asked.

"Same old. Getting up, working horses."

"You need a coffee break?"

She smiled. "I just might. Know where I

can get a good cup of Joe?"

"The Honey Bear Cottage. I like to go there around four."

"Funny. Me, too. I need a pick-me-up about that time."

"Maybe I'll see you there."

"Maybe you will." Michaela told him goodbye and donned the gorgeous, drop-dead-sexy rose-colored dress Camden had given her. She walked out into the front room of the suite. "Doesn't leave much to the imagination. Good thing I don't have big boobs, or I'd be falling out of this thing."

"For once, go with it. You look fabulous."

"I plan on it." Oddly enough she did want to look good, and although it had been one eventful day and she should be exhausted, a weight had been lifted. She knew that both Uncle Lou and Bean could now rest in peace.

They met Ethan in the lobby. Camden had done as she'd promised and arranged rooms for everyone. She had a date later on that evening with the manager.

Gosh, did Ethan look handsome in a light gray pinstriped suit and white shirt. Michaela's stomach sank.

"Look at you!" Camden said. "Didn't know you cleaned up so well."

"Thanks. I try."

"Where's the blushing bride?"

"She'll be down in a minute. Something about wanting to look perfect."

"Ah. I'm sure she will. I think I'll grab us some champagne before we head out." Camden winked at her.

Ethan smiled at Michaela and approached her.

"You okay?" she asked.

"Sure. Big step. A baby and everything."

"Yes it is."

"You do understand, don't you, Mick?"

No! she wanted to scream. *I don't understand why Summer is carrying your child and you're marrying her.* But the words that came out didn't match her feelings. "I do. You'll make a great daddy."

He hugged her. "Thanks." He kissed her on the top of her head. "You're my girl, you know."

She nodded. "I know."

"Always."

"Yep."

EPILOGUE

Sam was convicted for the murders of Uncle Lou and Bean, as well as for fraud. Michaela received her inheritance and used some of it to pay back all of the owners of the mares who'd had foals that did prove to be out of her stallion, Rocky. The AQHA did not pursue the charges, and Michaela did move on to her uncle's ranch. Camden also moved in with Michaela and refuses to ever get involved with a man again, especially one like Kevin Tanner. Kirsten was convicted of vehicular assault, and on top of some jail time must do community service, which entails roadside litter cleanup. As far as Michaela and the rest of her family, friends, and foes, look for the next segment of The Horse Lover's Mysteries in *Death Reins In*.

AUTHOR'S NOTE

As a writer of fiction, at times for the story's sake, I might take a bit of literary license. I realize that in *Saddled with Trouble* that I did a bit of this with Dwayne Yamiguchi's character. I have been to the NFR in Las Vegas several times and have grown up around horses, so I know what it takes for the men and women of rodeo to qualify to compete at the NFR. With Dwayne's position at Uncle Lou's ranch, I realize that he probably would not, in the real world, be an NFR competitor. To compete at that level would mean a rider must be completely devoted to that task only. I completely respect the men and women of rodeo and hope you enjoy reading The Horse Lover's Mystery Series.